MW00768113

Angel in the Sun

"And I saw an angel standing in the sun"
Rev. 19:17

"This symbol of an angel standing in the sun suggests not only that we should look for the spiritual in the material and the divine in the human, but that we should look for constructive elements even in destructive experiences."

From a sermon by Dr. Harold Cooke Phillips
Pastor, Cleveland First Baptist Church (circa 1945)

By Dub Graham

authorHOUSE®

AuthorHouse™
1663 Liberty Drive
Bloomington, IN 47403
www.authorhouse.com
Phone: 1-800-839-8640

This novel is a work of fiction. Any references to real events and people, businesses, organizations, and locales are intended only to give the fiction a sense of reality and authenticity and not to describe any actual conduct or to imply anything about the nature or history of any actual person, organization, or locale. Any character's resemblance to an actual person, living or dead, is entirely coincidental.

© 2009 Dub Graham. All rights reserved.

No part of this book may be reproduced, stored in a retrieval system, or transmitted by any means without the written permission of the author.

First published by AuthorHouse 9/14/2009

ISBN: 978-1-4389-9936-4 (e)
ISBN: 978-1-4389-9934-0 (sc)
ISBN: 978-1-4389-9935-7 (hc)

Library of Congress Control Number: 2009906173

Printed in the United States of America
Bloomington, Indiana

This book is printed on acid-free paper.

To the more than one million Special Olympic athletes in more than one hundred countries around the world.

Acknowledgements

I am grateful to my son, Laurin and his wife Christine, both physicians, for tutorials on the causes and symptoms of Down Syndrome. I also thank my other children and their spouses, John and Lisa Graham and Sally and Joe Helweg, for their support and encouragement. My thanks also to friends who read the manuscript and made suggestions: Sally and Tom Badger, Brandy Cerbone, Ann Connell, Jean Crowe, Emily Eisele, Sarah Gallienne, Jean Graham, Carl and Peggy Hibbert, Betty Ann Lennon, Mary Charles Sisk, and Bill Patterson, and to Susan Siegman for proof reading and copy editing and Michael Fortson for designing the cover.

The idea of a book about a child with Down Syndrome originated early on an Easter morning several years ago while I was having coffee and a sausage biscuit at a Hardees restaurant. A little Hispanic girl, who appeared to have Down Syndrome, came to my table and stood staring at me. Slightly annoyed at first, I started to turn away. Then another child, perhaps a slightly older sister said, "She wants to hug you." Suddenly I received a hug that was so warm and genuine that I have never forgotten it. Inspiration also came from my friend, Carl Hibbert, Jr., a three sport National Special Olympics champion. Carl leads an active and happy life that has included challenging church mission trips to Haiti and Mexico, as well as several places in America. Now 30 years old, he is among the most active and popular young adults I know. I was also encouraged by my son, a pediatrician, who finds his patients with special needs among his most endearing.

Chapter 1

IT WAS NEAR MIDNIGHT and Donald Hazelhurst had waited impatiently since early afternoon. A nervous young father shared the small, sparsely furnished room for a while. But hours ago, he rushed out when the doctor told him he was the father of a handsome baby boy weighing eight pounds and ten ounces. Don now waited alone.

Don didn't like hospitals. Even maternity sections were depressing—the smell of freshly scrubbed floors, long hallways with bare walls painted a bland color, and heavy doors opening into sterile rooms with narrow, uncomfortable beds, a couple of chairs, and little else other than institutional trappings. His dental office might not be the most cheerful place in the world, but it didn't have the claustrophobic feel of hospitals.

He sat at the end of a couch flipping through the pages of a two-year-old *New Yorker*, skimming the cartoons. Suddenly, he threw the magazine on the table beside the couch and walked across the hall to the delivery room. He pressed his ear against the door. The only sounds he heard were those of people talking quietly.

He started to crack open the door and glance inside, but his wife, Sabrina, had insisted that he not be present during any part of her labor or delivery. Now was no time to upset her. When she told him she was pregnant, he was surprised, because when the last of their

1

two children was born fourteen years before, she had vowed there would be no more.

INSIDE THE DELIVERY ROOM, Dr. Paul Sabantini pulled a tiny red infant into his large hands. A muffled sound emerged from the baby's mouth, but no distressful cry like he was used to hearing.

"Congratulations," said the doctor to a groggy Sabrina Hazelhurst, as he handed the infant to Nurse Naomi Parker to be cleaned, weighed and measured. "You have a baby girl."

Naomi, a middle aged nurse with three children of her own, took the tiny child in her hands and turned away, wiping it gently, as she had done with three other newborns earlier in the shift. "She's gorgeous," Naomi said, repeating the description she used about all babies.

Sabrina, still groggy, didn't hear the words of the nurse or the doctor, but she knew the tiresome journey was over. There would not be another. This time her tied tubes would assure it.

"Meet Dr. Jenkins," Sabantini said. "He's a resident in pediatrics and will be taking care of your baby until you go home."

Sabrina opened her eyes and saw a young man with short sandy hair standing beside Sabantini. He was no more than five feet, eight inches tall and looked barely old enough to shave. Standing beside Sabantini made him appear even younger.

Dr. Sabantini was tall, with thinning gray hair and a completely white mustache. To Sabrina, he was like a caring grandfather. She chose him to deliver her children because of his reputation as the best OB-GYN in Charleston, and because she didn't want a doctor from her hometown of Florence having intimate views of her while she was pregnant. Now, at nearly age 65, Sabantini was winding down his practice, only taking former patients like Sabrina.

The young doctor took Sabrina's hand, and though he had barely glanced at the baby, said, "You have a beautiful daughter. I look forward to checking her over."

Naomi Parker, in her twentieth year as an OB-GYN nurse, had never tired of her job in the delivery room. She knew that not all newborn babies looked alike, but some things about this child were different. This baby's nose appeared flat, her eyes were turned up at the outside edges like she was laughing, and she didn't cry, though a strange sound came from her mouth like she was trying to. Only a few times in her experience had Naomi seen such features, and she was concerned about what they might mean. As she cleaned the child's feet, she saw something else unusual—a gap between the big toes and the other toes large enough for another toe.

"Five pounds, four ounces, and 14 inches," Naomi said as she handed the child to the nervous young pediatrician.

While Jenkins held the baby, Sabantini took a tiny hand between his thumb and index finger and turned it up to look at the palm. Jenkins also looked and swallowed hard.

"Your baby is in good hands with Dr. Jenkins," the older doctor said. "I'll be by to check you tomorrow before you go home. In the meantime, try to get some rest."

As Sabantini left the room, Jenkins put the baby beside Sabrina with her tiny mouth next to a nipple. The infant had difficulty trying to suck. Jenkins knew he had work to do, but first he wanted to talk to Sabantini.

"CONGRATULATIONS," SABANTINI SAID as he opened the door and almost struck Don who stood there waiting. "You have a new daughter, five pounds and four ounces. The delivery was easy and your wife is doing well."

"Very small? Is she…is the baby OK?"

"She's fine. Dr. Jenkins will check her over good and talk with you and your wife in the morning."

Don rushed into the room, almost running into Jenkins who was coming out.

Sabantini was walking down the hall when Jenkins caught up and pulled at his sleeve. He had not worked with Sabantini before and the two barely knew one another. Jenkins was beginning to resent the older man, who seemed unconcerned.

"Did you notice the single crease on the palm of her hand?" Jenkins's voice was shaking.

"Yes," Sabantini seemed unmoved, and Jenkins disliked him more.

"Does it mean…does it mean?" Jerkin's breaths were close together and his voice was weak and seemed to emerge from deep in his throat.

"Most likely," Sabantini responded. "But you'll need to do the necessary tests to confirm it."

Jenkins continued to follow Sabantini down the hall. "Shouldn't we…shouldn't we alert them?"

"No. You shouldn't tell the parents until you're sure yourself."

"I've…I've never had to tell parents their child isn't normal."

"I suggest you not use the word 'normal' when talking to the parents," Sabantini said. "The more normal the child is treated the closer to normal she'll be."

Jenkins stood in the hall for several minutes after Sabantini had gone, uncertain of what his next move should be.

"Anything wrong, Doctor?" a passing nurse asked.

"No, no. Nothing's wrong. I'm just tired, I guess."

Suddenly, he rushed down the hall and ducked into the first room where he saw a computer. He nervously typed in "Down Syndrome," and clicked the search button.

Chapter 2

DON SAT ON THE EDGE OF HIS WIFE'S bed. One-day-old Carol Ann slept quietly in her crib at the foot of the bed.

Dr. Jenkins pulled a chair up close where he could look at both parents. "I'm sorry to tell you that your child has Down Syndrome," he said while trying to hide the stage fright sound of his voice.

Sabrina began to cry uncontrollably. She had never heard of the condition, but assumed it meant the baby wasn't normal. Don put his arms around her, but she pushed him away saying. "Don't touch me! Don't put your hands on me!"

Jenkins waited a few minutes for Sabrina's emotional outburst to subside. When it didn't, he continued to talk softly, as if it was a rehearsed spiel that was required of him. "Down Syndrome occurs in about every 800 to a thousand births. It has its origin in the genes. Every cell contains a number of chromosomes, or small particles, which determine the characteristics that are inherited from the parent. Normally there are 46 chromosomes, 23 from each parent. The person with Down has an extra chromosome, making 47 in all. This causes a disruption to the growth of the baby as it develops."

Don's stomach felt like it was on fire, and he could hear his heart pounding. A retarded child? Not a child of his. It couldn't be. He seemed to recall that years ago someone at a family gathering mentioned that one of his mother's nephews had been born a Mongoloid. He was placed in an institution shortly after birth and the family seldom talked about him.

Jenkins continued. "The extra chromosome can come from either the mother or father, it's impossible to tell which. Neither parent is to blame. The condition arises from an unavoidable genetic accident that occurs when the egg or sperm is made during the initial cell division."

Questions raced through Don's mind. "How much care will she require? Will our other children accept her? What about extended family, the neighbors, schools?" As hard as he tried, he couldn't see her fitting into their life.

Sabrina was experiencing more anger than sadness. Being six years older than her lover, Mike McMillan, and having teenage kids was enough baggage. Add the responsibility of caring for a handicapped child and she could kiss her chance of continuing her affair with Mike good-bye.

MIKE MCMILLAN WAS ONLY FOURTEEN when he first saw Sabrina. Mike's father, Leroy McMillan, was the most popular race car driver at the time. So he was selected to crown then 20-year-old Sabrina, the newly elected Miss Southern 500. Thousands of fans at the Darlington Motor Speedway stood and cheered as Leroy walked to the ceremonial platform followed by his son Mike carrying the crown on a satin pillow. Mike was mesmerized by the beauty of the young blonde princess, and when she leaned over and kissed him lightly on the forehead, he felt warm vibrations racing through his body all the way to the tips of his toes.

From that time on, Mike would look through the crowd of race car fans cheering his father, hoping for a glimpse of the lovely

Sabrina. Sometimes he would spot her standing with thousands of others, smoking, drinking beer, and yelling at the top of her lungs as Car 27 streaked by. He would stare at her for what seemed like hours fantasizing about making love to her. Often at night, he would lie awake squeezing his pillow, imagining it was the beautiful blonde lady.

Eight years after Sabrina was crowned at the Speedway, Leroy McMillan was shot and killed in a hunting accident. Sabrina and all of his other fans were devastated, and they quickly turned their adoration to his son.

Twenty-two-year-old Mike was perfect for the role. Tall, with sandy hair and blue eyes, he was even more handsome and charismatic than his father, and just as good a race car driver. From time to time, Mike would see Sabrina among the crowd, swarming around him after a winning race. She was as beautiful as the day she kissed him when he was fourteen. When he learned that she occasionally did house decorating as a diversion from caring for her two children, he had his secretary call and ask her to decorate the condominium he was buying in Myrtle Beach. It was to be his private retreat with no one knowing about it, including his wife.

MIKE HAD WATCHED AS SABRINA went about the condo measuring for carpet and making notes. She was dressed in fashionable beach shorts, and when she climbed the step-ladder to measure for drapes, he looked closely. He wanted to snatch her down from the ladder and love her madly right on the concrete floor. He didn't need to. They were soon sitting side by side on a carpet sample on the uncovered floor with decorator books spread out between them. Sabrina was asking his opinion about colors and fabrics. When he stopped answering, she turned to find his eyes focused on hers. She put down the book she was holding and took a deep breath. Neither would remember who made the first move, but soon they were in each other's arms kissing passionately. Mike was pushing her gently onto the concrete floor. But she didn't feel the concrete pushing against her back. All she felt was his heavy body against hers. He pulled off her shorts and tossed them aside. As he was pulling her panties down he whispered, "I get to keep these. All pants I take off, I keep as trophies."

"You've probably got drawers full," Sabrina mumbled as she rose to meet him.

Their affair continued intermittently until she became pregnant with Carol Ann. When Sabrina mentioned marriage, Mike would remind her that they were already married to other people, and say, "Not so fast. I need to catch Angela in bed with someone before I ask for a divorce or else, she'll take everything I have. But it shouldn't be long. I have a detective on her." If he ever caught her, he never acknowledged it to Sabrina.

SABRINA REGAINED HER COMPOSURE. "Do we have to take the baby home? Can't we place her in an institution?"

"You can of course," Jenkins answered. "There are some very good ones. She would be well cared for and you could visit her anytime you like. But you should seriously consider taking her home. Now days, most parents of children with Down Syndrome choose to raise them in the same way they raise their other children. Except for a different appearance and some slowness in learning, they're pretty normal. Parents and siblings find them as lovable as normal children, in most cases, even more so. Sabrina listened, but she didn't agree. The faster they could get the baby into an institution, the better.

Don went around the bed and picked up the sleeping baby. She woke up and started crying. He held her closer. The louder she cried the more upset her mother became.

"Make arrangements! You can afford it. Find the most expensive, prestigious home for handicapped children and get her in it!"

Little Carol Ann started crying louder, as if reacting to her mother's words of rejection. Don looked at the tiny creature and nestled her more firmly in his arms. He was hurting, but the little body in his arms was alive. She was human, breathing, feeling, needing love and affection as much as if she were perfect. The thought of handing her off to a group of strangers was making him ill. Would she be better off? Perhaps, but Don knew *he* wouldn't.

When the baby stopped crying, Sabrina started again, almost shouting. "She'll never be able to look after herself. You're fifteen years older than I am. Suppose you die twenty years from now. Our other children will be grown and have families of their own. They won't want her with them, and I won't care for her. It's better to put her somewhere while she's a baby than when she's grown."

Don replied, quietly, but firmly. "We're going to raise this child in as near normal a manner as possible."

It was the first time in their marriage he had stood up to his wife and made a decision that she was against.

Chapter 3

FOURTEEN-YEAR-OLD JEFF and his twelve-year-old sister rushed outside the moment they heard the car turn into the driveway. The nurse who was to help care for their new sister followed.

Sabrina got out of the car, carrying the baby completely concealed by a blanket. She mumbled "hello" to Jeff and Megan as she walked by them and into the house. They followed closely behind. Their mother went directly upstairs to the nursery and put the baby in her crib, the blanket still concealing her face.

"She needs changing," Sabrina said to the nurse as she turned to go downstairs and light a cigarette.

Megan ran to the crib and picked up little Carol Ann. The nurse reached to take her. "Not until we see her," Megan said as she sat down in a chair cuddling the child in her arms. Her heart pounded as she pulled back the blanket and looked at her little sister for the first time. Jeff leaned down, and also looked. He swallowed hard. Megan looked startled. After the nurse took the crying baby to change, Jeff and Megan looked at each other in a painful way, and then at their father who was standing over them.

Jeff was feeling a deep sense of disappointment, like he had opened a present on Christmas morning expecting it to be something beautiful and exciting only to find something ugly and unappealing.

He and Megan looked at each other, again, in a painful way. Neither could speak.

"Come downstairs and we'll talk," said their father who was standing near the door watching his children's reaction.

Sabrina ground out her cigarette as the others entered the den. When she saw the dampness in Megan's eyes and the distressed look on her son's face, she said to Don in an angry voice, "You didn't tell them when you called from the hospital? I can't believe you would wait until they saw for themselves!"

Don didn't answer but pulled his chair in front of the couch where Jeff and Megan sat. "When you get to know her," he said, "you'll love her as much as you love each other." He told them that little Carol Ann had Down Syndrome, recalling as best as he could the words of Dr. Jenkins, explaining the cause and the differences to expect.

Megan cried, more from anger than disappointment. Why had her father not told them? What had the family done to deserve such fate? When she had learned her mother was expecting another child, she had been embarrassed, knowing everyone would suspect that because of her father's age and the age of the older children, the pregnancy was likely an accident and perhaps unwanted. Now she faulted her parents for letting it happen.

"Don't call me for supper," said Megan, as she went upstairs to her room then closed the door behind her.

"I've got to meet some friends," Jeff said as he disappeared out the door.

The reaction of his children was as painful for Don as learning he had a child with Down Syndrome. No arrangement had been made for dinner, and he knew that unless he prepared it there would be none. But the thought of food sickened him. A feeling of hopelessness overcame him. He went upstairs and started to his room. As he passed the nursery, he paused and looked in. The nurse was relaxing in a chair by the Crib and pretended not to notice. He went in and picked up his sleeping daughter from the crib, and held her close.

Sabrina pushed back in her chair and put her feet on an ottoman. She was feeling as much anger as Megan, but she suppressed any feelings of guilt, even over the extra matrimonial affair that had caused her pregnancy. It was fate that had it in for her. After all, even her first two children, though she loved them, were disappointments in some ways. While drawing smoke deep into her lungs, she reflected on what she had been dealt: three children, none of whom she considered normal.

JEFF AND MEGAN WERE good looking and intelligent, but were not interested in stock car racing, or any of the things their mother enjoyed. Jeff had liked to play with his sister's neglected dolls and other toys, while she preferred playing with his football. She could kick it farther than any boy in the neighborhood, and she could climb trees like a scared cat.

Sabrina tried to change them. She made Jeff go out for little league baseball, but he was so afraid of the ball that he quickly backed away from the plate with every pitch, and he would run away when a ball came toward him. The other boys laughed at him and called him a sissy. After a few practices his mother let him quit.

Meanwhile, Sabrina enrolled Megan in ballet class. Nothing was more boring to the little girl than trying to dance around on her toes, and she found the prissy little girls in her class obnoxious. When she socked one with a right fist for snickering at her clumsy attempt to do some simple steps, she was expelled from the class. Jeff begged to take his sister's place, and since the class needed boys, the teacher agreed to let him replace her.

Chapter 4

WITHIN A YEAR'S TIME, JEFF AND MEGAN had bonded with their little sister. They excitedly watched every new move she made—when she was first able to turn over and when she first pulled herself up in her crib.

Carol Ann's first steps were a thrill to all of the family, especially Jeff and Megan. They loved for her to run back and forth between them, while they slowly moved farther apart until the distance became too great for the child to cover. They proudly reported her progress to their friends, unconcerned, even unaware that their sister's progress was slower than that of the average child.

When Carol Ann turned five, Don wanted her to go to a church supported pre-school program where she would associate with normal children. But Sabrina insisted they send her to a local center for handicapped children. Most of its students were badly handicapped and full time residents. At first, Don resisted, fearing that if anything happened to him, Sabrina would leave their daughter in the school permanently. But when the school agreed that she could continue to live at home and attend as a day student, he consented.

By the time she was six, only her father still called Carol Ann by her name. To everybody else she was "Huggie Bear." She liked to hug everybody she met, even strangers, so Megan and Jeff started saying,

"You're just a cuddly little huggie bear. Carol Ann liked it and told people who asked that her name was "Huggie Bear."

Jeff once took her to dance class where she watched intently. Later she showed the family how the dancers pranced around on their toes. Her mother seemed unimpressed, but the others laughed and clapped, and when she finished, Jeff picked her up and swung her around as she laughed and begged him not to stop.

Sometimes she worked as a bat girl at Megan's softball games. The players and spectators loved her. On hot days Megan and Jeff took her in the pool with them. She soon learned to dog paddle the length of the pool. Her father would stand by the pool and cheer her on.

Jeff and Megan were never embarrassed by their little sister or her tendency to hug everybody, or her loud off-key singing as she sat between them in church. If their friends ever thought of her as different, they didn't show it, and appeared to enjoy having her around. In fact, most people treated Huggie Bear as if she were normal, though there were the occasional curious looks from strangers and sometimes even finger pointing and laughing by other children too young or too uncouth to know better.

One of the most hurtful incidents occurred on Christmas after her sixth birthday. It should have been Huggie's happiest day of the year. Santa brought her a small bicycle with training wheels. Jeff and Megan walked beside her as she rode the bike on the sidewalk to the park. With training wheels, she didn't need anyone to hold her up, but they held onto her shoulders to make sure she didn't veer into the street.

It was eerily quiet on the cold crisp morning, since most families were in their homes going through their Christmas rituals. Only a few people were out. A man was talking on a walkie-talkie to a little boy across the park, and a small girl, about four years old, walked a Cocker Spaniel puppy with a Christmas ribbon tied around his neck.

When Huggie saw the cute little puppy, she hopped off her bicycle and ran toward it. As she reached out to pet it, the little girl screamed, "No, no! Go, go!" The man with her, apparently her father, said. "It's okay Nan. Let her play with Mopsy." When he stooped down to hold the puppy for Huggie to pet and looked at her face for the first time, he suddenly snatched up the puppy and grabbed the little girl's hand and led her away, saying, "Time to go, Nan."

Jeff and Megan kneeled beside their crying sister and wrapped their arms around her. Megan whispered, "You have Buffy. He's more fun than a dog." Buffy was a kitten rescued from a storm sewer, a short time before.

JEFF GRADUATED FROM THE SCHOOL OF THE ARTS the year Huggie was eight years old. Soon after, he left for New York to try out with a ballet company. He and Huggie clung to each other so long at the airport that he almost missed his plane. He promised her that he would be home for Christmas and that their father would take her to New York to see him dance.

Soon after Jeff left, Megan dropped out of college and moved to Whitefish, Montana. She wanted to live in a place where the air was pure and the summers were not so hot and humid. She would also find that there is a lot to do there, like skiing and snowboarding in the winter, white water rafting and camping in the summer, and big game hunting in the fall.

After being in Montana for two months, Megan called home to tell her family about her friend, Sam. Her father didn't approve of young people of the opposite sex living together before they were married, but he was excited to hear that Megan was finally interested in a male, that is, until Megan described Sam. "She's the best ski instructor on the mountain, and in the summers she takes her canoe over the highest rapids on the Flat Head River...and she likes big game hunting. Last fall she killed a bear and a long horned sheep."

Don and Sabrina listened on separate phones. Both had a sinking feeling. Don was the first to speak. "So Sam is a lady?"

"Yes," Megan said, sounding annoyed. "Sam is short for Samantha."

JEFF AND MEGAN CALLED HOME often during the first several months they were gone. Sometimes they talked to Huggie for as long as half an hour, telling her of their experiences, but mostly listening to her tell them about hers. As time passed, the calls became less frequent. Megan was working at a restaurant, and with a three-hour time difference, by the time she got off work it was near midnight in Florence. Jeff practiced until late into the evening and was so tired when he got home that he usually went straight to bed.

Huggie was no longer a happy, bubbly, cheerful little girl. Sabrina became more aware of her daughter's needs and began to spend more time with her. As the days grew shorter and the holidays approached, Don and Huggie began to feel like they were again a part of a happy, though smaller family circle. They talked about Christmas and how wonderful it would be to have the whole family together again. But shortly before Thanksgiving, that hope vanished.

First, there was the call from Jeff, beside himself with excitement. He had been selected for a major role in "The Nutcracker." Huggie and both parents listened on separate phones, expressing their happiness at his success. Then came his casual reminder that it would mean he would be on tour during the Christmas holidays and unable to come home.

Huggie put down the phone, and without saying a word, walked toward the stairs. By the time she reached them, the tears were flowing as she sprinted up the stairs and into her room. Don left Sabrina to finish the conversation with Jeff and ran after her. She threw her arms around his neck and placed her cheek firmly against his.

For the next half hour, Don held Huggie close to him as she cried. He couldn't imagine her more upset if she had been told Santa was dead and there would be no Christmas.

The next day Megan called to say her job at the restaurant would require her to work during the holidays. "You know we are at the foot of Big Mountain, one of the largest ski areas in the west. Christmas is our busiest season. Sam is booked solid with lessons everyday from the weekend before Christmas through New Year's Day. We won't have anytime for ourselves." She giggled as she added, "At least we'll be making good money."

This time Huggie didn't cry. It was as if she had expected the news and had already cried about it. When Don went to her room, she was in bed on her back with the covers pulled up under her chin. She was wide awake, staring at the ceiling. Buffy was curled up at her feet.

DURING THE DAYS THAT FOLLOWED, Don tried to assure Huggie they would still have a fun Christmas. "And on Thanksgiving," he said, "we'll eat at the club. Remember the buffet they always have with all the things you like? And afterwards we'll watch the Christmas parades on television."

The night before Thanksgiving, Sabrina talked on her cell phone for what seemed a couple of hours. Don didn't mention the long conversation, but Sabrina sensed a need to explain. "I was talking to my sister," she said. "Since she always talks so long, I used my cell. I didn't want to tie up the house phone. One of your patients might call."

The following morning, Don got up early and went downstairs to get the pancake mix ready. Huggie followed, carrying a wiggling Buffy in her arms. After giving her father a good morning hug, she opened a can of cat food and dumped it into Buffy's dish. Don had taught her how to use the electric can opener. Learning wasn't easy, but she was determined to do it, and could now feed Buffy without Don's help.

As Don placed a small pancake shaped like a kitten on Huggie's plate, he said. "Can't eat a big breakfast. Remember, we're having lunch at the club. You have to save room for turkey and dressing, and all the things you like"

Huggie laughed as she poured syrup on the little pancake. As she started to devour her pancake, Sabrina appeared carrying a small bag. Huggie ran to her for a good morning hug. "Pancakes," she said. "Mine is a kitten. What do you want daddy to fix for you?"

Sabrina dropped the bag and briefly hugged her daughter. "I've got to meet my sister in Charleston for lunch so I need to be on my way."

"But…but I thought we were going to have lunch at the club," Don said in a shaky voice, "together as a family."

"You and Huggie go and enjoy. I'm sorry but my sister needs me to be with her for a couple of days. I packed my clothes and put them in the car last night while you all were asleep. I didn't want to disturb you."

Don was speechless. "Her sister needs her? How could she possibly need her more than her daughter?"

Huggie forgot her half-eaten pancake and locked her arms around her mother's waist. "Don't go, please don't leave us," she cried.

For a moment, it appeared that Sabrina was moved by her daughter's grief, but then she forcibly removed her hands from around her waist and ran out the door. She then stuck her head back in the door and shouted loudly enough for her crying daughter to hear, "I'll be back for Christmas, Huggie dear."

Chapter 5

DAWG BRINSON PULLED HIS CADILLAC into the parking space nearest the back door of the Brinson Law Building. The space wasn't marked, but everyone knew it belonged to Dawg, as did the sprawling one-story building that covered half a block in downtown Darlington.

If wealth and power were measures of success, Brinson was successful. He had accumulated a fortune during 40 years of suing deep-pocket defendants for injured or maligned clients, and gouging rich husbands in divorce cases. A huge man of over 250 pounds on a six-foot-two-inch frame, he had long black hair, which he kept slicked back with the aid of a thick hair conditioner. Bushy eyebrows shadowed large brown eyes that could be intimidating to witnesses that he cross-examined. Though his name was James Earl Brinson, he preferred to be called "Dawg." He claimed people started calling him that because he tore into opposing witnesses on cross-examination like a pit bulldog.

PEOPLE AROUND DARLINGTON didn't know much about Brinson's early life. They assumed he had gone to law school somewhere and that he was licensed to practice law because that's what he did. Some had heard him say he came to Darlington because it wasn't overly lawyered and the mainline railroad ran through it. "I knew I could sue the railroad and get a settlement every time a train came through," he once said.

After practicing alone for a few years, Brinson hired another lawyer to prepare pleadings and other necessary paperwork he didn't know how to do. He added other lawyers from time to time, promising they would make good money but could not expect to become partners. "If you want to own a piece of a law firm or have a say in how it's run, you need to go somewhere else."

During his early years of practicing law, Brinson spent more time visiting hospitals and attending funerals than he did in court or in his office. He developed friends in the local Railroad Brotherhood, among sheriffs and deputies, local police, funeral directors and African-American preachers—anybody he thought could refer him clients.

After a few run-away verdicts for railroad workers injured on the job, he began to get referrals from other parts of the country. Since railroads could be sued any place they did business, plaintiffs' lawyers sought out areas noted for friendly juries. Few anywhere were as friendly as those where Brinson practiced, so he began getting referrals from across the country.

Some people regarded Brinson as a champion bigger than life. Even some who disapproved of his methods tended to regard him as a kind of folk hero. He became so popular that he was elected to the state senate while in his early years of practice. After a few opportune deaths and reelection failures, he became the senior member and Chairman of the Judiciary Committee. Whether it gave him unusual influence with judges was questionable, but he cultivated the idea that it did.

Not everybody loved Brinson. Railroad and insurance lawyers, and some judges, knew him to be unethical and an embarrassment to the profession. But because of his popularity, few would publicly criticize him, knowing they would be accused of being jealous. Only once over the years was he cited to appear before the Ethics Committee.

It had long been whispered that he tried to illegally influence jurors. The one time he was formally accused, the evidence showed a conversation with the neighbor of a man who had been called for jury duty. "Gus, I'm doing a little checking on your neighbor, Arnold. He's been called for jury duty next week and I got a case he may be sittin on."

"Dawg, you know Arnold as good as I do. He's honest as the day's long. Tell you something and you can take it to the bank."

"Oh I know he's honest, but Jake Dobson, the man I'm suing goes to the same church as Arnold, and they're brother Masons, just like me and you. My client's a negra tenant farmer. Jake's truck bumped him in the rear during the ice storm we had two winters ago. Probably needed some weight in the back. It didn't do any damage to my client's old car and the cops didn't give Jake a ticket."

"Then how come you're suing him?"

"'Cause a week or two after the wreck, my client's neck began to hurt. His chiropractor says he got a whiplash injury that's permanent. His neck's liable to hurt him the rest of his life, 'specially when it rains."

"Well I 'spec Jake's got insurance. Why ain't they paid your man?"

"They offered him a little settlement, but not nearly enough. And they hired a doctor from over in Florence to examine him. I'm sure they paid the doctor a bunch of money to testify there's nothing wrong with him."

"Well, Arnold was over in his yard a while ago I 'spec he's home. Why don't you go talk to him?"

"'Cause the law don't allow a lawyer to talk to jurors outside of court. That's why I'm here. And it doesn't let you mention insurance in court. The fact is Jake's insurance will pay any verdict up to $50,000. As long as the jury don't give more than $50,000, it won't cost Jake anything. Now, I'm not asking you to say anything to Arnold about this. It'd be unethical for me to do that, and as you know, I'd never do anything unethical. But if you were to decide on your own to tell him, it'd be all right, and I 'spec you feel like I do, that it's something Arnold would want to know."

Dawg claimed that since he had not contacted the prospective juror directly, he had done nothing wrong. He was given a written reprimand, which he had framed and proudly hung on his office wall.

BRINSON DIDN'T GO THROUGH THE DOOR leading to the reception area, but instead, went directly to his private quarters. He was the only person with a key to the outside door that opened into a short hallway leading into his office. Another door at the back entrance to the office opened into the reception area for Brinson's office, which was occupied by his secretary, Miss Ginny Beam.

Miss Ginny had worked for Brinson since he started practice in the small South Carolina town. Like Brinson, she was nearing her seventies but had no intention of retiring. She had never been married and had no family. Working for Dawg Brinson and serving his eccentricities was her life, and she believed she was the only person in the world who could do it. She did little typing, channeling all but the most confidential information to other secretaries in the office. When it was necessary for her to type something, she did it at home on an old upright typewriter. She had never learned to use the expensive computer sitting on her desk. Her job was simply to look after Dawg. He called her the keeper of his gate and often said, "No one comes to me except through Miss Ginny." She managed his calendar, saw that there was a constant supply of hot coffee, ran errands and passed along his orders to others in the office.

Her most important job was to change tapes on a recorder kept out of view in a drawer of Brinson's king sized desk. Every word spoken in the office was recorded. At the end of each day, Miss Ginny labeled the tapes with dates and filed them in a vault in the wall behind the desk, concealed by a mahogany panel that swung open when pressed on one edge. No one except her and Dawg knew about the tapes.

BRINSON WAS JUST SETTLING BACK in his large judge's chair when Miss Ginny appeared with a large mug three-fourths full of steaming black coffee. She stacked a large stack of mail on the desk, part of a larger stack that had come addressed to Brinson. The remainder had been sent on to other lawyers or discarded.

Brinson pulled a fifth of I. W. Harper whiskey from a desk drawer and finished filling the coffee mug with it. "Any mail worth my reading?" he asked.

"Not much," replied Miss Ginny. "Here's a letter from a lawyer in Chicago who wants to talk to you about associating in a case where a railroad brakeman had his legs cut off when he slipped and fell under a moving box car. He's looking for a friendly place to file suit."

"I'll call him," Brinson said. "In the meantime, mail him our brochure and make sure it's been updated to include our latest large settlements. How 'bout appointments?"

"Only one. At ten o'clock you're scheduled to talk to a young woman applying for a job."

"Oh yes. Brenda Horton, I believe her name is. She's been working with the Seigal law firm over in Columbia. For some reason she wants to move here."

"She sounds nice enough over the phone," Miss Ginny said. "But you know it's strange; she sounds a little culled."

"Colored's not what we spose to call 'em now, Miss Ginny. 'Member back when to be nice we had to call them Negroes. If you called one black, he'd fight you. Then that became what they wanted us to call 'em. Now I hear they want to be called African-Americans. Anyway, the Horton girl's black."

Miss Ginny swallowed hard but didn't say anything.

Brinson could tell she was startled and quickly said, "You know, Miss Ginny, times are changing. In some of the cases I try now days over half the jurors are black; and a lot of 'em are women. I got fourteen lawyers working for me, all white and all men. I need a black and a woman to roll out once in awhile. This may be a chance to get both in one swoop."

BRINSON HAD JUST STARTED his second cup of coffee laced with I. W Harper whiskey when Miss Ginny coldly announced the arrival of Brenda Horton.

The tall, slender black lady walked into the office with an air of confidence that surprised Brinson and annoyed Miss Ginny. She was attractive, and even Miss Ginny couldn't deny that. She had smooth, dark skin, lips that had been touched subtly with color and long dark hair that had been styled by someone who knew what they were doing. Her snugly fitting gray slacks and smart dark jacket suggested she was more clothes conscious than most women lawyers Brinson recalled seeing.

Brenda smiled, extended her hand, and with just enough of an accent to add charm to her voice said, "I'm pleased to meet you, Mr. Brinson."

Brinson took her hand, and held it for a few seconds, seemingly mesmerized by the dark eyes that seemed to penetrate his.

Brenda dropped his hand and glanced around the office. Dawg had still not spoken. "Nice office," Brenda remarked.

Brenda was intrigued by the walls of rich mahogany panels, expensive looking chairs and sofas tastefully arranged throughout, and an oriental rug that added richness to the large office. There were no windows but the walls were covered with paintings that were undoubtedly originals. She wanted to ask what professional decorator did the office, but before she could say anything further Brinson spoke for the first time.

"Me and the president of the railroad are the only people in the South with an office this nice, and the same railroad paid for both of 'em."

Brenda chuckled softly and sat down in a large stuffed chair across from Brinson. It seemed the thing to do, although she had not been asked to have a seat. She waited for the first question.

"How come you want to leave Columbia to live in a place like this, and Seigal's law firm?" asked Brinson. "He's got an uptown kind of law practice, I understand. Old Jacob Seigal and I were in law school together. He was at the top of the class and I was at the bottom. But I've made more money, and he never ran for anything. I been a state senator for nearly thirty years."

"Well," Brenda began, "as for the first question, I need to get closer to home. My mother lives over in Florence. She's getting old and I need to get closer by. I also need to make more money. Mama worked as a maid all of her life. None of the people she worked for paid social security taxes, and she has nothing. My sisters try to help, but they're also domestics and make little money, and they have families of their own to support."

She paused briefly as Brinson took a big swallow from his coffee mug. Neither he nor Miss Ginny had offered her coffee.

"I would also like to get out of Columbia. I've lived there since I was in the third grade, and for reasons I won't go into, I think it would be good for me to live somewhere else for a while."

Brinson wondered if she was the girl who shot and killed her father when she was a teen. It turned out he needed killing so nothing was done with the child. The senate was in session at the time and he was in Columbia. He recalled that the Columbia papers were filled with the gory details, but he didn't recall having seen it mentioned in any local paper. He decided not to pursue the matter. A little family killing wouldn't ruin her chances with his firm

"Well if you want to get away from Columbia," said Brinson, "this is a good place to do it. It ain't far from Columbia in miles, but in other ways it's about as far away as you can get. But if you want to make more money, I can't promise that you would do that here. I got fourteen lawyers working for me and I don't pay them anything. They get to eat half of what they kill. The other half goes to me for expenses and stuff, you know."

"I should be able to bring in some work," Brenda said. "My mother and both of my sisters are elders in their church. All of the people there are working people, and I'm sure they'll refer some worker's compensation and personal injury cases to me."

Brinson quickly changed the subject and asked what he considered the most crucial question of the interview. "You ain't one of them activists are you?"

Brenda knew she should leave the interview at that point, but instead she said. "That's what some people would call an indelicate question, Mr. Brinson."

During the pause that followed, Brinson drained the remainder of the bourbon-laced coffee from the cup.

Brenda continued. "I've never burned a bra or thrown a brick through a store window, but that doesn't mean I'm not sympathetic with women's issues or issues of race. I think activism should stop short of violence. But I appreciate what many who are called activists have done. I suspect that without them, I wouldn't be sitting across the desk from a successful white male lawyer in the South discussing a job with his firm, as a professional."

Brinson didn't like the answer, but at the same time, he didn't want Brenda walking out of the office and accusing him of being a racist or against women's rights. "Please don't get me wrong. Some of my best friends are black, and of course, I got nothing against women 'cept for the three bitches I been married to."

Brenda was imagining what the wives must have been like. Each was probably pretty and most likely blonde, with the help of something in a bottle. They were likely many years younger than Brinson and not very bright. Being the trophy wife of a rich man would be their highest achievement.

The interview didn't get any better, and the longer it lasted the more incensed Brenda became. Finally, she got up, and without offering her hand or saying good-bye, she walked to the door, turned and said, "It's probably wise that you not offer me a job. And should you do so, it would be wise for me not to take it." She stepped through the door, but as if an after thought, stuck her head back inside and said. "Just remember, Dawg, in the unlikely event I do come to work here, don't expect me to take any shit off you!"

Chapter 6

AS SOON AS HE PUT THE PHONE DOWN, Dawg Brinson called out excitedly to Miss Ginny. "Find the girl! Tell her to get in my office immediately."

Within minutes, Brenda sat across the huge desk from her boss. In the six months she had been working for him, he had not asked her to do anything illegal. Some of her assignments were questionable from an ethical standpoint, but were not the type that would risk disbarment or imprisonment. She had a premonition this was about to change.

Brinson looked directly into his associate's eyes. Before he spoke, he wondered again why he had offered her a job. Surely, there were other black women lawyers who would be subservient like the men who worked for him. Perhaps it was because she was good looking and sexy. But at times like these, his needs were for someone who would do what he asked, and it would not be for sex.

Brenda was wondering, as she often did, why she had accepted the job. It was the most illogical decision she had ever made. It was as if she had had an uncontrollable and irresistible urge to show up in the Brinson office on January 2nd. She wondered if she or Brinson were more surprised when she walked into his office that morning.

Miss Ginny had not been surprised, but rather disgusted, and from the beginning, ignored Brenda, as though she wasn't there.

Dawg got right to the subject. "You heard about that bad wreck last week between Bennettsville and Cheraw that killed three children and their daddy? Left a widow and three remaining children. I just got a call from the widow's preacher. She wants me to represent her."

"Everybody around here has heard about it," Brenda said. "It's such a tragedy…and such a shame that Mrs. Smith, the widow, and her remaining children don't have a claim."

"Don't have a claim! What do you mean don't have a claim?"

"The car veered into the path of the beer truck. Skid marks, debris and where the vehicles ended up show that."

"Nothing shows nothing 'til a jury says so!"

"And the only witness is the beer truck driver who's lucky to be alive. He says that…"

"Says to who? The newspaper, that's who, and what a witness says to a newspaper and what he says in court after Dawg's through cross-examining him are two different things."

"But there aren't other witnesses to contradict him."

Dawg looked annoyed but listened. He had not asked for a recitation of the evidence, just whether Brenda knew about the accident, which he asked about just to get the conversation started. Of course, she had heard about the accident. Everyone in the sand hills and low country had.

"The widow needs help," Dawg said. "Not only does she have to deal with the loss of her husband and three children, she has to take care of the younguns she has left. She has nothing, and the beer company's so rich. It serves no useful purpose, though I do enjoy their products from time to time."

"Not often," Brenda was thinking. "Not when there's a bottle of I. W. Harper whiskey within your reach."

Dawg continued. "You know even if the daddy was mostly at fault, if we had just a little evidence. What's it called? A scintilla of evidence that the beer man contributed to the wreck, we could get the case to the jury. With a widow left with three children and a rich beer company as the defendant, Katy, bar the door."

"Even if there were an eyewitness, how could it help?" Brenda asked. "The physical evidence makes it clear the beer truck had no chance to avoid the collision."

"Depends on what a witness would say," Dawg said. "A good eyeball witness could get that car back on the right side of the road. Suppose he'd testify he was in the area hunting and saw the wreck, but it was so horrible he couldn't talk about it for weeks"

Brenda sat silently, wishing she were not hearing what Dawg was saying.

Dawg continued. "Suppose we could find a witness who'd say it was the truck what was in the wrong lane. The car changed lanes to avoid a head on collision, and the truck then swerved back to its lane into the path of the car."

"But the truck's skid marks show it never got out of its lane." Brenda interjected.

"Aw don't worry about skid marks. By the time I get through cross-examining the investigating officer, there ain't gonna be no skid marks. And should they have pictures showing skid marks, they'll turn out to be old marks caused by some other vehicle."

Brenda braced herself. She didn't know what was coming next, but she knew she wouldn't like it.

"You have some brothers don't you?" Dawg asked.

"Yes, I have three. Two left home before I was born. I've never met them. I think one of them might be dead—shot, or killed in a fight. My brother who still lives over in Florence doesn't hunt. He doesn't even own a dog. Besides, he's a convicted felon so I don't think he would make a credible witness."

"Don't have to be a brother. You know a lot of people in the black community. Maybe you can find someone who'd be sympathetic to a widow and her children. Needs to be somebody who wouldn't worry 'bout a wealthy beer company having to pay them some money the beer people'll never miss."

Brenda was incensed. Not only was Brinson asking her to participate in a felony, he was seeking a perjurer from the black community, likely because he thought they would be more willing to lie.

Trying to conceal her outrage, she said in a steady voice, "I can tell you that I don't have any friends who would lie under oath and run the risk of going to prison." Then she added. "Have you considered your white friends? My people aren't the only people who will lie, you know."

"Don't get upset," Dawg said while trying to hide his frustration. "I was just thinking that because the widow and children are black, maybe a black person would be more sympathetic with them."

"It really doesn't matter, Dawg, what color a witness is. If they get on the stand and lie under oath, they're guilty of a felony, and a lawyer who puts them up to it is guilty of subordination of perjury. I wish we hadn't had this conversation."

"Don't lecture me. I been practicing law since long 'fore you was born and I've always tried to help people hurt by a big company with a lot of money."

Brenda wanted to ask, "And in every case, you take half of the compensation. So is it the poor you're willing to cheat to help, or is it yourself?" but held her tongue instead.

Dawg tried to stay calm. "Go visit the Smiths. I understand they're half starving to death. Maybe if you saw that first hand, you wouldn't be so worried 'bout the beer company having to pay them some money. I know the president of the beer distributorship. He has a big house on the ocean at Myrtle Beach. And I hear he goes to Las Vegas a lot to gamble. Probably loses enough in one weekend to support the Smiths for years."

"I would love to visit the Smiths," Brenda said. "And I would like to take them some groceries, maybe help them get on welfare. I'm sure they're in need. But the law treats everyone the same, rich and poor alike. In this case, the question is one of fault. Wealth, poverty or lifestyle is immaterial."

"You're lecturing me again," Dawg said. "And I don't need lectures. Why don't you get your ass outta here and back to work? And you better be glad you got work to do. Just 'member, I can put you out on the street at any time…and that might happen sooner than later. If you want to stay and feed at Dawg's trough, you won't mention this conversation to nobody."

Brenda got up to go, regretting that she accepted a job with the Brinson firm. But it wouldn't be easy to get another job or start a practice.

"Did you hear what I said about not telling anybody about this conversation?" Brinson called out.

Brenda didn't answer as she left and closed the door behind her.

Chapter 7

DR. DONALD HAZELHURST had just injected Novocain into the jaw of a patient he was preparing for a root canal when the letter carrier stuck his head in the door of the clinic and called out. "Sorry to disturb you, Doc, but I got one here you gotta sign for." Jim Camp, the letter carrier, had delivered mail to the Hazelhurst dental clinic for over twenty years. He and the dentist were good friends.

As Don quickly signed for the letter, Camp said. "I hope it don't mean trouble."

Don glanced at the letter. It was from the Brinson Law firm in nearby Darlington. No wonder the letter carrier was concerned. Everybody knew the reputation of Dawg Brinson for suing doctors and dentists. He bragged that he could get a million dollars out of any doctor who delivered his client an ugly baby.

"The patient's ready, Dr. Hazelhurst," his nurse called out from the treatment room.

Don started to drop the letter on his secretary's desk. He had plenty of insurance, so if he was about to get his first malpractice claim, it shouldn't be a big deal. But when he noticed Camp standing by to see what kind of trouble the letter contained, he ripped it open. His eyes had barely focused on it when the blood drained from his face and he turned as white as a sheet.

Don managed to complete the root cannel on his sedated patient, but before he did, he told his secretary to reschedule all appointments before the New Year, saying, "It's only two days until Christmas and we don't have a lot scheduled between the holidays. We all can use some time off so we'll just close the office for a few days."

Mrs. McCoy, Don's secretary/receptionist, could tell something was wrong and she knew it had to do with the registered letter. But she did not ask any questions.

IT WAS MID-AFTERNOON BEFORE Don summoned the courage to call his lawyer cousin, Dwight Andrews. Several hours before, he had spread out on the bed with his head buried in a pillow.

In a voice that seemed a long way away, Don read the letter to his cousin over the phone.

> *Dear Dr. Hazelhurst:*
>
> *Please be advised that I represent your wife, Sabrina, who is seeking a legal separation to be followed by a divorce. You, or a lawyer of your choice, must get in touch with me within seven days from the date of this letter. If I have not heard from you by then, I will assume you are not interested in negotiating an amicable settlement and I will file a civil suit to protect the rights of my client. In the meantime, do not try to contact your wife in any way.*
>
> *Sincerely Yours,*
> *(s) James E. Brinson*
> *The Brinson Law Firm*

If Dwight Andrews was surprised, his voice on the phone didn't show it. Perhaps it was because he and almost everyone else in Florence knew that Sabrina had been running around with a handsome young stock car racer for many years. Only Don, her husband, didn't know and Dwight didn't want to be the one to tell him.

Dwight and Don were near the same age and were always in the same class in school, but they were never close. Dwight was outgoing and popular. Don was an introvert and kept to himself, seldom dating or going to parties. Dwight joked that his cousin probably became a dentist because with his hands in patients' mouths he wouldn't have to converse with them.

During Don's single years, Dwight and his wife occasionally invited him to dinner parties to meet some of their single friends. He would listen politely to stories and jokes told by the guests but offer none of his own. Dwight joked to his wife, "Maybe it's because he has nothing of interest to talk about. People wouldn't be interested in hearing him describe a root canal."

After returning to Florence from dental school, Don settled in a stately old house two blocks from his office, once owned by an uncle. The estate sold it to Don for a bargain price when no one in the family wanted it.

Don's activities, other than work, were limited to singing in the choir at the First Methodist Church and occasionally joining a brother and his family for Sunday dinner. He may have wanted a wife, but he didn't aggressively pursue one. The parade of casseroles brought by from time to time eventually stopped when he showed no interest in the eligible ladies bringing them by. Finally, when Don was 36, Sabrina came into his life. She was only 21 at the time.

"CAN YOU ARRANGE FOR ME to see her, or at least talk to her?" Don was begging."

Dwight listened sympathetically though he knew that this was a dead one. No one had expected the marriage to last. That it had lasted 26 years was due more to the race driver friend not wanting to pay the high price to get out of his marriage than any desire on the part of Sabrina to save hers.

Another reason there would be no reconciliation was Dawg Brinson. When he got a client with a wealthy husband, he wasn't about to lose the chance to gouge the rich spouse for a big fee. And Don was wealthy, not just from the money he had earned, but also from inheritances from his wealthy family. Brinson would keep Sabrina in seclusion until negotiations were complete and final papers filed.

"I'll try to arrange it, but don't count on it," Dwight answered. "Live one day at a time. I know it seems like the end of the world now, but all things pass. Sabrina has no grounds for leaving you, so she won't be entitled to alimony, only an equitable distribution of the assets you accumulated during marriage. Megan and Jeff are adults and now on their own, so there'll be no question of child support unless Sabrina gets custody of Carol Ann. Since she's ignored her in the past, that's not likely to be an issue. Speaking of Huggie Bear, I assume Sabrina left her with you."

"Yes," Don replied. "And she'll be devastated. I need to pick her up from the Center, but in the emotional state I'm in, I'm afraid I'll start crying when I see her. She'll want to know what's wrong and if I tell her there'll be a very unpleasant scene."

"Don't go there today," Dwight said. "I'll get Geraldine to send one of her girls by to pick Huggie up."

DON WAITED ANXIOUSLY IN THE DEN. He was particular about the people he trusted his daughter with, and wished he had asked Dwight more about Geraldine's daughters.

Geraldine was in her early thirties and working for Don's mother when he was born. She liked to say that she raised him, which she practically did. While she spent time with Don and his brothers, her own sons had to raise themselves. They didn't do a good job of it. One went north and was shot and killed during a drug dispute. A second dropped out of school after a few years and drifted around until he finally disappeared. No one knew if he was living or dead. John Henry, the youngest son, took a locksmith course at the community technical college. He used the skills he learned to break into most businesses on the south side of town. For that, he spent ten years in prison and another four years on supervised probation. The girls, Ruby and Rose followed their mother's footsteps doing domestic work and became well respected help.

Geraldine was still working for the family when Don left for college, and he saw her only occasionally when he came home on weekends. He remembered hearing that she had a child after her others were grown, and seemed to recall hearing that she gave the child away.

Geraldine and her daughters worked some for Sabrina in the early years of their marriage, but Don was always at the clinic and never saw them. He remembered that Sabrina fired them, as she did everyone who worked for her, always saying, "you just can't get good help anymore."

AS TIME PASSED SLOWLY, DON BECAME CONCERNED. He was getting ready to call the Center to see if Huggie had been picked up when the doorbell rang. Huggie jumped in his arms as soon as he opened the door. She kissed him repeatedly while saying, "Luff you, luff you." It was moments later before he noticed the attractive, well dressed black girl who had been holding his daughter's hand. It wasn't one of Geraldine's daughters. Too much class, he thought.

"I'm Brenda Horton," the young lady said. "Geraldine's youngest child."

"She Benda," Huggie said as she broke loose from her father's embrace and turned to hug Brenda. Brenda dropped the bag of sandwiches she was holding onto the floor beside her as she embraced Huggie in a tight squeeze.

"I'm sorry we're late," Brenda said. "I live over in Darlington. When Mama couldn't get in touch with one of the other girls she called me. It took a little time to get to the Center from over there, and then we stopped for sandwiches. Mama said I was to prepare dinner, but I can't cook. We went by Hardees. Huggie said it's her favorite restaurant."

After an embarrassing period of silence, Don, said, "Please come in."

Brenda picked up the bag of sandwiches and stepped inside. She continued by Don and put them on the dining room table. Without saying a word, she got out three plates, napkins and water glasses and placed them neatly on the table. Then she went to the refrigerator and returned with a carton of milk and a large bottle of coke. She poured a glass of milk for Huggie and divided the Coke between her and Don.

"Hope you like double cheeseburgers," Brenda said as she put one on Don's plate and shook a large helping of fries from a carton. "Condiments," she said as she dumped several packets of ketchup, mustard and mayonnaise on the table.

Brenda then sat between Don and Huggie and ate her salad and a couple of fries she took from Don's plate. Don thought it unusual. Certainly no one else in Geraldine's family would have made herself so at home at the house of a Hazelhurst. But he took no offense. In fact, he enjoyed having her there. Her presence and his curiosity about her were replacing some of the sad thoughts he was having about Sabrina. And Huggie was having such a good time. She had not once asked about her mother.

"What do you do?" Don asked.

"I work for the Brinson Law Firm in Darlington," she answered. "I moved from Columbia about a year ago to be closer to home. Mama's getting feeble and the other girls are busy with their own families. As you probably know, my brothers never amounted to much. Guess they ran wild while mama was looking after you and other white children."

The Brinson Law Firm? Don thought to himself. But then he realized that whatever Geraldine's daughter did for the firm, it was unlikely she would know about his case, unless she was a secretary. He couldn't imagine Geraldine having a daughter who did anything other than domestic work.

Huggie finished her hamburger and climbed onto Brenda's lap. Since she was smaller than most eight year olds, she wasn't too big for laps. She buried her head onto Brenda's shoulder and was asleep within moments.

Brenda gently carried Huggie upstairs and tucked her into bed. Don followed and watched, silently saying a prayer of thanks that Huggie had still not mentioned her mother and seemed happy to be with the young girl she had never seen before that evening.

Brenda cleaned the table, rinsed the dishes and placed them in the dishwasher. Don started to help, but then remembered that domestic workers expected to do work like that without help from those employing them. But Brenda was unlike other domestic workers he had known. She was pretty and trim, and articulate in her speech. She certainly didn't look like someone hired to clean a law office. Her dark well-pressed slacks and smart looking jacket looked professional. Perhaps she worked at the law firm as a typist or file clerk. Or maybe she was a secretary after all.

Don followed Brenda to the door and asked as she stepped outside, "What do you do at the law firm? Are you a secretary?"

"No," she answered. I'm a lawyer. Are you a secretary?"

Don was embarrassed that Brenda had driven away before he remembered he had not paid her. In fact, he had not even thanked her.

Chapter 8

THE PITCHER OF MARTINIS Sabrina mixed when she got out of bed at eleven in the morning was almost empty. It was now mid-afternoon. She couldn't remember if she had added vermouth to the half fifth of 90-proof gin she had poured into the pitcher, or whether she had eaten anything. All she could remember was that the phone had not rung since Mike McMillan called three days before. "If he's left me, I'm in deep shit," she whispered to herself.

She staggered to the glass door opening onto the balcony of the tenth floor condo she had shared with Mike since Thanksgiving. Pressing her nose against the cold glass, she listened to the waves crashing onto the beach below. The fog and mist was so thick she could barely see the beach. A single figure wearing what appeared to be a raincoat and a ski hat was following a dog playfully chasing after a seagull that had landed on the beach. The bird quickly soared away and disappeared into the fog over the ocean. She wondered if there was any place lonelier than a deserted beach on a cold, foggy winter day.

Sabrina made her way back inside to the kitchen. The only food she found in the refrigerator was a frozen pizza. She put it in the oven and turned it on high without remembering to set the timer. She staggered to the great room and flopped down in a large upholstered chair. She leaned back, lifted her feet onto the ottoman in front of the chair and lit a cigarette. As she pulled the nicotine filled smoke deep into her lungs she cursed the fate life had dealt her.

IF SHE COULD HAVE BEEN CROWNED Miss South Carolina, it might have led to a career of modeling or acting. She was pretty enough to win, but the talent part of the contest did her in. She had tried to recite *The Stone,* by Ann Morrow Lindberg, but forgot the third verse and mumbled through the rest. The interview part of the pageant was even more of a disaster. Her coach had anticipated contestants would be asked what they planned to do in life. He and Sabrina had considered several possibilities such as "Save the Whales," but few people in South Carolina were interested in whales. The ministry perhaps? But what if she was asked where she attends church. A teacher, a chiropractor, a writer? A writer, for Christ's sake. Suppose she was asked what book she had read lately. What about a lawyer? Not a lawyer interested in making a lot of money, but one dedicated to representing indigent defendants?

"Bullshit," her coach said. "Nobody likes lawyers." But after a moment of reflection he said, "On the other hand, people like lawyers who prosecute criminals. Sometimes they even elect them to high offices such as governor or congressman."

Sabrina carefully memorized her answer. "I want to be a lawyer, the kind who prosecutes people. Criminals are being coddled. Drugs are everywhere. Marijuana smoking needs to be stopped. There are a lot of honest, hardworking judges and prosecutors, but we can do better. I want a South Carolina where people don't have to worry about being robbed by some pothead or somebody crazy from cocaine or some other drug."

Her coach took a long drag on a marijuana cigarette and handed it to Sabrina who sucked a long draw into her lungs. They congratulated each other on their choice for her career.

Whether or not the answer impressed the judges, Sabrina and her coach would never know. But the audience gave her an enthusiastic ovation.

Unfortunately, there was another question which neither Sabrina nor her coach anticipated. "Where do you plan to go to college and law school?"

She knew of the University of South Carolina and Clemson, but she had heard the schools were rivals. If she said either one, she might offend judges who had attended the other.

Then she had an answer. 'I'll go to college at the University of South Carolina, but Clemson is also a good school, so I plan to go there to law school." She learned later that the snickers in the audience were because there is no law school at Clemson.

SABRINA GROUND OUT THE CIGARETTE in the ash tray on the table by her chair and took a couple of swallows from the pitcher of martinis. Her thoughts continued.

She still might have made it in modeling or acting if she could have gotten to New York or even Charleston, after graduating from high school. But with so little money, she made it no farther from her tenant farm home near McBee than Florence. She got a job as a night clerk in a Holiday Inn. She enjoyed the work, but within two years was fired after a robber cleaned out the cash drawer while she was entertaining a guest in his room. By the time an employment agency got her an interview with the Hazelhurst Dental Clinic, she was desperate.

"Dr Hazelhurst needs a receptionist while his girl is on maternity leave," the lady at the employment agency told her. "The job is temporary and doesn't pay much, but Dr Hazelhurst is a respected dentist and a job with him will look good on your resume."

Sabrina waited in the small office shivering as she listened to the sounds from the dental drill across the hall. The office was bare except for a college diploma on the wall behind a small desk.

The drilling stopped and soon Don appeared. "I've got a moment before the filling material is ready," he said. "From your application it looks like you can do the job. Doesn't require much typing. It's mostly answering the phone and greeting patients. You'll need to open the mail, send out bills make deposits and pay the few bills that come to the clinic. Oh yes," he added, "and this is important. You'll need to take care of the appointment calendar."

She waited for questions, but there were none. As Don got up to return to the treatment room, he said. "Today's Friday. Why don't you think about it over the weekend and let me know on Monday if you want the job."

Sabrina followed him into the treatment room and said, "That's mighty kind, Dr. Hazelhurst, but please don't give the job to anybody else over the weekend."

Sabrina sat in her six-year-old Honda Civic for a moment before turning the key. The windows were down because the air conditioner was broken and she had no money to fix it. A hot August breeze drifted through the car, gently shuffling her long blonde hair. Though it was hot and humid, it felt like a spring day as she repeated to herself. "A job, a job, I've got a job!"

She looked down the street and saw what in her excitement she had not noticed when she drove up. Huge beautiful oaks lined each side of the street. Their long branches, thick with leaves and draped with strips of gray moss, shadowed the street and the sidewalks on each side. Lovely old homes sat back from the street on large lots. In the other direction, the homes were smaller and closer together. Though neat and well kept, they portrayed a less affluent neighborhood. The small one-story, redbrick dental clinic sat on a corner lot that seemed to separate the two distinct sections. It looked out of place in either neighborhood.

She wondered if Dr. Hazelhurst and his family lived in one of the beautiful stately old homes. He wore no wedding ring, but that could have been because he chose not to wear one while working with his hands in people's mouths. She smiled as she drove away.

Surely he's happily married, she thought, because he didn't undress me with his eyes as most men do. I won't have to worry about his trying to get in my pants. Not that I would mind that for the right boss, but I've seen turnips with more sex appeal than Dr. Hazelhurst.

SABRINA WAS AWAKENED BY HER COUGHING. The condo was filled with smoke and smoke detectors in every room were screaming. She struggled from the chair where she had been sleeping and rushed onto the balcony to get some fresh air. She heard sirens. Fire trucks, she thought. She leaned over the balcony and heaved. Thoughts of jumping and ending it all were interrupted when the front door crashed open and the condo filled with firemen.

"Would you believe a burnt pizza?" one of the firemen shouted. "Folks probably stuck it in the oven and then went out to eat forgetting they had a pizza cooking. They'll be surprised when they get home."

Sabrina curled up in a hammock on the balcony and closed her eyes. She was still so mellowed by the pitcher of martinis that the cold damp breeze hardly fazed her. An hour later, she was awakened again.

"What in the hell?" Mike was shouting. "This place smells like the inside of a smokestack! And what happened to the door?"

Then he saw Sabrina stagger in from the balcony, shivering from the cool outside air.

"Where the hell you been?" She shouted to him.

Mike looked at her in disgust. He wondered if she had been drunk the whole time he was gone. He also wondered how much longer he could put up with this drunken menopausal bitch.

Chapter 9

"BENDA, BENDA? WHERE'S BENDA?" Huggie cried as she stood by her father's bed.

Don slowly rose up to look at the clock. It was almost nine. Since he had canceled all his appointments until after the first of the year, there had been no need to set the alarm for the usual five-thirty. It was almost that time before he had finally drifted off to sleep.

Huggie jumped in the bed and gave her father a tight hug still asking, "Where's Benda."

"Brenda has gone home," Don said. He wanted to add, "She'll be back," but knew he couldn't honestly say so. He had no idea whether they would ever see her again. He pulled on a robe and stepped into his bedroom slippers. "Let's get some breakfast," he said as he took his daughter by the hand.

"I ate breakfast," she said. "I feed Buffy, too."

Huggie picked up the cat and crawled into a chair beside her father as he tried to eat a small serving of Raison Bran. After the second spoonful, he gave up.

AFTER DROPPING HUGGIE OFF at the Center, Don drove the three-year-old Buick Century toward Interstate 20. From there, he drove south to the third exit where he turned and drove for a couple of miles before turning onto a rural road. He had no planned destination. It was as if he were trying to escape, driving away from the sad thoughts that overwhelmed him. He didn't see the occasional farm house with smoke rising from the chimney, nor did he notice the truck load of chickens that followed close behind him for several miles before passing and leaving chicken feathers floating in his path. Finally, he pulled to the side of the road, though he had no idea where he was. He placed his head on the head-rest and closed his eyes. His mind was flooded with memories.

AFTER A FEW MONTHS, IT WAS OBVIOUS Sabrina could not do the simple things she was responsible for at the clinic. Sometimes she entered an appointment date on a card given to a patient and a different date in the office appointment book. There were times when no patients showed and other times when as many as three appeared at once. Even more troubling was her tendency to misplace bills, or in some instances, pay them twice. And she was never able to balance the checkbook.

When Don told her he would have to let her go, she cried. "I need a job. I have to have a job."

What she really wanted was a good provider. But there were few eligible men in the area, and her plan to hook up with a wealthy race car driver had not worked out. The ones who had taken her out were married and were only interested in sex.

Sabrina was shaking all over, trying to suppress her sobs so others in the office would not hear her.

Don started to take her hands in his and to comfort her, but he couldn't summon the courage. Finally, he said. "I'll help you get a job. In the meantime, I'll find something for you to do and continue to pay you. But it can't be here in the office."

Two days later, Don arranged his appointments so he had time to take her to lunch. They walked three blocks to the small drugstore owned by his friend Doc Sharpe. Doc's wife ran the small lunch counter. The four stools at the counter were taken, so after Sabrina ordered a BLT and Coke, and Don a grilled cheese sandwich on brown bread and a vanilla milk shake, they went to a table in a dark corner away from customers.

"I'm wondering if you would be interested in decorating my house," Don asked. "I've never gotten around to upgrading it and it remains pretty much as it was when I moved in several years ago. The living room is empty. There's an old couch in the den, a recliner I picked up at a yard sale, and a black and white television that I had in college. The only thing of value is a 33 RPM record player and a collection of classical records. The whole inside needs painting and the yard also needs work. The water in the pool hasn't been changed in years. I would pay you the same as I'm paying you now and you could work at your leisure while you look for a permanent job."

Sabrina didn't try to conceal her excitement. "I considered taking a course in interior design after high school, but was told there would be no jobs around here. People who can afford professional decorators go to Charleston or Charlotte." She nibbled around the edges of her sandwich while continuing to talk. "Can we go by the house after lunch? I can hardly wait. I've always wanted to see the inside, to see how you live."

Don blushed. "Tell you what, we won't have time to go by after lunch, but if you have no plans for after work we can go by then."

SABRINA EXCITEDLY WENT FROM ROOM TO ROOM with visions of fine furnishings dancing in her brain. "I can see velvet wallpaper here in the den. It'll give it a rich and warm look. And there will be a large desk with a judge's chair. The recliner must go. We'll replace it with a comfortable all-leather chair and ottoman. We'll need built-in book cases, and you need to get a modern stereo system, perhaps with speakers built into the book cases."

She then went to the windows and gazed outside. "And window treatments. It may be a little tricky in the den. Plantation shutters might work. But they'll need to be stained a dark color to blend with the velvet wall covering."

For the next three nights, Don walked at Sabrina's side as she went through the house making notes for each room. She never asked for his recommendations or for his approval of her plans. Neither did she seem to hear his suggestion that she go to a local furniture store to find the furnishings. "There's this place on King Street in Charleston, I've heard about," she said. "And in Charlotte, there's Mecklenburg Furniture. It's advertised in all the design magazines I've been studying. We might also consider looking in Atlanta and New Orleans. I know they must have great places there."

BEFORE SABRINA COMPLETED decorating the house, she was running it. Without telling Don, she cancelled her apartment lease and moved her few belongings into the guest bedroom. She fired the maid who came once a week and hired a cleaning service, saying she didn't want a maid who might tell neighbors what was going on in the house.

In addition to completely redoing the house, she had the back yard landscaped. The pool got new tile, and a heating system was installed that would permit its use for most of the months of the year. A bath house was added and an attractive fence enclosed the large back yard. Shrubbery and trees were planted and the entire yard was covered with an expensive sculptured Bermuda grass.

Although he was never asked for suggestions, Don liked what Sabrina had done with the house and yard, and he didn't complain about the expense. When the project was complete, he agreed to have an open house to celebrate its completion.

THE HOUSE WARMING PARTY WAS ONE OF THE LARGEST SOCIAL EVENTS in the history of Florence. The dining room at the country club might as well have closed for the night, and the Wednesday night services at the most prestigious churches canceled. Everybody who was anybody was at the Hazelhurst house.

Guests were met at the curb by valets who parked their cars. Candles lined the walkway to the front porch. Don and Sabrina welcomed guests in the foyer and invited them to tour the house before going to the back yard where they would find food and drink. Two waiters dressed in tuxedos stood to the side with trays of champagne and wine, which they offered as the guests started their tours.

Sabrina was dressed "fit to kill," having been given a blank check by Don to pay for being fully outfitted by Razooks in Pinehurst. Don dressed more modestly, but fashionable. Sabrina had gone with him to the finest men's store in town and selected a silk blue blazer, expensive designer slacks, and a light blue shirt with a silk tie that matched perfectly. She also had him purchase a pair of alligator slip-ons, and insisted he wear long black socks that covered the calves of his legs. "Those short anklet things you always wear are gross," she said.

Torches lit the back yard along the side and back fences. Candles floated in the pool. A string quartet from the Columbia orchestra played softly. Bars on each side of the yard were stocked with beer and wine. Trained bartenders from Charleston, wearing tuxedos, stood ready to serve exotic cocktails, though, they knew from experience that most people would ask for beer or bourbon and branch water.

Two long tables were piled high with food and at the end of each table a carver, dressed in a white uniform, stood ready to carve huge slices of lamb, ham or roast beef. As they started through the line, guests were handed a china plate and silver wrapped in cloth napkins. Tables and chairs from a rental place in Myrtle Beach were arranged throughout the yard. A rolled up tent rested on the side of the yard just in case of rain. But the weather was clear and comfortable on that late April night.

As guests left, they paused to rave about the house and yard. Some asked for Sabrina's business card.

"I don't have a business address yet," she told them. "But Dr. Hazlehurst will know where to reach me."

"A decorating career for her," Don was thinking. "Maybe that answers the question of where she goes from here."

IT WAS AFTER MIDNIGHT before the last guests left, and though the caterers remained busy packing and cleaning, the house seemed strangely quiet. Don and Sabrina kicked off their shoes, relaxed in the den and happily congratulated each other for a successful party. Don sipped a light beer and Sabrina worked on her third vodka martini of the evening.

Finally Don said, "I have a full schedule at the office tomorrow. I'm so keyed up, but I better go to bed and try and get some sleep."

Half an hour later, time enough for Sabrina to finish her fourth martini and smoke a couple of cigarettes, Don heard the click of the hallway light. For several moments light from the hallway drifted underneath his bedroom door. She forgot to turn off the light, he thought. She's tired and probably intoxicated too. As he rolled over on his side and closed his eyes, he heard the door to his room slowly open.

Light from the hallway filled the room. Sabrina was standing in the doorway wearing a short satin gown that came only slightly below her waist. Her panties were clearly exposed. She stood there just long enough for Don to become aroused. Then she walked toward the bed while unbuttoning her half gown and let it slide to the floor. For a moment, she stood by the bed. Don was breathing hard as he looked at her standing only a few feet away and wearing nothing but bikini panties. She curled her thumbs inside the elastic and pushed them down as she stepped out of them one foot at the time and then they dropped to the floor. Don lifted the top sheet and she slipped under it and pressed her warm body against his.

Don had slipped out of his pajama bottoms. He never wore tops. He was breathing so hard he could barely talk, but in a voice shaking with passion, he said, "I've never done this before. I may not be very good at it."

Sabrina replied, "Please don't apologize for what you've never done so I won't feel a need to apologize for things I have done."

FOUR WEEKS AFTER HAVING SEX for the first time, Don came home to find Sabrina in bed. "I've been sick all day," she said. "It's horrible. My stomach, dry heaves. I feel miserable."

He heated a bowl of soup in the microwave and took it to her, along with a glass of soda water. She took a sip of the water, but didn't touch the soup.

"Should I call one of my brothers?" Don asked. "I'm sure either would be glad to come over and check you, and maybe give you something that will bring some relief."

"No, no," she said. "I'll find a doctor in the morning, but it won't be at the Hazelhurst clinic. There should be an OB-GYN in Sumter. Maybe I'll go to Charleston. This is a private matter between the two of us. We don't need any of your family or friends to know until we're ready to tell them."

Sensing that he was missing the obvious, Sabrina said in a disgusting manner, "Don, I'm pregnant!"

Don was speechless. Conflicting emotions collided in the center of his stomach, sending fragments of shrapnel throughout his body. His picture of marriage and children had never wavered. First would be a marriage—a very proper and lovely wedding in a church filled with family and friends followed by reception at the country club. He and his bride would run through a shower of rice and rose petals to a limousine, which would take them to the airport to be flown to their honeymoon in some gorgeous part of the world. A couple of years later, his wife would whisper softly, "Darling I have some great news. We're going to have a baby."

After a few moments, Don leaned over Sabrina, wanting to take her into his arms and assure her that he was thrilled that they were going to be parents.

Sabrina held up her hands and turned away. "Please, please, leave me alone and sleep in another room." He could hear her heaving as he walked away.

THE WEDDING COULD NOT HAVE BEEN SIMPLER. Don wanted to exchange vows in the lovely garden in back of the house. But when the magistrate and the two witnesses he brought arrived, it was raining. So he and Sabrina stood with witnesses they had never seen before in front of the magistrate who read the language and asked for the vows to be repeated. There was no more than the minimum required by the state for the magistrate and the two witnesses to sign the marriage certificate. As soon as it was signed, the magistrate stuffed the hundred-dollar bill Don handed him in his pocket and left. Don handed each of the witnesses a twenty and they followed behind the magistrate.

After sitting silently in the den and smoking two cigarettes, Sabrina went up to bed. She didn't pause to kiss her new husband. She didn't even say good night.

JEFFREY WAS A BEAUTIFUL BABY, perfect in every respect, as was Megan, who followed two years later.

DON WAS AWAKENED BY THE FLASHING BLUE LIGHTS of a car that had pulled up behind him. He rolled down the window as a large African-American deputy sheriff approached.

"Anything wrong, sir?" the deputy asked. "We've had some calls that a car was parked here beside the road with someone in it, asleep, dead, or maybe just drunk. You aren't drunk are you, sir?"

"Oh no, Sheriff. I took some pills for this cold I have. Guess they made me kind of drowsy."

The deputy had his face inside the car, sniffing to see if he could smell any alcohol. "May I see your driver's license?" he asked. Don handed it to him.

"Donald A. Hazelhurst. Are you one of the Hazelhurst doctors over at the clinic?"

"No, sir," Don replied. "I have two brothers and a cousin who practice there. I'm a dentist." Then he fibbed: "Since it's so close to Christmas, I'm not working, so I was riding around looking for a tract of timber I saw advertised in the paper. I thought I might be interested in it as an investment."

After repeated assurances, Don told the deputy that he was all right and that he felt like driving.

The deputy turned to go. "You be careful, Dr. Hazelhurst. We don't want you dozing off and having a wreck."

Don looked at the clock on the dashboard. It was five-thirty. He didn't know how long he had sat there dozing while being tormented by thoughts of his life with Sabrina. He backed his car into the main road, uncertain which direction to go. A dim purple glow from the setting sun filled the sky behind him so he knew he was headed east. Soon, he saw a sign indicating that I-20 was a mile ahead. He realized he was late to pick up Huggie and he increased his speed.

It was just after six o'clock when he pulled in front of the Center. Mrs. Travis, a member of the staff, stood in the cold with Huggie. Don apologized for being late as Huggie jumped in the car and gave him a tight hug and kiss on the cheek. He knew he needed to tell people at the Center that her mother had left, but that could wait.

Chapter 10

THE ONLY FIRM MEETING AT THE BRINSON LAW OFFICE each year was on Christmas Eve. It was so Dawg Brinson could divide up the Christmas lists among the lawyers and staff and send them to deliver presents. Two vacant offices were filled with fruit, candy, liquor, wine and beer, tobacco products, children's toys and items that Dawg or Miss Beam had purchased. The gift lists included judges and prosecutors, sheriffs and their deputies in Darlington and the surrounding counties, policemen, ambulance drivers, hospital orderlies, chiropractors, bail bondsmen, funeral directors, and anybody Dawg thought was in a position to refer injured clients.

Dawg opened the meeting in a mocking tone. "Welcome to our annual meeting and Merry Christmas. I hope y'all can catch up on your work by nine or ten o'clock tonight so you can spend some time at home with your families. As you know, this is the time of year I get you together to thank you for all you done for me this past year, but to especially thank you for all you're gonna do for me this coming year."

There were a few chuckles, but for the most part everybody sat quietly, hoping to get the meeting over as quickly as possible so they could get home to their families. Dawg's talk of working until late was a joke. Except for being paid well, not being accountable for the hours worked was the most attractive feature of working for the Brinson Law Firm. The only measure of success was the fees generated. A lawyer who worked 500 hours a year was worth more than one who worked 2000 but brought in less money.

Dawg continued, still trying to be humorous. "The floor's open for business. Anybody got a complaint or suggestion can speak now or you can keep quiet knowing you'll get another chance to speak at next year's meeting."

There were a few more chuckles, then shock and surprise as a voice came from the back of the room. "There are some issues that need discussing."

Everyone turned to see the firm's only woman and only African-American staring directly at Dawg.

"We're the only firm in the area that doesn't do pro bono work. There are a lot of indigent people in the area who sometimes need a lawyer. And you don't have to be an African-American or Hispanic to be an indigent. I took a call this morning from a Brantley Cole's wife. I guess Miss Ginny referred the call to me because no one else was here at the time it came in. Anyway, Mr. Cole's in jail on a simple drunk charge, and without help, can't get out until after Christmas. I could find a magistrate and have him released in my custody, but I'm not allowed to work without pay."

"Other lawyers do free work," said Dawg. "What you call it?"

"Pro Bono," Brenda replied.

"Yea, pro bono. Lawyers do it for two reasons. First, they think that whoever they represent free is gonna hire 'em if they get run over by a truck or hit by the train, or slip and fall in the Piggly Wiggly. But whenever anybody gets hurt bad, they go to the lawyer who'll get 'em the most money. In this state, that's me. The second reason is that if lawyers put in enough hours working for free, the Bar Association will give them a pretty certificate to hang on their wall. It amazes me that some people will run across the Cooper River Bridge in Charleston just so they can get a tee shirt saying they done it, and some lawyers will do hundreds of dollars worth of free work just so they can get a certificate saying they done it. I don't need nothing to put on the wall."

As the meeting broke up, Dawg called out to Brenda. "I know Brantley Cole. That's probably why his wife called this firm. I'll get him out of jail, but it won't be for free. Go to my office and wait. I'll be there in a minute to give you instructions."

BRENDA WAITED IN DAWG'S OFFICE while he finished giving delivery instructions to some of the younger staff and lawyers. She knew she had angered him and braced herself for being told on Christmas Eve that she no longer had a job.

Dawg didn't speak when he first came in the office but went straight to his desk. He opened a drawer and pulled out a half-full bottle of I. W. Harper whiskey. He pushed the bottle across the desk in front of him and said, "Can I offer you a drink?"

"I think you just did," Brenda said, "and my answer is, 'thanks but no thanks.'"

Dawg turned the bottle up and took two large swallows. There was no water or other chaser.

His face, already red, turned more so as he took a couple of deep breaths and looked directly at Brenda. "Why do you always have to be such a smart ass? It hasn't been many years ago that what you said would have been considered sass, and I coulda slapped the shit out of you."

"You miss the good old days, don't you Dawg? And what I said in the meeting would have been uppity and you would have fired me. You may be going to do it anyway. Is that why you asked me to come by your office?"

"No, not at all. I wanted to wish you a Merry Christmas and say that I want the two of us to get along better. You're a pretty girl. Why don't we go on a little road trip after Christmas? I know Christmas is a big deal for you folks and I want you to enjoy it. But there ain't much going on between Christmas and New Years. I got a friend who owns a hotel at Myrtle Beach. It's not a five star, but we could hole up there a couple of days. I could teach you to drink liquor and you could teach me some of the tricks you folks are good at. My friend'll see we get the best food available. Steaks you wouldn't believe!"

Brenda was steaming to the point she was tempted to pick up the letter opener on Dawg's desk and go for his jugular. "I'm a vegetarian." She said and then changed the subject. "Do you know Dr. Hazelhurst over in Florence?"

Dawg wanted to get back to the subject at hand, but after reflecting briefly asked, "Is he that dentist with the funny looking kid?"

Brenda answered. "Well he does have a child with Down Syndrome. How she looks, I guess is in the eye of the beholder."

"Don't know him," Dawg said. "But I represent his pretty wife. I hear he's mighty rich. Well, I look forward to relieving him of some of his wealth, maybe all of it. You know I don't usually feel sorry for men in marriage trouble. I been in enough of it myself, so I figger if I hafta take it, others should, too. But I kinda feel for the dentist. He ain't done anything wrong, and he loves the blonde bitch that left him. And she left him with that dumb kid that ain't even his. There are two other kids, but they're grown and gone someplace far off. It's just as well. I hear both of 'em are queer."

Brenda decided to let the subject drop.

"I'll be handing out bonuses after Christmas. We can go to the beach and celebrate your bonus while we relax in our hotel room."

"Let's cut to the chase," Brenda said. "Will my bonus be more if I shack up with you at the beach for a few days?"

Dawg began to breath harder. He took her answer to mean that for enough money, he would get to do what he had wanted to do since the first day Brenda walked into his office. She would be surprised at how much he would be willing to pay.

He reached for the bottle of I. W. Harper. "Your bonus should increase by..." He paused to think, not wanting to come up short. "Your bonus will increase at least $20,000."

"So," Brenda said, "$10,000 a day. I know you can afford the money, but are you sure you can get yourself in condition to receive what you're buying?"

Dawg giggled. "Oh I know what you mean. But they got pills now. Ah, the miracles of modern medicine."

Brenda felt unclean being around the repulsive, vulgar old man. But she would play out his game.

"Twenty thousand dollars," Brenda repeated, as if she was seriously considering Dawg's preposition. He was too dumb and too drunk to realize she was saying it in mockery. "If I accept your proposition, Mr. Brinson, what does it make me? I think it's better to stick to one profession at a time. I'm not a whore. I'm not a maid. I'm not a secretary. I'm a lawyer. It's an honorable profession, though there are some people in it who aren't."

Dawg was mad but held his temper. He knew he could not match wits with his bright, young, sober associate. But he wasn't too drunk to be concerned that Brenda might tell others of his conduct. People would believe her because it was the sort of thing they expected him to do.

"Brenda, please forget we had this conversation," Dawg said, slurring his words. "It's Christmas. The drinks are flowing and old men say foolish things. The real reason I asked you to come to my office is that I have some special baskets prepared for the Smith family and I want you and Miss Ginny to deliver them. You remember the Smiths, the widow and surviving children of the man killed by the beer truck. I told Miss Ginny to make sure their baskets were overflowing with toys for the younguns, a frozen turkey and other stuff. I hope it'll make their Christmas a little better. It's such a shame. The beer company hasn't even said they're sorry."

Brenda left without responding. She didn't plan to mention Dawg's conduct to anyone, but she was making no promises.

Dawg called after her as she got to the door. "Would you ask Miss Ginny to step in here a minute? There's something I need her to do before you all go."

BRENDA WAITED FOR MISS GINNY to return from Dawg's office. She said nothing to Brenda when she returned, but went to her desk and dialed a number on the phone.

"Miss Cole, this is Mr. Brinson's law office. He wanted me to call and let you know that he will have Mr. Cole out of jail and home by tonight. He just needs to make a couple of phone calls. He's sending out a Christmas basket and hopes you have a nice Christmas. And please have Mr. Cole call and make an appointment with Mr. Brinson after Christmas as soon as possible."

I should have known, thought Brenda. Dawg needs a witness who will lie about the Smith case and one who won't recant. Brantley Cole needs money desperately, and once he lies under oath, he can't afford to recant. He already has several felony convictions and another could send him to prison for most of the rest of his life.

MISS GINNY HELPED BRENDA gather the baskets going to the Smith family. Brenda tried to start a conversation but the old lady didn't answer, pretending not to hear.

Brenda's Z3 sports car was not large enough for them and the baskets. "Maybe we should call a taxi," Brenda said laughing. There were no taxis available in Darlington on Christmas Eve.

Miss Ginny didn't laugh and replied with frustration, "I'll get my car."

Brenda watched as the old lady went to an old 1980s style car, which was parked next to the building in the space next to Dawg's Cadillac.

Dawg must consider her second in importance to him, Brenda thought. She put the baskets in the back seat and got in the front seat next to Miss Ginny, who looked straight ahead and didn't speak as she gunned the old car into the street, almost running over a couple walking their dog.

A policeman coming out of the station across the street laughed. It's just a matter of time until that old lady takes somebody out, he thought.

Miss Ginny continued to ignore Brenda who tried not to take offense. She knew it was hard for an old lady who had lived in the South all of her life to adjust to having an African-American working in the same office as a professional.

THE OLD CAR PULLED UP TO A SHOTGUN HOUSE in the middle of the worst slum in the county. Black smoke poured from the chimney. Brenda noticed rags stuffed in the windows where the glass had been broken out. If the house had ever been painted, it was so long ago that all signs of paint were gone. The roof had wooden shingles, most of which were rotten. There was no porch. A large rock in front of the front door served as a step.

Brenda knew she had been selected to help with deliveries to the Smiths so she would be overcome with pity and look the other way while Brinson defrauded the beer company and its insurer.

Miss Ginny quickly jumped out of the car and pulled the baskets from the back seat onto the ground. Then she jumped back in the car and locked the door. She was frightened to be in that part of town.

As soon as she knocked on the door, Brenda heard what sounded like several pair of bare feet rushing to the door. It flew open and there stood three children, half dressed and wearing no shoes. The two boys looked to be around ten and twelve. A little girl appeared no older than six. Brenda shoved the basket through the doorway and went back to the car for the second one. When she returned, a frail looking black lady of around forty was holding the door open for her. The children dug into the first basket and crammed fruit cake into their mouths as if it might disappear if not eaten quickly.

"Come in," the lady said. "I'm Maybelle Smith."

Brenda took her outstretched hand and said, "Merry Christmas. I work for the Brinson Law Firm and Mr. Brinson asked that I bring you these baskets. There's a frozen turkey in one. You will want to take it out and put it in some water so it'll be thawed by tomorrow."

"My Lawd have mercy," Maybelle Smith said. "Bless Mr. Dawg's heart. This'll be the only Christmas we have. Since the beer truck killed my husband and three of my children, times have been mighty hard. We had to move into this shack. I get a little money from the welfare, but not nearly enough to live on."

Brenda looked around the shack. A few thousand dollars would do so much for the Smiths, and the beer company and its insurance company would never miss it. She briefly wondered how it could be all that wrong to help someone in such desperate need, even if it required some cheating to do it.

BRENDA SAT QUIETLY AS MISS GINNY drove back to the office, still not saying anything or making any gesture that suggested she knew Brenda was there. Brenda's thoughts were no longer on Miss Ginny, but on the Smith family where there was a different kind of suffering from Miss Ginny's obvious loneliness. She wanted to help them, but there would be time to decide how after Christmas.

There was another family where there was pain and suffering of another kind. Should she block them out of her mind, or show up at their door tonight to wish them a Merry Christmas?

Chapter 11

SHOPPING WITH HUGGIE ON Christmas Eve reminded Don how rich a blessing his daughter was. She skipped through the department store from counter to counter excitedly suggesting gifts—a bright red scarf for her mother, and a yellow tie for her father. Don pretended not to hear as she whispered to the clerk which tie she wanted. He seldom wore ties, but he would wear this one, no matter how tasteless it was.

"We've got to get a present for Benda," Huggie said.

Don didn't protest, though he thought it unlikely they would see Brenda again. Huggie picked an indescribably ugly necklace from a counter piled high with fake jewelry. "Don't wrap it," she told the clerk. "I wrap it myself."

After having dinner at Hardees, they stopped at the grocery store where Don planned to buy a rotisserie chicken for their Christmas dinner. It wouldn't be a turkey, but Huggie would be so excited she wouldn't care, and Don had no appetite.

The hot counter where the cooked chicken and roasted pork usually were was cold and empty, probably because people didn't buy pre-cooked items for Christmas. At the deli section, they struggled through the crowd lined up to get turkeys and hams they had ordered weeks before. The pressed ham and turkey in the deli didn't look appetizing, and clerks were too busy to wait on them.

With Huggie still tightly clutching her shopping bag, on their way out, they passed the frozen food section. Don reached in and pulled out two frozen turkey dinners.

THE TREE WAS PLACED in a corner of the den where it could be seen while sitting on the couch in front of the crackling fire. After wrapping gifts, Don and Huggie popped corn in an old fashioned popper. Huggie held the long handle and kept the basket filled with yellow kernels over the hot coals her father had raked to the front of the fireplace. She jumped up and down and yelled, "Yuck, yuck," as the kernels exploded into a fluffy white mass.

They settled onto the couch with a bowl of popcorn resting between them. The tape of "Frosty the Snowman" was in the VCR. As Huggie was getting ready to push the button on the remote, the doorbell rang.

"Benda, Benda," she shouted as she rushed to the door. When she opened the door, Brenda was standing there holding a large package. Huggie led her into the den, talking rapidly in short choppy sentences about the tree and the gifts she had bought and wrapped herself. She picked up Brenda's gift and offered it to her.

"How sweet," Brenda said. "First I want you to see what I brought you. She broke away from Huggie and shortly returned with the large package she had dropped at the door.

Huggie jumped up and down, clapping. "Can I unwrap it now? Can I?"

"Brenda may want you to wait until the morning. It isn't Christmas yet, you know," Don said.

"I want her to open it whenever she wants to," Brenda said in a tone that suggested that the matter was between her and Huggie.

Huggie had torn off enough wrapping paper to see that it was a stuffed bear almost as large as she was. She quickly ripped off the remainder of the paper and shout, "Huggie Bear! He Huggie Bear!"

"He already has a name," Brenda said. "See the tag around his neck? It says, 'Theodore Bearington.' I think he may want you to call him 'Teddy' for short."

Huggie would have none of it. "He Huggie Bear," she said.

"But I thought you were Huggie Bear," Brenda laughed. "How will you know whether your mo…How will you know whether people are talking to you or the bear?"

Huggie thought for a moment, realizing Brenda had a point. "Then I just call him 'HeBear,'" she said. She squeezed the bear and said, "Luff you, luff you." Then she dropped the bear and ran to Brenda, hugged her and said over and over, "Luff you, luff you."

Don was afraid that when Brenda saw the tacky necklace she would be offended, thinking it was what prominent whites thought African-Americans would love. But as she gently removed it from the box, her eyes dampened and she said, "This is the most beautiful gift I've ever received. I'll wear it often, and when I do I will think of you, Huggie."

Don made hot chocolate while Brenda and Huggie popped fresh popcorn. The three sat together on the couch with Huggie snuggled up close to Brenda while holding HeBear on her other side.

An hour later, after Don and Brenda had tucked Huggie into bed, Don walked Brenda to her car parked on the street in front of the house. He started to give her a good night hug, but thought better of it as a car passed and slowed down. Neighbors weren't used to seeing an expensive sports car driven by a young African-American lady parked in front of the Hazelhurst house.

"Merry Christmas," Brenda said as she slid onto the seat.

"And to you, too," Don said, holding the door open, waiting for her to put the keys in the ignition.

"And get some rest," Brenda said. "Huggie will have you up early in the morning."

"I know," Don replied. "And there's work left to do. I hope I can have the train and other toys put together before she gets up. This is the first year my older daughter hasn't been here to assemble the toys. I don't know that I have the skill to do it."

Brenda pushed the door open, shoved Don aside, and started toward the house. "Come on, I'll help."

TWO HOURS LATER THE TRAIN was in place and circling through the den, into the hallway, through the dining room, and back into the den. Don had watched Brenda assemble it as well as other toys.

When she finished and started to leave, Don said, "Let's have a glass of wine before you go. I have a bottle of white in the refrigerator and a bottle of red in the cupboard."

"I would love a glass of wine," Brenda said as she went toward the refrigerator. She opened the freezer door, hoping Don would think it was by mistake. Two frozen turkey dinners were all that were inside. The refrigerator contained only the wine, a few beers and some milk.

They sat on the couch with a couple of feet of space between them. Neither spoke as they gazed at the sparkling fire.

Several minutes went by. "I've known about your family all of my life," said Brenda. "Before I went to Columbia to live with my father

I often went with Mama or one of my older sisters when they worked for one of your brothers in his huge home. I suspect that few if any in your family remember me, or even that Geraldine had a bastard child when she was nearly fifty."

Don didn't know how to respond so he sat quietly.

Brenda continued. "But your wife might remember me. When I was about eight or nine, she was having trouble with her cleaning service and asked Mama to help her for a few days. Mama didn't want to because after Mrs. Hazelhurst fired her and my sisters several years before, she told all over town that she had had enough of that lazy, no account crowd. Made it harder for Mama and my sisters to get work. But Mama needed the money so she agreed to help if she could bring me along because she had no one to leave me with.

"It was miserably hot and I spent the first day watching Jeff and Megan splash around in the pool. The next day, without Mama noticing, I slipped on an extra pair of pants under my flimsy dress. When Mrs. Hazelhurst drove off with the children in the car, I slipped off my dress and one pair of panties, and got in the shallow end of the pool. It was the first time ever I had water to cover my entire body.

"I had planned to abandon the wet panties in the bushes, put on the dry panties and my dress and be out of the pool before Mrs. Hazelhurst and the children returned. But the water felt so good on that scorching hot day, I stayed in longer than I should. Before I knew it, the car pulled back into the driveway. I jumped out of the pool and tried to hide behind the shrubbery, but it was too late. Mrs. Hazelhurst saw me and I guess the sight of an almost naked little black girl in her children's swimming pool was more than she could handle. She snatched me from behind the shrubbery and dragged me into the house where Mama was working. I don't remember what she was saying, but she ordered Mama to take me, get out of the house and never set foot in there again. She wouldn't even let us get my dress from beside the pool, and she never paid Mama, although she had worked a day and a half.

"I remember walking home wearing nothing but wet panties. I cried all the way thinking Mama would blister my bottom when we got home. But she didn't. She took me in her arms, pulled me close and whispered, 'I love you. Everything's going to be all right.' She had tears in her eyes."

Brenda laughed. "I've always wished I had peed in that pool. But I'm sure she had it drained and disinfected before she let the children get back in it."

Don placed his hand on top of Brenda's and whispered, "I'm so sorry. I never knew. Sabrina never talked to me much and the children never mentioned the incident. They were probably too embarrassed by their mother's tantrum."

Brenda raised the wine glass to her lips. She no longer sipped but took the two large swallows that remained without bringing the glass down. Don, who was holding his beer in his left hand, turned up the bottle and drained what remained.

"More wine?" Don asked. "I'll put another log on the fire."

"I must go," Brenda said. "It's past two in the morning. Since it's Christmas, I'm staying with Mama. If she wakes up and sees I'm not home she'll be worried.

"I'm worried about your driving home alone," Don said. "Shall I follow in my car to make sure you get there safely?"

"Oh no," Brenda said. "Stay here with Huggie. When I get inside the door at home, I'll call you. You don't need to answer. I'll hang up after the second ring and you'll know that I am there safely. Should I not call within fifteen minutes, call the police and suggest they have a cruiser check by the house."

For the second time that night, Don held the car door open for Brenda. This time she quickly slid under the steering wheel and drove away.

Chapter 12

HUGGIE WAS STANDING by her father's bed long before daybreak. "Christmas, Christmas!" she said loudly while jumping up and down. Don rolled out of bed. He needed to go to the bathroom, but that would have to wait. He followed his daughter down the stairs and into the den.

Huggie stopped at the bottom of the stairs, stared at the presents, then started toward the train.

"There'll be plenty of time for the train later," Don said. "Let's open some of the presents first."

The package from Megan was a cowboy suit; the one from Jeff was a Barbee doll in a ballerina outfit.

Don watched his daughter go from present to present for an hour before he went to the kitchen to start the pancakes. If she noticed there was no present from her mother, she didn't mention it.

HUGGIE SAT AT THE HEAD OF THE TABLE with HeBear on her right. She insisted he also be served a pancake. Don put two on her plate, one carved like a bear. She wouldn't eat it, but put it in the freezer to keep as a toy. She ate the other one and also the one in front of HeBear, pretending he was eating it.

After spending all morning with her Christmas presents, Huggie was getting tired. Don slipped a Christmas video in the VCR and flopped down in his leather chair. Huggie watched for a few minutes before she was asleep on the rug in front of the TV. The frozen turkey dinners were in the oven, but would not be ready for another hour. Within minutes, Don was also asleep.

Huggie woke up on the first ring of the doorbell and staggered to the door. Don followed.

Brenda, wearing the necklace Huggie had given her, was standing at the door, looking bright and happy, and holding a large basket. "All right troops," she said, "time for Christmas dinner. Christmas is not a time to eat frozen dinners. You need real turkey and dressing, ham, baked sweet potatoes, turnips and collards, and oyster casserole. Maybe even a little chicken bog. And for dessert, fruit cake and pumpkin pie."

Don and Huggie watched in disbelief as Brenda walked by them, carrying the basket of food to the dining room table.

"Brenda, you shouldn't have done this," Don said.

"Why not?" Brenda answered with a laugh. "We folks on the southeast end of town need to look after the underprivileged, especially on Christmas. My family may be half starving, and not have a pot to p…" She looked at Huggie and then turned to Don and continued. "You know what I mean. But on Christmas, we always have more than we can eat. So Mama wanted you all to have this. It's better than letting it go to waste. Sorry we don't have cranberry sauce for the turkey. We use strawberry preserves that Mama cans in the spring. These collards are a little cold, but it'll only take a minute to warm them in the microwave. They're great, especially if you have the right kind of vinegar to pour on them."

Brenda poured coffee from a thermos and set it in front of Don. "Mama's coffee will put hair on your chest," she said. She then poured half a cup for herself. "Thanks for inviting me to have Christmas dinner with you," she said in jest. "But I'm already stuffed. I'll just sit here and watch you all eat. If you don't eat like you are starving, it'll hurt my feelings."

Don and Huggie had no difficulty in assuring her feelings were not hurt.

After she finished eating, Huggie gave Brenda a hug, and returned to her toys in the den. Don and Brenda remained at the table sipping coffee.

"Have you ever considered sending Huggie to a public school?" Brenda asked.

"Oh no," Don said. "Neither Jeff nor Megan attended a public school. In this day and time, people who can afford it send their children to private schools."

Brenda was taken aback knowing that a lot of whites considered public schools in the area inferior because they were predominantly black. But she tried not to show any reaction. "Well, you could put her in a private school then," she said. "She needs to associate with normal children and get normal schooling. I've checked the Internet on Down Syndrome. The more normal the lives of children with Down Syndrome, the more normal they are." Then she added, "And another thing. I haven't seen a computer in the house. Are you not online?"

"Not here at the house. There are computers at the office. I've never learned how to work them. Sabrina wasn't interested. Jeff and Megan had computers in their rooms and took them with them when they moved away."

"Huggie would love a computer, and she could learn to use it. She could send and receive emails and there are a lot of computer games that are educational."

They cleared the table. Brenda wrapped some of the left over turkey and ham in plastic and put it in the freezer. She put other left over food in the disposal. After rinsing the plates and placing them in the dishwasher, she picked up the basket. "Well, Doctor Hazelhurst, I need to be going. Tomorrow's a work day."

Huggie was sound asleep among the scattered gift wrappings under the tree with HeBear clutched to her chest.

"I can't leave without telling Huggie good-bye and I don't want to wake her," Brenda said

"This means you'll have to wait awhile," Don said. "Have a seat. I have a little wine left. I'll get you a glass."

Don returned from the kitchen with a glass of wine for Brenda and a glass of water for himself. He sat on the end of the couch near Brenda's chair. They sat quietly for several minutes. The only noise was the heavy breathing of Huggie asleep amid the Christmas gifts and discarded wrapping paper under the tree.

Don spoke first, choosing his words carefully. "In the last few days you've done so much for Carol and me, at a time when we needed someone desperately. You've made her Christmas special, and you've cushioned my fall into a valley of deep despair. I wish there was something I could do to repay you."

Brenda's eyes dampened. "If you reach out to somebody with an act of kindness, expecting it will be repaid, it becomes like a commercial transaction and the joy of doing it is gone. Whatever I do for you and Huggie, I do also for myself."

"I would enjoy knowing more about your past." Don said. "I won't ask, but if you feel like sharing it with me, I'll listen, and nothing you can tell me will change how I feel about you."

"Oh, I don't mind talking about my background, but it's not a pretty story. Everybody around here knows most of what there is to know about the prominent Hazelhurst family. So, I guess it's only fair that you know more about me. There are no similarities.

"My father was a railroad worker in Columbia. When the great flood took out a section of the railroad track across the Pee Dee River, his crew was sent here to repair it. It took several weeks, and the railroad pulled some sleeper cars onto an abandoned side track here in town for the workers to live in. It also provided a diner car where the men could eat breakfast and dinner and be given a boxed lunch to take with them for lunch. Mama was one of the local women hired to cook. She and my father became friends. He was much younger and they never planned to marry, but they did have an affair. Mama thought she was too old to get pregnant, but she was wrong, which was fortunate for me, or unfortunate, depending on how you look at it.

"From the beginning, my father acknowledged I was his child, and sent checks for support. He also visited often and we would go to the movies or to the park. When I was six, he took me to Disney World. I adored him. When I was ten, he asked Mama if I could live with him. She agreed because he could do so much for me. The schools in Columbia were better. He had a nice house in a nice section of town and a good salary. It was like I had fallen into a pot of honey. I made a lot of friends, had nice clothes, ate well and was given generous amounts of spending money. Daddy insisted I take dance lessons, swimming lessons, even tennis lessons. I became quite good in all of them.

"But there was a problem. My father started treating me as if I were his wife instead of his daughter. When I first moved in, he wanted me to sleep in the bed with him. He said he didn't want me to be frightened. Even though I was a child, I thought it strange, especially since there were two other bedrooms, one of which he had decorated with all sorts of frilly things. He called it my bedroom and that's where I kept my clothes and personal things, but not where he would let me sleep. When we had visitors he would show them the room and tell them it was my room.

"From the beginning he slept close to me. I would move to the edge of the bed and he would reach out and pull me back close to him After about a year he started giving me what he called massages, and then, well I'll skip a lot of stuff. When I was twelve, I went to my own bed. He begged me to come back to his, and when I wouldn't, he started sleeping in mine. Although he repeatedly abused me, I was thirteen when he raped me. I cried and begged him to stop but there was no stopping him. When it was over, I was crying and bleeding profusely. He tried to be kind. He brought towels and told me everything was going to be all right. He said he was just trying to prepare me for my husband.

"I was too embarrassed to tell anyone, even Mama. I was also afraid no one would believe me. It continued every couple of nights.

"Finally, I decided to run away. I planned to slip a bag of clothes out and hide it in the hedges. I had enough money for a bus ticket. I planned to leave the next day, after school. In the meantime, I could not bear to think of it happening again.

"I took his 45 caliber pistol from the drawer in his room where I knew he kept it and put it under my pillow. I never planned to shoot him, just to scare him away.

"When he came to my bed that night, I begged him, 'Please Daddy, please stay away.' He wasn't about to stop. He had no pants on and he was steaming. I pulled the gun from under my pillow and, holding it with both hands, pointed it directly at his face. He yelled something like, "What the hell you doing with my gun!' and lunged onto the bed grabbing for it. I don't know whether I pulled the trigger or he grabbed it and caused it to accidentally discharge. All I remember is a loud noise and a flash of light.

"For several minutes, I was so stunned I didn't know where I was. When I came around, my father's dead body was draped across mine. Blood was splattered all over the room, even onto the ceiling, and brains were draining from the hole in his head."

Don placed his hand on top of Brenda's.

"The police came. I was too hysterical to tell them what happened. They took me to a juvenile detention center and locked me up. It was three days before a lawyer came to see me. Mr. Siegel had been appointed to represent me, and he turned out to be an angel. He had a social worker interview me and insisted I be examined in the hospital. The examination confirmed that, not only had I been raped repeatedly, but that I was pregnant. Mama came and authorized an abortion. They removed half my insides, even removed my appendix while they were at it."

Don whispered repeatedly, "I'm so sorry. You poor child."

Brenda continued. "The story improves some, but there are other ugly parts. I have no libido and am turned off by the thought of sex. Not a good condition for someone who would love to have children. I had a boy friend for a while when I was in law school. It turned out he was more interested in sex than anything I had to offer. After he tried to rape me, I gave up on men. Now I'm having to deal with another mean one. Dawg Brinson is an ass in every way it is possible to be an ass. He knows no shame."

Paper began to rustle under the tree, as Huggie was waking up. She wiped her eyes and yawned as she walked in front of Brenda and opened her arms. Brenda leaned over and took Huggie in hers.

"You crying Benda. Why you crying?"

Don answered, "Maybe she's been laughing. You can get tears from laughing as well as from crying."

Huggie looked at her father and said, "You been crying, too."

Don picked his daughter up and sat her on the couch next to him. "It's Christmas, a time to be happy. Sometimes happiness brings tears just like sadness does. And we have so much to be happy about,"

Chapter 13

MIKE GUNNED THE HIGH POWERED Jaguar west on Highway 501. There were shorter routes to Interstate 95, but he was in no mood to drive his way through narrow roads and sleepy little towns where the power of his Jag would be meaningless. He was in a hurry, as if trying to escape, and he would make up in speed for the greater distance. But he had to be careful. With cocaine and marijuana under his seat, he couldn't afford to be stopped.

He planned to drive straight to Daytona, the site of the first race of the year and also the home of his crew chief and best friend, George Givens. He had a lot of fans but few good friends. George was the best among the few he had, like an older brother, or even a father.

At Florence, Mike got on I-95 and drove south. It was almost devoid of traffic late on Christmas Eve. He set his cruise control at 79, trusting that at less than ten miles over the limit he wouldn't be stopped. Soon he overtook two cars traveling side by side at no more than 60 miles an hour. He pulled in behind the car in the left lane and flashed his lights. Neither car changed positions. The drivers seemed to enjoy keeping him behind them with a running roadblock. He leaned out the window and yelled, "Get out of my way, you sons of bitches!"

Frustration soon turned to anger and instinctively Mike accelerated enough to tap the rear bumper of the car in front. Then he did it a second and third time, each time with a little more force. The car in front slowed and moved to the shoulder of the road. The driver was an old man, probably too old to be driving late at night, but not too old to see the "Car 49" on Mike's license plate. It would take only a brief glance to see it and know it was the car number of the state's most famous race car driver.

The road ahead was clear and Mike was no longer trying to stay close to the speed limit. Within seconds, the needle on the speedometer was bouncing off 110 mph. He saw no lights in his rear view mirror, so he began to breathe easier. Perhaps he could make it to Daytona in time to have dinner with George and his family. But as he passed the next exit, he saw a patrol car with blue lights flashing, moving rapidly down the ramp onto I-95. It fell in behind him with sirens blaring.

Mike thought of the drugs under his seat as he pushed the accelerator to the floor. Slowly, he began to put space between him and the trooper, but he knew that somewhere ahead, there would be a roadblock. He took the next exit and at the top of the ramp, turned left with his tires squealing. He quickly made another left turn onto Highway 301, hoping the trooper would not expect him to reverse directions and head back the way he had been driving.

There was no sign of the patrol car as he turned off 301 onto a rural paved road, and then left onto a graveled road, through a field, around an old abandoned house covered with kudzu, and into some dense woods. By the time the road emerged from the woods into a cleared area, it was little more than two ruts, which ended at the yard of a small old weather beaten one story house. A frail looking

Christmas tree stood on the front porch. A single strand of lights gave off the only light in the area.

Mike began to relax, feeling he was in such a remote and forsaken area he was safe from his pursuers. He turned around, drove back to the wooded area on the other side of the field, and pulled as far off the road as he could.

He took the marijuana from under the seat and rolled a joint. As he pulled the smoke deep into his lungs, he relaxed, completely sure he had lost his pursuers. Before he drifted off to sleep, he silently repeated a curse. Damn that woman's hide. Why did I ever get tangled up with her? All of this is her fault.

DAYLIGHT WAS BARELY BREAKING when Mike woke up on Christmas morning. It took a while for him to remember where he was and how he got there. Suddenly he saw something that sent shivers up and down his spine. A truck with search lights on the cab was sitting in the yard of the old house. He shivered as he realized it could belong to a late working wrecker driver who lived in the hovel. Suppose the driver called the sheriff or 911 to report that a car with license number "Car 49," was sitting on private property off the main road with someone dead, drunk or just asleep inside.

The wheels of the Jaguar were just settling into the two ruts of the road when a car with blue lights flashing came toward it. Several other cars followed with multiple lights flashing and sirens blaring. The lead car clearly marked "Sheriff" pulled up until its bumper touched that of the Jaguar. Mike recognized the other cars as belonging to the state patrol. It seemed like only seconds before the Jaguar was surrounded by troopers with their weapons drawn.

Two men from the sheriff's car ran to the driver's side. The younger, a deputy, stood a few feet away with what appeared to be a sawed off shotgun pointed at Mike's face. Mike reached for the drugs under the seat. It was too late. The older man wearing the sheriff's badge was knocking on the window. Mike rolled it down.

As if in a single motion, the sheriff reached inside, unlocked the door and snatched it open. Before Mike could speak, handcuffs were clamped around both wrists and the sheriff was pulling him from the car. He shoved Mike against the hood and made him lean over with his hands stretched across the hood and his legs spread. Mike could feel a weapon pressed hard against the base of his spine as hands reached first in one pocket and then the other, removing all contents. Then the sheriff's hands moved all over Mike's body, including between his legs and over his crotch. Six troopers, their weapons drawn, watched curiously as the world's number one stock car racer submitted to the humiliation.

There was a pause, which seemed to last for minutes. Finally, the sheriff said in a calm voice, "You can relax now, Mr. McMillan. I'm one of your fans, and was one of your daddy's before you. I 'member watching him go over the wall at Darlington in 1963. Sure thought he was a goner. But your old man was tough."

The troopers stared at Mike enviously like his fans do, but none asked for an autograph. One gave Mike a clue as to what they were thinking. "I was a fan of yours, Mr. McMillan, but what you did last night could have got me and some of my friends killed. Along with these other officers, I've spent all night looking for you, and here we are on Christmas morning missing the look on our children's faces as they find what Santa left for them."

The sheriff turned to the young trooper and said, "Mike did sort of get carried away, but let's not scold him. It ain't our job."

Mike felt better. The sheriff was a fan and his kind words suggested he was on his side.

The sheriff continued to sound sympathetic as he spoke in a soft voice, "By the way son, you don't mind if we search your car do you?"

Mike was about to say yes, when he remembered the drugs under the seat. Could he trust the friendly sheriff and the other officers to ignore them? Finally, he said in as polite a voice as he could, "I think I need to talk to a lawyer before I give you permission. I need to know what my rights are."

The sheriff shot back in a voice showing irritation, "You were read your rights, Mr. McMillan. Didn't you hear Deputy Greene here reading them to you while I searched you?"

Mike recalled some mumbling in the background, but he hadn't understood a word he heard. His mind had been on the huge hands of the sheriff and the humiliating search.

"Read him his rights again," the sheriff said to the deputy. "And this time, you better listen, Mr. McMillan!"

The young deputy held a flashlight over a card and read from it rapidly. The only thing Mike clearly understood was that he was entitled to a lawyer. Trying to avoid sounding arrogant, he said, "I can afford a lawyer and I want to call one now."

"There'll be plenty of time for that when we're done booking you," the sheriff said. "Right now we got to get a warrant to search your car. I sure hate to disturb Judge Webb on Christmas morning, but he's the only person left around here during the holidays who can sign a warrant. He'll be the judge to sentence you, and he'll be some kind of pissed when he learns you're the reason we have to interrupt his Christmas. But then, it ain't no skin off my ass."

IT WAS 8:00 A.M. when the phone beside Dawg Brinson's bed rang. His wife, who slept upstairs in a separate room, wasn't disturbed.

"Dawg here," Brinson answered.

An hour later, Dawg was making his way through television cameras and reporters camped outside the Florence county jail.

There were hundreds of questions, only one of which Dawg bothered to answer. "Are you going to represent Mike McMillan?"

"Depends on the color of his money," Dawg answered.

Moments later, Dawg sat in the small interview room across a table from a racing champion who was tired, scared and disheveled. Mike looked like anybody but the handsome young champion he prided himself on being.

"Thanks for coming," Mike said, "especially on Christmas morning."

"Christmas is no big deal at my house," Dawg replied. "No younguns, you know. To tell you the truth, it seems good to have something to do." He paused briefly before continuing. "I know you're in a heap of trouble, son. On the late news last night, they were telling about the officers chasing you. With your license plate having your race car number on it, everybody knew it was you they were after." Dawg continued. "I understand they have a warrant to search your car. Hope they don't find any drugs. Courts 'round here don't pay much attention to liquor. But drugs, well let's just say it riles 'em up as much as the Baptist preacher who caught two of his deacons sodomizing each other in a back pew during a prayer meeting."

"They may find a small amount of marijuana and a couple of sniffs of cocaine," Mike said, trying to conceal his anxiety.

"If they do, it'll be harder to keep your feet on the ground, son. But before we talk too much about the case, we need to seal our deal. I don't do much criminal work any more. Not enough money in it. At least not the kind of money I'm used to making. So I'm curious as to why you called me."

"I don't need a lawyer to prove I'm innocent. Even F. Lee Bailey couldn't do that. I need one to negotiate the best deal possible. I'll pay any size fine, stay on probation the rest of my life, do community service, anything but hard time. I've heard that you own some of the judges around here, so you're the best lawyer to help keep me out of prison."

Dawg blushed. "That ain't exactly true." Then he added with a little chuckle, "I do hold a first mortgage on some of 'em, but I can't say I own any outright. I understand what you mean though. I'm your best choice. Now let's see if we can come to terms. I'll have to have a retainer of a hundred grand to start with. Of course, you understand that's just the beginning. I'll bill you along the way as we go. And of course if you have to do time, I'll take that in consideration and my fee won't be as much."

"Anything," Mike said. "I just want to get this over with as quickly as possible."

"Whoa there cowboy," Dawg said. "We don't want a trial for at least a year. We need time to let the public cool down. The longer we wait, the more time it gives people to lose interest. So, I'll keep getting continuances. The TV reporters'll get tired of having to load up their equipment and leave the courthouse without a story and will stop showing up. So'll the press. One day a year or so down the road, I'll get a continuance at the beginning of court. Then after all the media people and everybody else has left, we'll change our mind and plead guilty. The judge'll announce a sentence we've already agreed to and we'll get out of there before you have to talk to anybody."

THE FOLLOWING MONDAY MORNING, Mike sat across the desk from Brinson, looking much better. He tossed a counter check on the desk. "Here's your 100K," he said. "Sorry I couldn't get hold of my accountant to get a check with my name printed on it. But I think the bank'll recognize my signature and honor the check, even if my account doesn't have that much money in it."

"I ain't worried, son," Dawg said. "You're in enough trouble without giving Dawg a no-count check. And speaking of trouble, boy, let me read you the charges they put against you. I asked the D. A. if these were all the charges and he said they were for now. I asked him if they didn't need to charge you with bucking a sheep while they were at it. Anyway, you're charged with felony hit and run. The old man you bumped in the ass claimed it caused him to have a sore neck. And he also claimed some of the shine was knocked off the bumper of his old car, so you're also charged with hit and run involving property damage. The next one is speeding 120 in a 70-mile-an-hour zone. There's careless and reckless driving, failure to stop for a flashing blue light, and trying to outrun a police officer. All kinds of shit. I'll get some of these consolidated and some dropped. I can work with the traffic charges. The drug charges'll be tougher."

"Drug charges?" Mike asked as if surprised.

"The marijuana and cocaine weighed enough to support charges that you possessed drugs with intent to sell 'em. It don't take much for the law to presume you had more than enough for your own use, so you must have intended to sell some of it. I can probably get the charges reduced to just simply possession, but it's still serious. It might not amount to much if you were in Myrtle Beach or Charleston, but in this county people won't put up with drugs."

Mike sat quietly as Dawg continued. "During the next year or so you got a lot of work to do, son."

"What do you mean?"

"Well for one thing, you got to go to a lot of meetings about not using drugs and things"

"What!" Mike exclaimed, almost coming out of his chair. "I'm no pothead. Those drugs had been in the car for over a year. I hadn't had a joint in months, and I've never taken more than three or four snorts of cocaine in my whole life, for Christ's sakes!"

"Now, now," Dawg said, "that sounds kinda like 'I didn't inhale,' don't you think? And speaking of Christ, you gonna have to start going to church."

"I only been inside a church once in my whole life and that was to go to my daddy's funeral. Me and my wife didn't even get married in a church. We just went over to the marriage place in Dillon one Saturday night."

"Well you need to do these things because if the judge and the public think you're perfect, then why'd you do all those bad things? They'll think it was because you don't give a shit, and people don't have sympathy for somebody that don't give a shit. But if you got a drug or liquor problem, admit it, and overcome it, they'll cut you some slack. So we're gonna act like you have a problem, even if you don't. We'll say it was the drugs that caused you to act so bad. We need the director of the drug rehabilitation place to testify or sign an affidavit saying you've been clean for a year and have renounced drugs forever, and we need a preacher to say you've come to Jesus and repented all your sins."

Blood rose in Mike's face as he became more and more disgusted. He was tempted to say, If I got to go through all that chicken shit, I'd just as soon do time.

But Dawg wasn't finished. "You also got to do some volunteer work to show that you're a sensitive, caring person."

"Can't I just give money, or pay somebody else to help?"

"Naw, won't work. You got to get down and dirty. Work at a homeless shelter, serve meals at the Salvation Army, or adopt a youngun. I'll think of something."

Both sat silently for several moments. Mike was noticeably upset at the prospect of having to do so many boring things.

"Tell you what," Dawg said. "The Civitan Club helps support this center for handicapped children over in Florence. Sometimes I see pictures in the paper of some of them playing with funny looking kids. You can join the Civitan Club. We could get some good press. The champion race car driver pictured with all those poor little creatures. It'll help show you're a changed man."

Chapter 14

SABRINA HAD VOWED she would stay sober through the Christmas holidays, but when she woke up with a throbbing headache the day after Christmas, the vodka bottle on the table beside her bed was empty. So was the other side of the bed.

"Maybe he's asleep on the couch," she said to herself as she struggled out of the bed and staggered to the bathroom. She popped several aspirin into her mouth and sent them down with a single swallow of water.

She made her way to the kitchen, bumping into furniture along the way. Only two beers remained in the refrigerator. She pulled one out and managed to pop off the cap. She turned it up and let half of it flow into her mouth, swallowing as if dying of thirst. After catching her breath, she drank the remaining half without taking the bottle from her lips. She tossed the empty bottle toward the trash container, but it crashed onto the floor, sending glass flying everywhere.

Maybe he's taking a walk on the beach, she thought as she staggered through the den toward the balcony. Her attention was drawn toward the coffee table as she bumped into it. A white sheet of paper lying on the table with a hundred dollar bill on top of it caught her eye. She snatched up the paper and dropped down on the couch. She had needed glasses for a long time, but was too vain to wear them. Contacts were impractical since she wouldn't be able to keep up with them. Holding the paper at arms length and squinting, she was able to make out the written note:

> *"I've had enough. Sorry. Why don't you go back to your husband and your kid? Here's a little money. It should be enough to get you back to Florence. Be out of the condo within thirty days."*
> *Mike 12/24*

Sabrina was so incensed by the reference to "your kid," that it was several seconds before the hard fact sunk in. Mike was gone, and she had no hook to bring him back. Her looks were fading fast, liquor had destroyed most of her libido and Mike was likely repulsed by her drunkenness. She was alone without any way to support herself. Except for a few dollars in her purse, the $100 Mike left her was all she had.

"Your kid, your kid," she kept mumbling to herself. "The son of a bitch won't acknowledge he's Huggie's father and he's suggesting I go back to Florence. He knows I'll never return to Don. He makes me sick. I don't know why, but it doesn't matter. When you loath someone, you can't change your feelings by admitting there's not a reason why. Leaving Don was as much to get rid of him as to be with Mike."

She found some pink, perfumed, very feminine stationary in a bedside drawer in the guest bedroom. It was not hers, but the fact another woman might at some time have shared the condo with Mike didn't bother her. The important thing was that there was pen and paper, envelopes and stamps. She scribbled letters to each of her two older children.

SKI CLASSES DIDN'T START until 9:30. Sam was still sleeping when Megan slipped out of the apartment with her snowboard early on the last day of the year. The crush of holiday vacationers had meant double overtime for the servers at the Hibernian restaurant where she worked, so she had had little time for herself. Today she was determined to get in a couple of hours on the slopes before reporting to the restaurant for lunch duty.

The lifts started a couple of hours before they were opened to skiers, so members of the ski patrol, workers at the summit restaurants and others who worked on the mountain could ride up ahead of the crowds. All of the staff knew Megan as Sam's partner so no one stopped her as she got on the lift with her snowboard.

The lift ended at mid-point of the mountain. She snowboarded from there to the lift that went to the summit where it unloaded skiers almost into Glacier National Park. Sunrise was still several minutes away, but plenty of light already reflected off the freshly groomed slopes.

Megan was alone on the mountain, which was clear of cats and snowmobiles. She looked down the mountain, toward Whitefish Lake and saw nothing but the gray clouds, which had closed like a curtain behind her as she ascended on the chair lift. But she wasn't really alone. Snow ghosts, scattered throughout the snow-covered slopes, were poised as if guarding the mountain from unwanted intruders. Steamboat Springs has its barn, Vail its clock, and Telluride the old Sheridan Hotel and the bank which Butch Cassidy once robbed. Every ski resort has charming features that help distinguish it. At Big Mountain, it's snow ghosts. They form as fog rises from Whitefish Lake below and spreads across the mountain. It freezes as it hits bushes and branches of trees, leaving them looking like fluffy white clouds resembling whatever your imagination sees in them.

Megan spoke to some of the snow ghosts as she glided high above them, whispering softly, "Good morning, you guys." She recognized Tony the tiger, Willy, the whale, a camel, a giraffe, a gorilla, and her favorite, the Wizard of Oz. They looked so light and fluffy, it was tempting to ski up to one and wrap your arms around it, but though they were white and looked like snow, they were really ice, and in some places, as sharp as razors. Skiers were warned not to touch them.

When she skied off the lift, she paused to look at the sun rising over the mountains in front of her. She was on top of the world. Nothing could spoil the day. She headed for a black diamond slope with the snowboard making a sweet sound as it cut through the crust on top of the snow.

Megan was still on a Rocky Mountain high when she got to the restaurant four hours later. But as she was putting on her server's uniform, the manager handed her a letter. It had been delivered to the restaurant, which was the only address her mother had.

Dear Megan,

I've thought of you constantly, especially over the Christmas holidays, but I have been too sick to call or shop for gifts. You must know by now that your father and I are separated and will be getting a divorce. Until the separation agreement has been completed, I have no money. It hurts to ask you and Jeff for help, but there is no one else for me to turn to."

Mom and Dad separated? Megan shivered as the thought penetrated like a knife to the pit of her stomach. It wasn't that she was surprised. But when an institution like a family, even a dysfunctional one, crumbles, there is pain. Why didn't they tell me? How long has it been? Where's Huggie? If Mom has her, Dad will die, and Mom too, if she has to care for her.

Megan ran to the phone. Her hands were shaking so that it took three tries for her to punch in the correct numbers.

The phone rang in the Hazelhurst home three thousand miles away.

"Yes," Don answered softly. Usually Megan would be thinking. "Why the hell doesn't he answer more assertively, say, 'Dr. Hazelhurst,' or even a firm 'hello.'" But this time the emotions flooding her body left no room for trivial thoughts.

"Dad, Dad," Megan said as her voice broke. "I just got a letter from Mom. I'm, I'm so sorry. Why didn't you tell me?"

Her father replied. "I assumed your mother told you before she left, and then when I didn't hear from you or Jeff at Christmas, I hoped it was because you all were with her."

"No, no Dad. Neither Jeff nor I would ever take sides. We love you both. And Huggie? Please tell me Huggie is all right."

"Hughie's right here. We had a good Christmas. I know she misses her mother but she seldom mentions her. Maybe it's because of a new friend she seems to care for so much. Her name is Brenda. She's Geraldine's oldest daughter. She was especially kind to us during Christmas."

"Brenda? I remember Brenda. She used to come with her mother to help clean. She was a little older than Jeff and I. Something happened and Mom ran her and Geraldine off. I never knew what it was, but then Mom ran off most of the help she had. Is Brenda cleaning for you now?"

Don hesitated. There was no need to explain now. There were more important things to talk about. Besides, what could he tell

Megan about his and Huggie's relationship with Brenda that she would understand.

"Not on a regular basis," he replied, then quickly changed the subject. "How's your mother? Could you tell by her letter?"

"All she said is that she desperately needs money. I don't have money to send her, and I doubt if Jeff does either. Why are you not giving her money, Dad? It's so unlike you."

How could he send Sabrina anything when he didn't know where she was and her lawyer had ordered him not to contact her? He had suggested to his lawyer that they give her lawyer some money to pass along to her, and he had said, "That's not the way it's done. When it's time to write a check, I'll let you know."

Don wanted to explain this to his daughter, but he choked up and had a hard time saying anything. Finally, he was able to say in a breaking voice, "I'll call the bank right now and have them transfer $5000 to your account. You can send some of it, or all of it to your mother. And you can tell her that her credit cards are still good. I haven't cancelled them even though my lawyer suggested that I do."

IT WAS LATE AFTERNOON ON January 2nd when Jeff returned to his SoHo loft apartment after a six-week holiday tour with the ballet company. The apartment was lonely. He would like a companion, but he couldn't decide whether it be male or female. At times, he was tempted to start cruising gay bars, but thoughts of HIV and AIDS made him hesitate. Another reason he didn't start trolling the gay community was that he hoped he might meet a woman who would arouse latent heterosexual feelings he hoped existed somewhere deep in his soul. He wanted children, perhaps a son he could name after his father.

The mailbox was full and several packages were stacked underneath. The one on top was from Huggie. "Bless her heart. I can't wait to see the present she sent me." But before dealing with the packages, he pulled a double handful of mail from the box, anxious to see what bills were overdue. Some sweet smelling perfume from a letter in a pink, very effeminate envelope caught his attention. He recognized the handwriting as that of his mother. He ripped open the letter. Huggie's present would have to wait. Everything would have to wait.

DON WAS STARTLED by the emotional voice of his son on the other end of the line. "Dad, dad, I'm sorry, so sorry. I love you both and would never take sides. But Mom is the one who needs me most now. Do you know how I can reach her?"

"No," Don said, trying to appear calm. "Her lawyer has ordered me not to contact her. I couldn't anyway, because I have no idea where she is or how to get in touch with her. Her lawyer is James Brinson in Darlington. He might give you her number."

NO ONE ANSWERED THE PHONE at the Brinson residence. A call to the law firm got only a recording saying they would open for business the following morning. If only Jeff's mother had a close friend, or relative who stayed in touch.

What about the race car driver, Jeff wondered? She was such a fan of a particular driver. In fact, from time to time, he and Megan got whiffs of rumors that their mother was having an affair with him. But what was his name? They had met only once, after a race his mother had virtually dragged him to.

Within minutes of finding a list of race car drivers on the Internet, the name of Mike McMillan jumped out. That was it; he was ninety percent certain.

A search of telephone numbers for McMillans living in the Darlington area turned up several with the name Michael, Mike or with an "M" initial.

The first three dials brought curt answers. "No, no race driver lives here." The next two reached an answering machine.

A woman answered his fifth dial. Jeff could tell she was inebriated. "Why do you want to know?" She responded when asked if a race driver named Mike McMillan lived there.

"I'm trying to reach my mother, Sabrina Hazelhurst, and I thought that Mr. McMillan might know where she is. She's a fan of his."

"Fan!" the voice slurred. "She's his whore. They been shacking up for years. Have a condominium in Myrtle Beach. Tried to keep it a secret, but my lawyer's detective found it and hid a video camera in their bedroom. Caught them in the act. Your mama's a tramp."

Jeff almost threw up. But at least the conversation confirmed that his mother was in trouble. She must have had an affair with McMillan and he left her. Otherwise, why would she need money?

"Can you please give me the address and telephone number of the condominium?" Jeff begged.

"Of course, I got it from the detective. My lawyer told me to keep my ass away from there, but I guess there's nothing wrong with your interrupting their little party. Mike deserves some more trouble. I'm sure you've heard about the trouble he's already in: possessing drugs, trying to outrun cops, all kinds of things. It couldn't happen to a more deserving son of a bitch."

As Jeff expected, no one answered the phone at the condo. But he had the address.

Flight schedules required changes in Charlotte, then Columbia or Charleston, some even in Atlanta. He couldn't get there on a commercial airliner before the next day.

He pulled a phone number out of his billfold. It was written on a piece of napkin, which had been in his billfold since shortly after he came to New York. Ernest ("Ernie") Fletcher was a well-known bachelor and patron of the arts, especially ballet. He was heir to an oil fortune and had never had to work. Although he had never formally come out of the closet, his sexual orientation was well known. Jeff met Ernie at a party for the ballet company shortly after Jeff joined. Ernie jotted his number on a napkin and handed it to Jeff, saying, "Call me, young man, if I can ever do anything for you."

ERNIE WAS EXCITED TO HEAR Jeff's voice and happy he would ask him for a favor. He didn't ask why he needed to get to Myrtle Beach so quickly, but simply said, "Go to General Aviation at LaGuardia and ask for my pilots, Jim and Nelson. I'll call and make certain they have my jet ready."

Jeff quickly threw his shaving kit and a few items of clothing in a backpack and headed out the door. The mail and packages remained unopened on the kitchen table.

Chapter 15

JEFF WAS GETTING READY to ring the doorbell when he noticed the door was ajar. The lock had not been repaired since the firemen broke in. Moments later, he burst into his mother's room and saw her lifeless body stretched across her bed. He reached for the phone before going to her. "Probably an overdose," he said to the 911 operator.

An offensive odor, like a toilet had overrun filled the room. Sabrina was lying face down. Jeff rolled her over and breathed a sigh of relief when he noticed she was breathing, though barely. He shook her and got no response, so he gathered her in his arms. When he lifted her from the bed, he saw that the place where she had been lying was badly soiled, as were her clothes.

Jeff dragged his unconscious mother to the bathroom and into the combination tub and shower. He held her up against his body and turned the cold water on full blast. He was unmindful that he and his clothes were being drenched as he held her face up so it would catch the full force of the flowing cold water. She began to shake and to breathe in short, gasping breaths.

As he turned the water off, he heard a siren approaching from a block away. He quickly carried his mother into the guest bedroom and put her on the unsoiled bed. When he went to her bedroom to get fresh clothes, he saw two pill bottles on the nightstand beside the bed and put them in his pocket.

Before Jeff could remove his mother's clothes, two medics with a stretcher ran in. Within seconds, they had Sabrina strapped to the stretcher and were headed out the door. Jeff ran after them and handed one of them the pill bottles. "Please take these. The emergency room doctors may find them important."

Jeff stood in the doorway almost in a trance as he listened to the siren fade into the distance. He glanced at his watch and was surprised to see that it was slightly after midnight, only a few hours since he read his mother's letter. Another hour and it would have been too late. It may have been anyway. He picked up his backpack, which he had dropped by the door. Even in his haste to pack, he had put in a change of clothes. He pulled off his soaked clothes and threw them in the washer. After putting on a dry pair of slacks and a shirt, he walked onto the balcony and breathed in the ocean air. The pure cool air was quite a contrast to the foul smell inside the condo.

After about thirty minutes, he called the hospital and identified himself as the son of the lady admitted to the emergency room with a drug overdose.

"Your mother has been revived," he was told. "But she'll have to stay here for two or three days, or longer if someone doesn't agree to be responsible for her bills."

IT WAS MID-MORNING, and Don was grinding away on a molar when Mrs. McCoy stuck her head in the room. "Your son's on the phone. Says he desperately needs to talk with you."

Don handed the drill to his nurse and whispered to the patient, "Excuse me. I'll be right back. You can probably use a breather anyway."

Jeff skipped the details and got right to the essentials. His mother was in the hospital recovering from a suicide attempt. She was expected to recover, but had no place to go from the hospital. She has no money and no insurance. She's told people at the hospital that not getting paid would serve them right for having revived her.

"She's mistaken about not having insurance," Don said. "We're not divorced. In fact, we aren't even legally separated. No separation papers have been signed. She's still covered under my family policy. Wait at the hospital. I'll cancel my appointments for this afternoon, and Carol and I will be there within a couple of hours. I'll handle your mother's expenses."

SABRINA LOOKED LIKE a different person than the woman Jeff drenched in the shower six hours earlier. She looked tired and sad, but had on a clean gown, her hair had been washed and combed, and she had on a touch of make up.

She didn't speak when Jeff came in, but she did open her arms. He bent over and gently took her hand in his. "I'm sorry," she whispered.

"Let's not worry about the past," Jeff answered in a soft voice. "Think only of the future, and always remember, you have three children who love you dearly and will always be there for you no matter what."

Sabrina pretended to listen, but her mind was elsewhere. Finally, she started talking, softly, as if to herself. "I'm in love with Mike. I have been for a long time. And he was in love with me. We planned to get married. Now he's gone. It hurts to be rejected by someone you love. He didn't even say good-bye. He left me a curt note telling me to be out of the condo within a month. He left me with only a hundred dollars and told me to go back to Florence, as if that were an option. He knows I'll never return to Don. The alternative, which I tried unsuccessfully, appeals to me more."

Jeff listened, but didn't respond. It wasn't a time to challenge his mother's feelings. But her words hurt. "I'll leave now, Mom, so you can get some rest. Dad and Huggie will be here for me shortly. I'll stay with them until you get well, and I'll visit everyday."

WHEN JEFF STEPPED OFF THE ELEVATOR in the lobby, Huggie ran into his arms. "Luff you," she kept repeating. As he put his arms around his excited little sister, he wondered how he and his sister could possibly have stayed away from home on Christmas.

Huggie picked up HeBear, which she had dropped to give her brother a hug. "This is HeBear," she said as she handed the stuffed bear to Jeff. "Benda gave him to me."

Before Jeff could ask who Benda was, he saw his father sitting in the business office across the hall in front of the desk of a serious looking woman, signing some papers in front of him.

As he took Huggie's hand and walked toward the office, he heard his father say to the woman, "Please see that she gets whatever she needs. I'll guarantee all of her expenses."

"Thank you Dr. Hazlehurst," the woman replied. "I have your address and telephone number. I'll be in touch if we need anything else. I expect she'll be here for another couple of days, and her psychiatrist will probably want to talk with you, or whoever in the family will be caring for her at home."

AS SOON AS THEY ENTERED the house, Huggie pulled her brother up the stairs and into her room. The Barbee Ballerina he had given her was sitting on the dresser. She showed him all of the costumes and slippers that came with the doll. Then she pulled him back downstairs to see her other Christmas gifts. He watched as she

105

rode her train around the circle three times, holding HeBear in her lap with one arm while alternating between ringing the bell and blowing the whistle with her free hand."

Jeff saw the new computer and said excitedly, "Great, now we can email each other."

"Santa didn't bring the computer," Huggie said. "Benda said we needed one so Daddy bought it."

It was near midnight when Huggie was finally tucked into bed and on her way to sleep.

On their way downstairs, Jeff asked his father, "Who is Benda who Huggie talks about so much? She must be a special friend."

"Brenda is Geraldine's youngest daughter. Geraldine had her bring Huggie home from the Center the day I got the letter from your mother's lawyer saying she would not be returning. I wasn't in any condition to go after her myself. They've became friends."

"Well, why don't you hire her to work here full time? As I recall Geraldine and her other daughters were pretty good maids and cooks, although Mom didn't get along with them. But then she didn't get along with anybody who worked for us."

"Oh, Brenda isn't a maid," Don said. "She's a bright, well educated young lawyer with the Brinson Law Firm in Darlington."

"What!" Jeff exclaimed in disbelief. "Geraldine has a daughter who's a lawyer? For heaven's sake, I really have been gone from here a long time."

MEGAN WAS JUST GETTING HOME from work when her father called. "It's great to hear from you Dad. But I hope nothing's wrong. It's after midnight back there, I'm sure."

"Well nothing to get alarmed about. But there is some news you need to know. Jeff is home and on the phone in the kitchen. I'll hang up and let the two of you talk. Your mother doesn't want me in her life, so the responsibility for her rests with you and Jeff. I'll help with money, but that's all I can do."

For the next hour, Jeff and Megan talked about their mother, at times with sadness, and at other times with anger.

"How can we forgive her for the way she's treated Dad and Huggie?" Megan asked.

"It isn't easy," Jeff said. "But we have to intervene and try to save her. Suppose we wash our hands of her. What do you think will happen?"

Megan was crying. "I understand. She'll end up dead, or shacked up with someone even more wretched than the race car driver who dropped her. But it's late and I'm tired. I don't feel like making any decisions now. I'll fly home tomorrow and we can talk further. I think there's a morning flight out of Kalispell to Chicago. If I can get on it, I should be able to get a flight from there to Columbia or Charlotte. I'll give you a call and you can meet me."

WHEN JEFF GOT TO THE HOSPITAL the next morning his mother had moved to a room where she could smoke. She was sitting by an open window puffing away and trying to blow the smoke out the window. It was blowing back into the room, leaving it as filled with smoke as a cigar bar.

"Good morning, Mom. How do you feel?"

"Not half bad," she replied in a somewhat mocking voice. "When can I get out of this damn dump? The doctors are idiots, the nurses suck, and the food is worse than the slop Geraldine used to serve."

"First we have to decide where home for you will be. It can't be the condo. I went by this morning. The locks have been changed and your belongings were in the hallway. I have them in the car."

Sabrina lit a fresh cigarette with the butt of the one she was finishing. She pulled the smoke deep into her lungs and exhaled slowly. "Just get me some money and I'll be all right. There's a hotel in Darlington where you can rent rooms by the week. I can stay there. There are a couple of race drivers who've always wanted to be with me, but knew better than to make any passes as long as I was steady with Mike. I suspect they've heard by now that Mike and I have broken up. Either one of them will support me until I can reach a settlement with that wretched sperm donor of yours."

"Are they married?" Jeff asked

Sabrina answered in a voice suggesting that it wasn't important. "Probably. Isn't everybody? I don't know and I certainly don't care. If they're married but would rather be with someone else, they shouldn't be married. Anyway, what they do is their wives' problem, not mine."

Jeff changed the subject. "Mom, Megan is flying home today. I'll pick her up tonight and she'll be here to see you tomorrow. She and I will decide what to do with you. I can assure you, it won't be to put you in a cheap motel in Darlington to commit adultery with race car drivers who are interested in only one thing, and after a couple of days will no longer be interested in that."

"What the hell do you mean?" Sabrina asked. "When did you and Megan get to be my guardians? I'll decide what to do with me."

"No Mom, you won't," Jeff said firmly. "You're addicted to alcohol and lord knows what else. You've attempted suicide and at this point in your life are unstable. We can petition a court to have you involuntarily committed to an institution. The doctors and nurses will file affidavits. Megan and I will testify, and we'll subpoena Mike and your lawyer. Your conduct is enough for the judge to order you committed."

Sabrina sat quietly, finding it hard to believe that shy and effeminate Jeff was taking charge. If she weren't so pissed, she would be proud of his new found assertiveness. She started to say something, but before she could Jeff had reached the door.

He turned and faced his mother. "Megan and I will be here tomorrow. We'll let you know where you'll be going when you're released."

"The only way I'll go to an institution is in handcuffs and chains," Sabrina said.

"That can be arranged, but I hope it doesn't come to that. Incidentally, Mom, Huggie will be with us tomorrow, too."

"I don't want to see her." Sabrina said. "Leave her with Don. Let him take care of her"

"Her father loves her and does a good job of taking care of her," Jeff said. "But she has two parents."

"I said Don, not her father," Sabrina said. "There's a difference."

Jeff was half way down the hall and didn't hear her last remark.

JEFF AND MEGAN SPENT little time exchanging pleasantries about each other's recent experiences. They were anxious to resolve the difficult question of what to do with their mother.

Megan's voice broke as she spoke. "Mom's not a very lovable person. She's selfish and uncaring, even about her family. But she's my mother and I can't stand to see her suffer."

"I agree, Megan," Jeff replied. "Let's try to suppress our emotions so we can make the best decision possible. There aren't a lot of alternatives. We can insist that she return here and live with Dad and Huggie. Dad would take her back in a minute, and would, pardon my French, take whatever shit she threw at him. But she hates him so much she would do anything to hurt him. Suppose she were to decide to give suicide another try. She might want to take him with her, maybe Huggie, too. I had a horrible dream the other night that she set fire to the house and it burned to the ground with all three of them in it."

"Let's scratch that possibility. What's next?"

"We can have her committed to an institution. She would never go voluntarily, and it wouldn't be a pretty picture."

Megan was picturing her mother, handcuffed and restrained, and being dragged kicking and screaming into a dark cold asylum or mental hospital. The thought started tears flowing again.

When he saw his sister's reaction, Jeff responded. "The only alternative is for one of us to take her home with us. I'm sure Dad would give us the money to hire someone to take care of her while we work."

"In winters, where I live, snow banks along the streets are three or four feet high," Megan said. "Mom hates snow and cold weather. Sometimes the wind coming off Whitefish Lake cuts like a knife and there's nothing there that would interest her. Also Jeff, I'm in a committed relationship that I will let nothing threaten. I'm sure Mom would find it repulsive."

SABRINA WAS SITTING in a chair by the window when her two older children walked into the room. She wasn't smoking and looked better than she had the day before. She was looking at an old copy of *The New Yorker* magazine.

"Megan," Sabrina said as she got up and embraced her daughter. "It's so good to see both you children." As she stepped back, Megan's damp eyes looked into those of her mother. Her blue eyes, as usual, were dry and cold, reflecting no emotion.

"Mom, there's another child you know," Megan said. "Huggie's waiting downstairs. Would you like to see her?"

Sabrina didn't answer immediately, and it was apparent she was choosing her words carefully. "Of course I would like to see her, but it might not be a good idea. I've always felt she would be better off in a home for children like her. I'll never forgive your father for not agreeing to it. I guess that since I've always thought that someday she would be in an institution, I've never bonded with her."

There was a lot that Jeff and Megan wanted to say, but neither spoke.

As if reading their minds Sabrina said, "I know what you're thinking. How can an institution, however perfect, make Huggie happier than she is at home? But it's not only Huggie you need to think about; it's also us. A child with Down Syndrome limits you in so many ways. I don't want to say they're baggage. That sounds too insensitive. But we would have been better off as a family with her somewhere else. Go ahead and bring her on up. I'll speak to her, but I don't want her climbing all over me."

HUGGIE SCREAMED WITH DELIGHT when she came through the door and saw her mother. Sabrina remained seated, but spread her arms as Huggie ran to her and threw her arms around her neck, squeezing tightly. Sabrina's arms remained spread and didn't embrace her daughter, who was crying with joy and kissing her mother on first one cheek and then the other. Sabrina stiffened her entire body and turned her head from side to side to dodge her daughter's kisses. She put her hands under each of her daughter's arms, lifted her out of her lap and pushed her away, almost causing her to fall. Huggie looked at her mother and burst into tears.

Megan picked up her sister and held her tight. Huggie buried her head on her sister's shoulders and continued to sob. Megan wept quietly, trying not to let Huggie see her. She gently placed her on the floor and took her hand in hers. As she led her from the room, Huggie looked at her mother who sat stoically, avoiding eye contact with any of the children.

Jeff looked at his mother. Her eyes were completely dry. His were not.

"It was a mistake," she said. "You all simply don't understand. I did the best I could."

Jeff fought to control his temper. He wanted to run from the room and never see his mother again. He wanted to say, "You're despicable. I'm out of here and I never want to see you again." But however angry he was, he loved his mother. "Mom, I have flight reservations for tomorrow morning. You'll be going to New York with me."

Sabrina smiled. It might not be like the New York of her dreams, but it would be better than South Carolina. She didn't answer, but picked up the old copy of *The New Yorker,* and started flipping through it.

Chapter 16

THE NEW YEAR was only four days old when Brenda pulled her Z3 into the yard of Maybelle Smith. She was afraid that seeing them again in such miserable and hopeless conditions would make it more difficult to discourage Dawg from becoming a felon in order to help them. But in the end, she couldn't stay away.

It was a cold morning and the two older children were outside pulling loose boards from the side of the house.

Oh my God, they're using their house for firewood, she said to herself.

Maybelle greeted Brenda from her chair pulled up close to the old rusty stove, their only source of heat. Old and dirty blankets were scattered around the stove. Since there were no beds, Brenda assumed the family slept on the floor, using the blankets as mattresses.

Strips of fatback were cooking in a frying pan on the stove. From her chair, Maybelle kept flipping the fatback and mashing the grease out. Brenda knew the routine. Flour and water would be added to the grease to make thick, greasy gravy to pour on biscuits, probably made with water, because there was no milk. A few biscuits soaked in the gravy, along with what remained of the strip of fatback would be breakfast for the family.

Brenda put a brown sack on the table. The children quickly gathered around it, each trying to get his head in the sack. One of the older children grabbed it and emptied the contents onto the table.

Maybelle, sitting by the stove minding the fatback, said. "Lawdy mercy, honey, look what you brought us. Jest what we need, what we been praying for: Flour, corn meal, rice, lard and canned beans. There's enough here to get us through the rest of the week. Did Mr. Dawg send all this?"

`"No. I've wanted to come out and make sure you folks were all right, and I didn't want to come empty handed. So I stopped at the Winn Dixie on my way over and picked up a few staples. I also got some all day suckers for the kids. You know they put the candy right by the check out counter. It's hard to get by without buying a handful."

The children spotted the suckers the moment the contents of the bag hit the table. Within seconds, they all had one in their mouth. They tried cracking them with their decayed teeth so they could chew them up and get them into their empty stomachs as soon as possible.

ON HER WAY THROUGH DAWG'S reception room, Brenda stopped at Miss Ginny's desk to admire a small vase of artificial flowers. She held it up in front of her face and said. "How nice. But not as pretty as the real ones you grow."

Miss Ginny pretended to be busy searching for something on her computer and didn't answer.

"Is Dawg in?" Brenda asked. "I need about an hour of his time."

Miss Ginny disappeared into the huge office. She came out in a few moments to say that Mr. Brinson could see Brenda briefly, but that he had an important appointment he would have to keep as soon as the client showed.

As usual, Dawg was holding a coffee mug between his two hands, but Brenda detected no odor of alcohol. It caused her to worry that she was taking a cold.

"I need to talk to you about Maybelle Smith and her children," Brenda said while settling into a large chair across from Dawg's desk. "I went by their house on my way to work this morning and took them a few grocery items. They're desperate."

"Well I'm glad you 'preciate the condition they're in. Maybe you'll start being on their side rather than on the side of the beer company. But, I'm gonna help them whether you object or not. I'm close to finding a witness. Got a fellow coming by this morning who may remember seeing the accident after I remind him of some of the facts, especially after he goes out and sees how bad that family needs money."

Brenda took a deep breath as she prepared to hit Dawg with her plan. "Dawg," she said in a soft voice, "do you ever think when the hearse goes by that someday you, too, will die?"

"What the hell you talking 'bout, woman? Sometimes I think you plumb crazy. Then at other times, like now, I damn well know it."

Brenda continued in a soft voice as if she had not heard Dawg's response. "I'd be willing to bet that the richest lawyer in the state has no estate plan. Probably doesn't even have a will. And he'll die someday, regardless of what he thinks. When he does, the government will get most of his money. It'll be embarrassing when people learn that the smartest man in the world left most of his millions to the tax payers. But I'll explain that he loved the IRS and wanted them to have most of his money. I suppose his lovely wife will get the rest.

There'll probably be enough left for her to attract some handsome young husband,"

"If you're talking about me, well I'd rather the government get my money than that bitch I'm married to. I'm getting rid of her anyway. I may have to pay her more than I paid the first two, but it'll be worth it. And there'll never be another one. Next time I'm tempted to get married, I'll just give a bunch of money to some woman I hate. Now, I still plan to have some affairs, and as you know, I'm willing to pay for them. But you started off talking about the Smiths. I don't understand what my money has to do with them. It's the beer company's money you should be thinking about."

"I have a friend in Columbia who's the best estate planning lawyer in the state," said Brenda. "She lectures to lawyer groups all over. Why don't you let me get you an appointment with her? One of her recommendations is likely to be that you establish a charitable foundation. You can fund it with a couple of million dollars and shelter some of the income that will keep flowing as long as you can keep suing people. The government would in effect be helping you to fund it."

"But once I put the money in the foundation it's no longer mine?" It was more of a question than a statement.

Brenda answered. "But you can control where the income goes. You can be chairman of the Board of Trustees. You'll need a couple of others on the Board, but you can select people who'll let you give to whatever charitable cause you wish. They'll know it's your money."

"Don't see what good that'd do me," Dawg said. "I'd have to spend time trying to decide who to give my money to. Whatever I gave it to would probably turn around and give it to somebody too lazy to work."

Brenda shot back. "Not at all. What started me thinking about this is the Smith family. Your foundation could support them. It might need to be through gifts to churches, or civic or social organizations, to be used for distressed families, but there are ways you could get it to the Smiths."

Dawg started to say something, but Brenda continued before he could, talking fast and hopefully persuasively. "The James Earl Brinson Foundation! Sounds great doesn't it? It would be good public relations. And it would make you feel good knowing that you are helping good causes. When you walk down the street, you can feel warm glances from people thinking, 'There goes Lawyer Brinson, a successful and wealthy man and a good citizen. He knows the importance of giving back to the community.'"

Dawg listened politely, seeming neither annoyed nor amused. "You got me confused with somebody else," he said. "You said public relations. The only public relations worth a shit in the law business is to make 'em pay. Sleazy insurance companies and greedy corporations, especially railroads. And you say it'd make me feel good when I walk down the street. I ain't walked down the street in twenty years and I don't intend to start now. The biggest, most expensive Cadillac they make takes me wherever I want to go, and I get a new one every year."

"There would be another advantage, Dawg. You could help the Smiths without risking your law license and going to prison. And if you are as rich as you want everybody to believe, you would never miss a couple of million."

Dawg didn't reply. He reached in the drawer and pulled out an I. W. Harper whiskey bottle. He turned it up and shook it over his coffee mug. Only a few drops came out. He threw the bottle in the trash can and began snatching open first one drawer and then another, reaching in and feeling around for a bottle that wasn't there. "Miss Ginny!" he shouted loudly enough for her to hear with the door closed.

Miss Ginny stuck her head in the door immediately.

"Need you to go to the store for me," Dawg said in a demanding voice.

Brenda felt for the old lady, having to go buy a product she despised at ten o'clock in the morning. What if some of her Baptist friends saw her?

"Tell Cole to come on in," Dawg said to Ginny as she turned to go.

As Brenda left, Brantley Cole came in. She wanted to say something, but when she tried to make eye contact, Cole turned and looked away.

"I DROVE BY BUT DIDN'T GO IN." Brantley Cole answered when Dawg asked if he had been by to see the Smith family. He continued. "I know they're in great need. So are other families. There're folks equally as needy for reasons other than the breadwinner colliding with a beer truck. Shouldn't we be thinking about doing something to help people in need general, rather than doing something for a single family? Something that wouldn't get us in trouble?"

Dawg ignored the question and moved to the subject of Cole's own poverty. "You and your family are also in need, but not as desperate with your wife working. And I'm giving you a chance to do something about it. You can become financially secure while helping the Smiths. The victim? A beer company that'll never miss the money since it's such a small amount to them, or its large insurance company, which I spec is Lloyd's of London. It's a place where wealthy British bet money that a certain company won't suffer a loss. If they lose, they have to ante up. Just like they were playing roulette in Las Vegas. Except they get paid in advance. Just like any gambler, they expect to win some and lose some. With millions of bets placed each year, the loss we are talking about is peanuts. There won't be any losers."

Cole was shaking and the palms of his hands were sweating. "But what about me?"

"What do you mean what about you? You'll be paid a lot of money for a good cause."

"And what about you?" Cole asked. "I can tell a lie. I've told my share. But each time I tell one it hurts. And I've never told one as big as what you are asking me to do. How about you, Mr. Brinson? Will your conscience be hurt?"

"Oh hell no. Don't look at it like telling a lie. Nobody saw the collision. Just keep telling yourself that you saw the collision and that it took place like you remember it. I used to represent a lot of criminals. Some who were as guilty as sin would plead not guilty and really get to believing they didn't do it."

"It's not just my conscious, Mr. Brinson. I worry about getting caught. One more felony conviction and I'm up the river for good. Won't get a chance to see my children grow up."

"Trust me," Dawg said. "If there was a chance we'd get caught, I wouldn't be considering it. I don't need the money, so why would I take such a chance if there was any risk to it?"

"There's another thing, Mr. Brinson. I don't do well under pressure. Suppose a sharp lawyer gets a hold of me on cross-examination and gets me so confused I agree to something that shows I wasn't anywhere near the accident when it happened. Everybody'll know I'm lying and I'll probably be charged with lying under oath, and they will try to beat it out of me as to why. What should I tell them?"

Dawg didn't answer right away. He was beginning to worry. He had been so sure that Cole would jump at the chance to make some money that he had not thought what may happen if he didn't. If he signed a sworn statement, there was no way he would take the risk of getting sent away, possibly for life. But if he didn't, what would keep him from getting drunk and telling somebody Dawg offered him money to lie?

Finally, Dawg said in a calm reassuring voice, "I understand your fear of being cross-examined, son. But that won't be necessary because we won't have to go to court. The case'll settle once the beer company and its insurance company know I have a witness. I may have to take less than I would win in court if everything went right, but that's all right. We can probably get a couple of million without a trial. The Smiths can live like royalty on their million and I'll give you ten percent of mine."

"A hundred thousand dollars! My family could also live like royalty with that amount of money. Can I have some time to think it over?"

WHEN COLE LEFT, Miss Ginny went into Dawg's office carrying a brown paper bag containing two-fifths of I. W. Harper whiskey. Her hands were shaking and the bag rustling.

Dawg handed her two twenty dollar bills and said, "Thanks. I hope this is enough to cover it."

Miss Ginny didn't reply but turned to leave. "Don't go yet," Dawg said. "Have a seat. Seems we're always so busy we don't ever have a chance to talk."

Miss Ginny sat in the leather chair in front of the huge desk. Her eyes avoided Dawg's. Her hands rested in her lap and Dawg noticed one was shaking visibly while the other held it, attempting to keep it from shaking.

"How come your hands are shaking so?" Dawg asked. "I hope you're not still nervous about going in the liquor store."

"It's nothing much," Miss Ginny said, her voice shaking. "When my mama was about my age she had the same thing happen. But it didn't affect her work. She was a seamstress and kept right on sewing until she died twenty-five years later. She could still thread a needle, even though her hands shook more than mine. So this won't affect my work. I can assure you."

"Oh I ain't worried about you doing your work. You got a job here as long as I'm here. You're the one person in this office I can trust. I trust you more than I trust my wife, or any of the wives I ever had."

Miss Ginny didn't find Dawg's comparison of her to his wives particularly complimentary because she knew he never trusted any of them. She sat quietly; waiting for what she feared was coming. Her boss was getting ready to ask her to do something that was wrong and it would not be the first time. This time, she had a premonition it would be serious.

"I need you to type a confidential affidavit," said Dawg. "You know, about the Smith family. I got a witness who saw the wreck what put them in the fix they're in. But it'll be controversial, and a lot of people'll think my witness is lying. It don't need to be made public. I think when I show it to the beer company lawyers, they'll settle. You met Brantley Cole, the man who was just in here. Well, Brantley was driving behind the beer truck before it crashed into the Smith's car. It drifted over into the left lane as it was meeting the Smith car. Cole thinks the driver of the truck probably went to sleep.

"Smith did the only thing he could do to avoid a crash. He couldn't turn onto the shoulder 'cause there wasn't room. So he turned quickly into the left lane, trying to change lanes with the truck. If the truck had stayed in the left lane they'd have passed safely. But the truck driver woke up and saw he was on the wrong side of the road, because he turned back into his right lane and right into the path of the Smith car. Weren't nothing Smith could do but say good morning to his maker.

"Cole said he slowed down when he saw the truck go over to the left lane, so he didn't run into the wreckage. He pulled around it slowly and saw all of the blood and gory mess, and knew everybody was dead. It skeered him so bad he panicked. He took off home and didn't tell nobody. Said he had nightmares for weeks afterwards. After a lot of time passed, he got better. He heard I represent Maybelle Smith and her family so he came to see me and told me what he saw."

Miss Ginny wasn't surprised. She had expected Dawg to come up with a bogus witness, but had hoped he wouldn't ask her to participate.

"I'll write out the statement in long hand," Dawg continued, "putting down what the witness told me. And of course, he'll review it to make sure I got it right. I'll need you to type it up and have him swear to it before you. With your notary stamp on it, it'll be just as good as if he swore to it before a judge."

Miss Ginny's hands began to shake faster, and her voice was shaking as much as her hands. "Maybe after you write out the statement in long hand, I can take it home and type it. I still have a real typewriter there. It may take me awhile, but I'll work on it nights and weekends."

"Nights and weekends?" Dawg wanted it typed in a couple of hours. And on an old typewriter? Anybody could tell it had not been typed on a modern computer and printed on the latest model laser printer, which might raise more questions.

"You'll need to learn how to type on the computer," Dawg said. "I'll get somebody to teach you. Maybe somebody that'll help you type it without reading it." He didn't have to wonder long who that could be. There was only one possibility.

Chapter 17

MAKING MISS GINNY LEARN to use the computer under the tutelage of Brenda was like locking her in a room with a hairy, smelly ape that at any moment might mistake her for an in-season female of the same species. Miss Ginny protested when Dawg suggested it, and even briefly considered quitting her job.

"I know the two of you don't get along," said Dawg, "but for just this once suck it up. I've already taken my chances with Brenda, and I don't want to spread the risk any more. I'll have a tough enough time keeping her under control. Why don't you tolerate her as best you can and when you're finished, as far as I'm concerned, you can tell her to go sit on it."

NEITHER MISS GINNY nor Brenda wanted people parading through the reception room to see them hovering over a computer with their heads close together, so they agreed to use the computer in Brenda's office. Miss Ginny arrived half an hour before Brenda. She closed the door behind her so others in the office would not see her there. The office made her uncomfortable.

Brenda's framed law license hung on the wall behind her desk. It was flanked on one side with her college diploma and on the other side by her law school diploma. Paintings, which to Miss Ginny looked to be little more than splotches of paint, covered the other walls. She could make out one that looked like a black female dancer, completely naked with private parts exposed. It was covered with a grayish mist, which she assumed was an attempt by the artist to camouflage it enough to avoid arrest for painting an obscene picture. Another painting was even more offensive. It looked like Christ ascending into heaven, but the surrounding angels were black and the figure obviously meant to portray Christ was even blacker.

It troubled Miss Ginny to be in a room with the uppity Brenda. In addition to that burden, she also had to endure a room filled with vulgar and sinful paintings.

The door burst open and Brenda came through carrying in one hand a cardboard box with Styrofoam cups filled with coffee. In her other hand, she carried a large brown bag.

"Good morning Miss Ginny," Brenda said in a cheerful voice. "Before we start work, there's breakfast to do. I recall you like your coffee plain, that is, without cream or sugar."

I like my coffee black, thought Miss Ginny, but I'm not going to eat a meal with this uppity and sinful black girl. Then she spoke up quickly. "I just ate a big breakfast. I don't want anything else to eat."

Brenda ignored her statement, put the coffee in front of her, spread out a napkin and placed a large cinnamon bun on it. It was still hot and was the sweetest smelling bun Miss Ginny could remember. It was all she could do to keep from devouring it quickly. She had skipped breakfast knowing that her churning stomach, caused by anticipating the day ahead, might not be able to handle food. It was no longer churning, but yearning for the sweet smelling bun.

Brenda was half finished with her bun and was obviously enjoying it immensely. "Better eat up, Miss Ginny. We can't get started until these are gone, and I can eat only one. Got to watch my figure, you know."

Miss Ginny couldn't take her eyes off the cinnamon bun in front of her, but she remained determined not to do anything that would make her beholden to Brenda. Besides, her generation didn't eat with black people. It might not bother young white folks, but older ones like her, those who had been raised right, still respected what they had been taught.

"Here, just taste it," Brenda said as she held the napkin and the bun in front of Miss Ginny's face.

Miss Ginny broke off a small piece and put it in her mouth. She was starving and couldn't remember when she had tasted anything so good. She took a small sip of coffee.

"Coffee's not half bad either, is it?" Brenda asked. "If you do well on the computer, I'll tell you where I got it. They have wonderful donuts, too."

Miss Ginny broke off another piece of the bun and ate it. And then another. Brenda pretended not to notice as she devoured the bun right down to the last crumb, and with a few large gulps, finished off the coffee.

The old lady's hands shook more than ever, but Brenda attributed it to nervousness. The shaking was so violent some of the coffee splashed from the cup as she raised it to her mouth. It wasn't just nervousness or age. Something was wrong.

Brenda looked at the shriveled old lady with pity. There were many things about Miss Ginny that Brenda wanted to know, but knew she shouldn't ask. Did Miss Ginny have any family or friends? If she needed help in the middle of the night, was there anyone to call? What about her finances? Has she put away enough to support herself in her old age? Does she have any pets? Maybe she should have a kitten, something warm and cozy to care for and love. Should she give her a kitten that Sinbad sired? She would get the pick of the litter.

THE MORNING PASSED QUICKLY. First, Brenda had Miss Ginny type some random sentences and bragged about her typing. "You're doing great, Miss Ginny. You haven't forgotten a thing."

Miss Ginny was pleased and surprised at how easy it was to type on the keypad.

Brenda showed her how to delete mistakes and type over them. "No more erasing," she told her. "Remember how hard it was to erase a mistake on an old typewriter, especially if you were making a lot of carbon copies?"

After an hour of practice, they were ready to start typing Brantley's affidavit. Brenda did the centering, and from time to time a spell check, but she was relieved that Miss Ginny could type well enough that Brenda didn't have to follow the script.

Shortly before noon, Dawg came in to say the affidavit needed to be completed by four o'clock. "Cole will be in then. He called this morning and said he was ready to go forward. I don't want him to have to wait. He might change his mind."

"No problem," Brenda said. "Miss Ginny is a much better typist than I could ever be, and she is such a quick learner."

Before going out for sandwiches for lunch, Brenda showed Miss Ginny how to exit *Word*, save the document on the computer, and pull up a search engine. When she returned, Miss Ginny was playing with the computer, almost spellbound. She had learned how to check the weather, news headlines, even the stock market report. She was like a child with a new toy.

By three o'clock, the affidavit was finished and ready to be printed. Dawg was in the office within seconds of being called. "We need only three copies," he said. "And as soon as you know the copies turn out all right, delete the statement from the computer."

"That's not many copies," Brenda said. "You'll need two for defense counsel, a couple for your files and of course you'll need to give Cole a copy."

Dawg looked at her like she was crazy, but didn't say anything. He didn't need to. Brenda knew he was thinking there was no way Brantley Cole was going to get a copy of his statement. He might lose it or get drunk and show it to somebody.

Miss Ginny moved the mouse as Brenda instructed until the arrow was on "*File*." She clicked twice, and was surprised at the long menu that popped up on the screen. Without further instruction, she moved the mouse until the arrow was on "*Print*." Brenda showed her how to select the number of copies and told her to click "*OK*."

"Follow me," Brenda said.

They went down the hall past a couple of associates' offices and into the supply room, which also housed two copying machines and two laser printers.

Dawg was standing by one of the printers with a stack of papers. "Come look, Miss Ginny," he said.

Miss Ginny took one of the pages and looked at it in disbelief. The words she had typed into the computer moments before were printed clearly, as good as if done by a professional printing company. She beamed as she took the sheets of paper to her desk, to arrange in order.

MISS GINNY HAD JUST RETURNED to her desk when the phone rang.

"Will you please tell Mr. Brinson that I can't make it this afternoon?" Brantley Cole asked.

"May I tell him why?" Miss Ginny asked.

Cole was silent for a moment while he tried to think of an excuse. "A job interview. I have an interview for a possible job."

"Mr. Brinson will want to know when you plan to come in. We worked hard to get the papers typed so they would be ready this afternoon. Mr. Brinson will be disappointed to hear they won't be signed today as he expected. And when he's disappointed, so is everyone else in the office."

Cole didn't answer.

When Cole hung up the phone, his wife asked, "Why did you tell whoever that was that you have a job interview, when you don't, and it looks like you're never going to have one. With your record, you're probably never going to get a job again, especially after being locked up right before Christmas. I'm getting sick and tired of having to support this family. My job at the dry cleaners barely pays a minimum wage. Not only do I have to wash and iron, cook and support two children, I have to support you. Sometimes, I'm tempted to tell you to take your things and get out of this house. It would at least mean one less mouth to feed."

Cole approached his wife and started to put his arms around her. She jerked away and left the room. The kind of money Brinson was talking about would let him get his life back together and save his family. Whatever the risk, he had to take it.

THE NEXT MORNING BRANTLEY COLE WAS waiting for Dawg when he got to the office. He had asked Miss Ginny to see the statement, but she said she didn't know where it was. "It's probably locked up in Mr. Brinson's desk," she said. "You'll have to discuss it with him."

Dawg was surprised but glad to see Cole. He greeted him warmly and told him to go into his office. Dawg followed after Miss Ginny handed him the stack of papers Cole had noticed at the corner of her desk.

Even old ladies sometimes lie, Cole thought. So maybe it isn't such a big deal.

Dawg handed Cole one of the copies. "Here read this. I want you to be familiar with it, but I can't give you a copy to take with you. As you read it, think of it as accurate. People can convince themselves that things happened that never did if they try."

While Cole was reading the statement, Miss Ginny came in with two cups of coffee. Her hands were trembling causing some of the coffee to splash onto the floor. "Cream or sugar?" she asked Cole.

"Both please," he replied.

She returned with small packages of sugar and powdered cream. As she tried to drop them into Cole's hands, hers were shaking so that they missed and fell to the floor. Cole didn't say anything, but quickly picked them up and poured their contents into what was left of his steaming cup of coffee. Dawg didn't notice the spilled coffee. He was concentrating on pouring a large slug of I. W. Harper whiskey into his own cup.

Cole read through the three-page statement three times. As Dawg suggested, he tried to believe he really witnessed the accident and that it happened as Dawg had written it. But he couldn't. Even the most gullible would know it was a lie.

The palms of Cole's hands were sweating. He was breathing hard and this heart had picked up an extra thirty beats. "Should I be tested on a lie detector, saying things like these, it would explode into smithereens," said Cole.

"You aren't going to be asked to take a lie detector test, son, and nobody's gonna question you. Stick with me, boy, and I'll make you somebody."

"Can I get an advance on my fee, Mr. Brinson? My family is really strapped for money. And maybe having some money in my pocket would make it easier for me to swear to these lies."

"Sorry, son," Dawg said. "You working a contingent fee, just like I am. We get paid when our client gets paid."

Dawg poured more liquor in his cup as he called for Miss Ginny. "Take young Cole out to your desk. Have him sign all three copies and swear that they're true. You notarize and sign the copies saying he appeared before you and swore they are true. You got a notary seal, don't you? And a bible? You need to have him put his hand on the Bible when he swears. You got a bible don't you?"

MISS GINNY PULLED a well worn bible from her desk drawer and put it on the front of her desk. "Put your left hand on the Bible and raise your right hand please, Mr. Cole," she said in a voice that was shaking. Cole's hands were also shaking.

"Do you swear...do you swear," she said. She struggled to remember the words of the oath. With a nervous laugh, she said. "I seem to forget the words. But I got a copy of the oath right here."

She opened her desk drawer and started shuffling papers as she buried her head among them. She found the oath, but when she looked up, Brantley Cole was gone.

Chapter 18

THE SEVEN TINY KITTENS swarmed over the mother cat's breast searching for a nipple. The larger ones pushed away their smaller siblings to get to the larger faucets. The mama looked suspiciously at Brenda and the veterinarian who were staring at her babies.

"I'm sorry to have to ask you to make your selection before they get larger," said the veterinarian, "because sometimes they do change. But since you get the pick of the litter, I can't let anybody else select until you have."

"No problem," Brenda replied as she picked up the smallest and checked out its gender. The kitten climbed up her wrist and curled up in her hand. "I'll take this one."

"Oh, but you get to take the best one. This little runt would place seventh out of seven."

"The more tiny and frail they are, the easier they are to love. I want one that will be impossible for a little old lady not to love."

Two weeks later, Brenda returned to pick up "Simmie." She put the kitten in a shoebox with enough small holes punched in the lid to assure the kitten would have enough air.

MISS GINNY'S COTTAGE was on a lot half the width of others in the neighborhood, but it was far back enough that the cottage sat back behind the back yards of the houses on each side. It was surrounded by a wire fence covered in vines.

Brenda nervously knocked lightly on the door, while holding the kitten tightly against her breasts with her other hand. The inside door opened and Miss Ginny stood looking through the screened door. She didn't utter a word of greeting, but stared at Brenda, waiting for her to say why she was there. Her left hand held her right one, trying to hold it still.

"I brought you a friend," Brenda said as she put the kitten against the screen in front of Miss Ginny's face. While crying softly, the kitten reached out with a tiny paw and scratched at the screen.

"A cat! A cat! I don't want a cat. They shed and get cat hair all over the house."

"Simmie won't shed. She's a Siamese. They don't shed."

Brenda was determined not to give up easily. She reached out and pulled on the screen door, intending to stick the kitten inside and see if Miss Ginny would touch it. The screen door was latched and Miss Ginny made no movement to open it.

"Okay," Brenda said. "I'll take her home with me. Should you change your mind, it may be too late. Once I get attached to Simmie, I won't want to give her up."

Miss Ginny didn't respond, or make any move to suggest to Brenda that she was a welcomed guest.

"If it wouldn't be too much trouble, could you give Simmie a small drink of water? She's thirsty and I'm afraid if we wait until we get home she'll be dehydrated. It's important for small kittens to get lots of water."

Miss Ginny didn't speak. After a moment, she unlatched the screen door and pushed it open. She had a look of annoyance on her face as Brenda glanced around the living room, hoping the trappings would give her some insight into the strange old lady. No lights were on and little daylight found its way through the heavy drapes that covered the windows.

Brenda noticed three large portraits on the wall above an old upright piano. The one in the center looked like an original oil painting of Jesus. On its left was a large portrait of a man wearing a gray Confederate Army uniform. The picture on the right was a man sitting in a chair and a woman standing behind him with her hand on his shoulder.

Miss Ginny pointed to the cabinet above the short kitchen counter. Brenda took a saucer from the cabinet, filled it with water, and placed it on the counter. She put the kitten down in front of the water.

"On the floor! On the floor!" Miss Ginny shouted. "I don't want a dirty cat on the kitchen cabinet." As she spoke, she snatched the saucer from the cabinet and put it on the floor. Her hands were shaking so that all of the water spilled from the saucer and splashed onto the floor.

Brenda put Simmie on the floor and the kitten immediately began licking up the spilled water. While Brenda was refilling the saucer with water, Miss Ginny went for a mop. She started mopping the floor aggressively, obviously overdoing it in an effort to send a message of her unhappiness to Brenda.

Simmie playfully grabbed at the strings of the fast moving mop as it was being pushed forward. The mop caught the kitten like it was on a shuffle board, sending her flying against the far wall. Simmie let out a yelp.

Miss Ginny dropped the mop and picked up the kitten. "I'm sorry," she said. "I didn't go to hurt her, but I can't let a cat mess up my kitchen." Her hands were shaking so badly that the little kitten's head bobbed back and forth as she handed her to Brenda.

Brenda had intended to make a last persuasive offer to Miss Ginny, confident that if she could get her to hold the kitten, even briefly, she would become so attached that she would not let her go. But as she watched the old lady's hands shake, she realized she was in no condition to care for a kitten. She wouldn't be able to pour her a saucer of milk.

SINBAD AND SIMON CAME RUNNING when the front door opened. They glanced at Simmie briefly with curiosity, but paid little attention to her until Brenda poured a saucer of milk and sat it on the kitchen floor. Before Simmie could lap up a second swallow, the other cats came running. Sinbad rudely pushed his daughter away as he and Simon finished off her milk with a few quick gulps.

Brenda poured another saucer of milk and placed it and Simmie in the pantry, and closed the door. Later, she would put two shoeboxes in there with her, one filled with kitty litter and the other would have a door carved in it so Simmie could get in and sleep securely. In a few weeks, when she was large enough to fend for herself, she could join her father and brother sleeping on the foot of Brenda's bed.

MISS GINNY DIDN'T SPEAK or look up as Brenda walked by her desk the following morning. Her eyes were on the computer screen. Since Brenda taught her how to pull up topics on the Internet, she had spent her spare moments looking up things that interested her. Whenever Brenda could, she would glance over Miss Ginny's shoulder to see what she was looking at. Once it was flowers; another time, birds; and one time it was a picture of a weird preacher by the name of Robertson.

This time, when Brenda sneaked up behind Miss Ginny and looked to see what she was looking, the computer screen was filled with pictures of little Siamese kittens.

WHEN BRENDA GOT HOME THAT EVENING, Sinbad, Simon and Simmie came running as soon as the door opened. She picked them up and with two under one arm and the third under the other, headed to the kitchen. She shook some dry cat food into each of their bowls, and then made a tuna sandwich for herself.

The light on the answering machine was blinking. While holding her sandwich in one hand and a Miller Light in the other, she punched in the light with her little finger. The first message was an important notification that she had been pre-approved for a new credit card. The second was congratulating her for having won an all-expense-paid trip to Disney World for her and her children. The next was from a carpet cleaning company.

Brenda regretted not recording the clever answer she carefully wrote out when she purchased the answering machine: "If you're calling about a bill, the check's in the mail. If you're calling for a contribution, I gave at the office. If you're calling to say I've won a free vacation, you should know that I'm still trying to pay for the last free vacation I won. If you're calling to offer me a new credit card, I suggest you first check with my bankruptcy lawyer. If you are a friend, leave your number and I'll call you back. But if you're calling for other reasons, please hang up and try another number."

After listening to the first few messages, Brenda started to delete those remaining. But something told her to listen to one more. It was a young voice pleading, "I miss you Benda. Will I never be seeing you again?"

TWO DAYS LATER, after going home from work, feeding the cats and eating a cold sandwich, Brenda drove to the Hazelhurst home.

The door opened after a single short touch of the doorbell. Don stood in the doorway with Huggie, barely as tall as his waist, standing in front of him. "Benda, Benda!" Huggie yelled as she jumped into Brenda's arms and buried her head on her shoulder.

"It's so good to see you," Don said while giving Brenda a partial hug. With Huggie in her arms, a full enthusiastic hug was not possible. Huggie released her grip and wiggled out of Brenda's arms. She took Brenda's hand and pulled her into the den.

"Look, look,'" Huggie said as she pointed to the new computer.

Don joined in. "We have you to thank for our getting a computer. It had never occurred to me that we needed one until you suggested it. We took a crash course at the community college, and there's still a lot for us to learn. But we've learned how to send emails. I've been tempted to call you and get your email address, but I didn't want to interrupt your work with a personal call. I finally let Carol call your home and leave a short message."

Don sat in his chair in the den pretending to be reading the newspaper, but actually listening to the conversation between Brenda and Huggie.

Huggie had brought HeBear from her room and put him on Brenda's lap. "Member HeBear? You gave him to me. He sleeps with me every night. HeBear has missed you, too."

"It's great to see HeBear again." Brenda said. "Let's get on the computer and find bears. Maybe we can find out what kind of bear HeBear is."

Huggie was fascinated with all bears, especially Pandas. She decided HeBear looked more like a black bear. "But he must be different, because he doesn't sleep all winter."

It was almost ten o'clock when Don told the two girls it was time for Huggie to go to bed. She didn't protest, especially after Brenda assured her that she would visit more often in the future. Brenda went with her to her room, tucked her into bed with HeBear snuggling close beside her, and kissed her good night.

Don waited at the bottom of the stairs for Brenda, and walked with her to the door.

"I'll come again," Brenda said. "Spring will soon be here and there's so much I would like to do with Huggie. Bike rides, picnics in the park, and this summer, I'll teach Huggie to swim. And you, Don, maybe I'll teach you to dance."

Before Don could respond, Brenda was out the door. He stood at the door for several moments.

"Don." She called me "Don" and not "Dr. Hazelhurst," he was thinking. It sounded good. But dance? Me learn to dance? Not likely at this age.

Chapter 19

HAD MIKE PETERSON BEEN FREE to move to a larger city, life would have been easier. But Dawg Brinson had ordered him to stay in Darlington where he could attend a drug rehabilitation support group, join a church and civic club, and establish himself as a reformed person. So he went to church every Sunday and despised it, though it wasn't as bad as the Civitan Club, where he found the members silly and the meetings boring. The thought of the club's approaching quarterly visit to the Center for Handicapped Children was especially depressing.

Drug rehabilitation counseling would have been easier if he had a substance abuse problem, but he had to fake one, not only with his counselor, but also with his support group. He was bored half to death listening to members of the group talk about how far they had fallen before seeing the light and starting to climb back. "To take it one day at a time," seemed the mission of each member of the group.

When his time came to confess, Mike wanted to say, Look folks. I got no problem with drugs or alcohol. I don't need to take it a day at a time. It'll be easy for me to resist drugs and alcohol until after my trial, because they never interested me much in the first place. I'm here only because my lawyer made me come. You see, I got caught with drugs under the seat of my car. It was no more serious than keeping liquor in a cabinet, and seldom touching it. I'm not addicted, but I know something about it. My girlfriend was a drunk. That's why I left her. In fact, the reason I had a lapse in judgment is that I was pissed at the bitch and trying to get as far away from her as I could, as quickly as I could.

What Mike actually said was, "My father was my hero. He was a champion larger than life, not only to his thousands of fans, but especially to his son. He inspired me and taught me the skills that made him such a successful race driver. But he was so much more than a mentor, or a coach. He was a loving father who always placed his family first. When he was killed in a hunting accident, my life came apart. I started drinking heavily. I tried to stay sober on race days, but would get falling down drunk as soon as the race was over. My crew noticed the odor of stale alcohol on my breath and started questioning whether I was endangering my career, and theirs, by excessive drinking. So I started using drugs, because they are harder to detect on a person's breath. I didn't limit my drug use to marijuana and cocaine. I took speed, yellow jackets, stuff I would buy without having any idea what it was or what it would do to you. I took anything I thought would take my mind off the death of my father.

"I believed that with the passage of time I'd get over my depression. But when I reached a point I no longer needed drugs to escape the reality of my father's death, it was too late. I was addicted. My body craved drugs, often drugs and alcohol together.

"On Christmas Eve, a few months ago, I remember being in my condo in Myrtle Beach, drinking and doing drugs with my girlfriend. The next thing I remember is the following morning and a sheriff is standing by my car many miles away and a long way from a public road. I had no idea how I got there. I was arrested and put in jail.

I learned that my car had bumped another car in the rear on I-95 and that I tried to out-run the troopers who tried to stop me. I was driving over a hundred miles an hour and got away. It wasn't until the next morning that the law enforcement officers were able to find me. I had drugs under the driver's seat and within easy reach. So, in addition to being charged with a lot of traffic offenses, I was charged with felony possession of drugs."

Mike also told the group that the church had helped change his life. "I've given my life to Christ. With His help and the help of God and the Holy Spirit, I will overcome. I'm willing to take my punishment and start anew. I hope someday to be able to race again. Please pray for me."

Mike didn't like lying, especially when it made him out to be weak and humble. But Dawg had said these were roles he needed to play to avoid prison, so he was left with no choice. In the meantime, he was beginning to feel for the first time ever that he would like to get drunk.

THREE OTHER CIVITANS AND MIKE were making their first visit to the Center. There they were ushered into a small conference room for orientation. They were met by the director, a lady in her late thirties who had started work at the center as a physical therapist shortly after graduating from nursing school. She had been the director for three years.

She held out her hand and firmly took Mike's hand. "I'm Roberta Campbell. Welcome to the Center."

Roberta was attractive in a plain sort of way. She wore no makeup, not even a trace of lipstick The corduroy slacks and cotton blouse she wore could have come from a thrift store, and her shoes, a pair of old sneakers, were well worn. She wore no rings so Mike assumed she wasn't married.

For thirty minutes, Roberta talked about the history of the center and its dedicated staff who happily worked long hours at minimum wages to serve the children. Then she talked about the children. In addition to badly handicapped children who lived there all of the time, a few lived with their families and spent only their weekdays at the center.

"For instance," she said. "We have an eight-year-old with Down Syndrome who has been a day attendee since she was a small child. Her father has decided to place her in a mainline school as soon as there's an opening. We'll miss her. She's the sweetest child. Everybody calls her 'Huggie Bear' because she likes to hug people. When she sees you, she will likely run to you and give you a warm hug. It'll be a wonderful experience."

Speak for yourself woman, Mike thought to himself. I won't enjoy it and hope I don't have to endure it.

After Roberta's presentation, Mike joined the group doing the laundry. The last thing he wanted to do was something that might require him to touch some of the "peculiar children." It was bad enough being in the same building with them. He had not seen any, but could hear some unintelligent sounds, some quite mournful. And there was crying, even shouting occasionally. And he could smell them. No matter how much the staff cleaned and disinfected, they couldn't prevent those who were helpless and incontinent from defecating and urinating in their clothes, and again on their bed as soon as they were cleaned and put down. To Mike, the place reeked from the odor of feces and urine.

Laundry duty proved too much. Mike didn't like handling soiled sheets and children's dirty smelly clothing. He was afraid he would get a dreadful disease from touching a damp diaper. After a few minutes, he told the others in the laundry he was going to help those cleaning the floors. "I'm a good scrubber and y'all seem to have everything under control here."

He didn't join the floor cleaners, but instead slipped out the door and down the street to a small park where he sat on a swing and smoked cigarettes until lunchtime.

AT NOON, MIKE SLIPPED INTO THE DINING ROOM to join the others. He knew he couldn't eat anything, not amid the noise, the odors and the total ugliness of everything he saw. He would fake eating, and afterwards have a double cheeseburger and a chocolate shake at Hardees.

Some of the children were strapped to high chairs. One had to have his head held up so he could be fed. Several of the Civitans volunteered to help spoon feed those who couldn't feed themselves. When Mike was asked if he would like to feed some of the children, he begged off. "I would love to, but I'm so clumsy. I'm afraid I might shove a spoonful of food too far down their throat and choke them to death."

He looked around and saw that other Civitans were helping in some way. He knew he needed to be engaged, but was determined it would not be in a way that would bring him in contact with the children. He went to the table where Roberta sat with members of the staff who were getting a break because of the help from the Civitans. He slipped onto one end of a bench beside her hoping others would think he was talking with her in an effort to learn more about the Center.

"Please join us Mike," she said as she slipped down the bench so he would have more room. Nodding to the others at the table, she said, "Meet Mike McMillan. Mike's a new Civitan. This is his fist visit here." She introduced the others. "Sadie is one of our cooks, and Ethel and Johnsie both work as teachers and therapists."

The lady called Ethel looked at Mike and said, "You know there's a race car driver with the same name as you, and his picture even favors you. That's quite a coincidence isn't it?"

Mike mumbled. "Yeah. Seems like somebody else mentioned that one time."

Neither Roberta nor the other ladies seemed curious.

A SMALL HAND AND ARM reached over Mike's left shoulder and placed a plate of food in front of him.

"Thanks, Huggie," Roberta said. Then turning to Mike, she said, "Huggie's the child I told you about who has Down Syndrome. She enjoys waiting on tables at lunch and does a wonderful job."

Mike was petrified and unable to speak. The urge to jump up and run away was overwhelming. What made it even worse was he could feel vibrations from the small body standing behind his left shoulder.

"Huggie wants to hug you," Roberta said.

Mike instinctively turned to his left, as Huggie, with her arms stretched out lunged toward him. He reached up, thrusting his arms between hers and spreading them quickly to keep her from wrapping her arms around his neck. At the same time, he moved back, got up from the bench, and ran from the building, leaving his food untouched, and a little girl frightened and crying.

Roberta put her arms around Huggie and pulled her close. She pressed her cheek against the child's tear-streaked cheek and whispered, "Everything will be all right, Huggie. We love you."

Other staff members and Civitans quickly gathered, asking what happened.

Roberta said in a calm voice, "When Huggie tried to hug Mike, he had an emergency of some sort and had to leave quickly and Huggie became frightened."

Robert Davis, the largest of the Civitan group at six feet-four inches reached down and pulled Huggie from Roberta's arms into his. She was still sobbing. Robert cuddled her in his arms with her head resting on his shoulder and her wet cheek against his. He looked back as he carried the crying child out the door and said, "Huggie's my sweetheart. She'll be all right."

The Civitans gathered around. "I'm sure Mike had an emergency," said Roberta. "Maybe it was a call of nature. I know he feels bad. Please don't mention this to him. I don't want him to be embarrassed."

Robert walked with Huggie around the building and into the flower garden in the back. There was a sign that read: "Please don't pick the flowers." It was early in the season and there were not many flowers. But Robert broke off a blooming azalea limb and put it in Huggies's hand. "This is for my favorite girl," he whispered.

"I SCREWED UP BADLY," Mike said as he barged past Miss Ginny into Dawg Brinson's office. Dawg, who had been dozing at his desk, was startled, but didn't protest when he saw his client was distressed.

"It was at the Center for Handicapped Children a little while ago. A child I fathered tried to hug me." Mike was trembling and fighting back tears. "When I looked in her face I lost it. She was ugly, so deformed. She looked like a creature from outer space. And I was responsible for her being alive. It was more than I could handle and I panicked. I thought if there is a God, it might be His way of punishing me. I jumped up and ran out. I guess I scared the kid 'cause she started crying. I know the Civitans are pissed at me. It would have been better if I'd never gone to that dreadful place."

"Just calm down," Dawg said as he poured a few splashes of I. W. Harper into his coffee mug. He held it up and gestured toward Mike. "I'm sorry I can't offer you a drink, but as you know, you aren't to drink until after your trial."

Mike's shaking had lessened, but he was still far from relaxed. "Sorry to barge in like I did, but I'm desperate to talk to someone and you're all I've got, Mr. Brinson."

"I understand," Dawg said. "No little children ever came walking up at my house, but I spec that if one which was dumb and ugly had, I'd a pitched a fit just like you did. But it does present a little problem for your case.

"Here's what we need to do, son. Write a letter of apology to the Center. Tell 'em you had been nauseated all morning. It must have been the left-over chicken bog you warmed over for supper last night. You shouldn't have gone to the Center, but you had looked forward to the visit so much that you tried to make it through. But it suddenly came on you and you had to go. You made it to the car when you threw up. Enclose a check for a hundred dollars and ask that they buy something for the youngun that you scared. You'll need to send copies of the letter to the other Civitans who were there."

Dawg paused, but Mike could tell he wasn't through.

"Tell you what else you need to do, just to be on the safe side. Meet privately with the president of the Civitan Club. Tell him how you were touched by the Center and the great job the folks there are doing. Give him a check for a thousand dollars made out to the Center and ask that he deliver it and tell them it's from someone who wishes to remain, what do you call it? Anonymous? Tell 'em you don't want anybody knowing you done it."

"But I don't understand. How can it help me if everybody doesn't know I made the gift?"

"Oh, they'll know," Dawg said with a grin. "The president of the club'll tell a few of his close friends, in confidence. Meanwhile, the trustees of the Center will want to know and they'll be told. In confidence, of course. And they'll tell some of their friends. Pretty soon, might near everybody'll know you did it and they'll think more highly of you for not wanting to get credit for it. You see, by asking that to remain a secret, you'll leverage the benefit you'll get."

"You're brilliant, Mr. Brinson. I'll happily give a thousand dollars if it means I won't have to go back to that place again."

"We'll come up with some good excuses for your not going," Dawg said. "Maybe you need to plan to be sick or something."

Chapter 20

BY THE TIME WINTER turned into spring, Brenda and Huggie had become as close as sisters. Don was ambivalent about Brenda's role. Was she like a daughter with a sibling who came along years later? Or was she something more? When he welcomed her or said good-bye with a friendly hug, he worried that sometimes he held her too close and for too long. But she never pushed back or protested.

AT BRENDA'S SUGGESTION, Don had the backyard pool drained, scrubbed and refilled. By early May, Brenda was coming two or three afternoons a week and on weekends to teach Huggie to swim. She was soon swimming so well Brenda wanted to get her on a swim team. It would be an opportunity for her to associate with other children and would be another step toward getting her into the mainstream.

Don was excited when Brenda mentioned the possibility to him. He thought of the youth swim teams at the country club. His older children had been interested in other things and never participated, but he recalled sometimes hearing happy cheering around the pool while having dinner on the veranda.

Don called his brother, Jim, a former president of the club.

"Yes," Jim said. "The club has a swim team for all ages of youth. They compete with teams from other clubs and with some municipal teams."

There was a pause and Don knew his brother was thinking about what to say next. He finally, spoke with hesitancy. "You know Don; I doubt that Huggie would enjoy the swim team. The other kids have been swimming most of their lives, and have taken lessons. I wouldn't want Huggie to have her feelings hurt because the other children are better swimmers."

Don waited silently knowing his brother wasn't through.

"I hesitate to say this," Jim continued, "but you know how people around here are, and a lot of them don't know Huggie. Some people would be surprised to learn that there's a handicapped child in our family. And another thing, you would have to go with her to practice and all the meets. As busy as you are, that's asking a lot. Why don't you just take her to the municipal pool on weekends, let her play around in the water. She'll enjoy that a lot more."

"Does the club require a parent to be with the child at all times?" Don asked.

"Not necessarily a parent," Jim replied, "but a responsible adult. I'm sure that in your case, it would have to be you since you have no one else available".

PARENTS, COACHES AND OTHER SWIMMERS watched in amazement as the different looking little girl darted through the water like a seal, easily finishing ahead of all the others in her age group. No one finished close to her in the freestyle, and she also finished well ahead of the half dozen others in the breaststroke. She didn't like swimming on her back, so she withdrew from the backstroke competition.

Huggie wasn't aware she was a faster swimmer than other children her age until she heard Brenda tell Don that evening what a star swimmer his daughter was.

"I swim fast, I swim fast!" Huggie repeated excitedly.

Don thanked Brenda for taking Huggie to swim practice in the afternoons. "I know this is taking time away from your law practice and probably costing you money."

"Not really. Most of my cases scheduled for trial this summer have been settled so I have some free time. But in case I'm unable to get away some afternoon, perhaps you should recruit another parent to take Huggie to practice or to a meet."

Other parents with children in the swim program were much younger, even of another generation, and Don knew of no one he could call on.

THE LETTER FROM THE CLUB'S swim committee chairman was a form letter addressed to all members, but Don knew he was its target.

> *Dear Member:*
>
> *It is necessary that we make firm the club's policy requiring a parent or other responsible adult member of the club to accompany each child on our junior swim team to all practices and meets. It is not acceptable to send your child with your maid or other family servant.*
>
> *Thank you for your understanding and cooperation.*
>
> *Jason Dilbert, Chairman of the Swim Committee*

Dilbert was sent to Hazelboro several years before as District Manager of Bottom Dollar Store, a discount chain selling low scale items, mostly to low income people, many of whom were minorities. He lost no time in becoming a big man about town. He joined the Rotary Club and solicited places on the Board of Directors of the Chamber of Commerce and the United Way. His wife was elected president of the PTA at their children's private school and they joined the church with a "white Cadillac" reputation.

Years earlier, the Dilberts would have had to wait to become members of the country club. But financial challenges at the club had opened the doors wider and they were accepted as members soon after moving to the area. Dilbert asked to chair the swim committee because he had two children on the team.

Unlike his brothers, Don had never resented newcomers trying to run everything as soon as they arrived. Any efforts that were helpful, he commended, whatever their motive. And he certainly welcomed them to the country club. It was no Augusta National and it didn't have a waiting list like some of the prestigious clubs in larger cities. New members helped pay the bills. However, the letter from Dilbert brought forth a feeling of resentment. His assumption that Brenda was a maid was especially appalling. But it would do no good to protest. Some club members would not want anyone black on club property unless she worked there. It was a white-only club and was likely to remain that way for many years, even though discriminatory restrictions had been removed from its charter and bylaws. While Don was considering what to do, the phone rang.

"Dr. Hazlehurst, this is Jason Dilbert, Chairman of the Swim Committee at the club. I know you by reputation though we've never met. When my family and I came here three years ago and were looking for a dentist, you were highly recommended. But since we had young children we decided to go to Dr. David Thomas, who is nearly our age and has young children like we do."

"I'm flattered that someone recommended me, but somewhat surprised." Don said. "People who are from here know I haven't taken any new patients in years, unless they are children whose parents have been patients of mine for a long time. I refer anybody who moves here from out of town to Dr. Thomas. He's not from around here and has plenty of time."

Dilbert didn't reply immediately, obviously realizing that "old Florence" was trying to put him in his place. Had Don been active as a club member, Dilbert would have been careful not to insult him.

While Dr. Hazlehurst was a respected dentist from a socially prominent family, he was not among those considered socially elite himself. His reputation was not helped when his wife left him with their handicapped child. Dilbert didn't feel he could hurt his chances to become socially prominent.

Dilbert got right to the point of his call. "Your daughter swims so much faster than others in her age group that some people are wondering if she might be older than her stated age. She's naturally smaller, but since she looks different than most children, it isn't easy to judge her age. We need a birth certificate in case someone challenges her age when we begin competition. Can you send us a copy?"

"I can, but I won't." Don replied emphatically. "Unless, every parent is required to do so, as well, which they probably aren't because you don't suspect their children of cheating. But you must suspect the father of a handicapped child, whom you likely find too unattractive to represent the club swim team."

"Oh no. I don't suspect that. But if the question of age comes up at one of our meets, we want to be able to respond. And to be frank, the question has arisen among some of our members. Some parents with children in the same age group have raised the issue. It just doesn't seem normal that a handicapped child can swim so much faster than others of the same age, especially when one in the age group was state champion last year."

Don's heart beat faster and his anger continued to rise. "Is the champion who can't keep up with a child who has Down Syndrome by any chance one of your daughters?"

There was a momentary silence and then a click. Jason Dilbert had hung up.

DON GOT TO HIS OFFICE half an hour early. His receptionist/ secretary, Mrs. McCoy, was already there to receive calls or early arriving patients. Don pulled up a chair in front of her desk. "Can you take a letter I dictate, or should I write it out for you in long hand?"

While secretarial duties were a part of her job description, Mrs. McCoy was seldom asked to type letters. "My shorthand is kind of rusty," she said, "but why don't we try. Just talk slowly."

"The original is to the president of the country club. Copies are to go to the all members of the Board, the members of the swim committee and the chairman of the Bottom Dollar Stores in New York.

"I hereby resign from the Magnolia Country Club in Florence because of insults to me, my eight-year-old daughter and a young lawyer friend who happens to be an African-American woman. My daughter, Carol Ann, made the swim team in a couple of categories. I would like to think the club would be honored to be represented by the granddaughter of one of the founders of the club, and from a family that through the years has furnished more members and support to the club than any other family.

"*The first problem arose when the swim committee, or at least its chairman, decided it unseemly for our young lawyer friend, who taught my daughter to swim, to accompany her to the club for practice. In fact, Jason Dilbert assumed she was our maid, undoubtedly because of her skin color.*

"*The second problem was Mr. Dilbert's demand that I furnish a birth certificate to prove that my daughter is only eight years old. He claimed that because she has Down Syndrome, it's impossible to tell her age by looking at her. He didn't ask other parents for their children's birth certificates. Apparently, he thinks the Hazlehurst family is the only family capable of lying.*

"*I am sending a copy of this letter to the Chairman of the Bottom Dollar Stores as a courtesy. It seems only fair that should there be a boycott of his stores by African-American customers and parents of handicapped children, he should know why. None of us like to be insulted.*"

During the years she had worked for Dr. Hazelhurst, Mrs. McCoy had occasionally seen him sad, and even frightened, such as the time he discovered that his patient's blood wouldn't clot after having a tooth pulled. But she had never seen him angry. After typing a draft and handing it to him, she said, "Why don't you take this home and think about it? Tomorrow will be soon enough to mail it."

Don didn't take issue with her suggestion.

HUGGIE, TIRED FROM her strenuous workout in the pool, went to bed with HeBear shortly after dinner. Don and Brenda sat on lounge chairs beside the pool as Don tried to decide how to tell

Brenda that he was getting out of the club, meaning Huggie would no longer be swimming on the team.

Brenda was telling him about the upcoming meet. "It's at the club late Friday afternoon. Huggie will be swimming the freestyle and the breaststroke and will surely win. You should come and help us celebrate. It'll mean a lot to her to have you there cheering for her."

Don began to worry about how Huggie would be affected by his resignation from the club. She wouldn't understand the reasons and would be disappointed to learn that she couldn't swim at the club anymore. Perhaps he should swallow his pride and simply furnish proof of her age. Or he could ignore Dilbert's request. He wouldn't have the nerve to kick Carol off the team. Don's family might be embarrassed by the child's abnormal looks, but they knew her age and wouldn't tolerate a newcomer like Dilbert questioning the word of a Hazelhurst. Dilbert wouldn't dare do anything that would bring forth the wrath of so prominent a family.

But there was the question of Brenda. Someone would need to go with Carol, and Brenda couldn't return to the club without the risk of further insults. On that issue, Don's family would likely be on Dilbert's side.

Don handed the draft resignation letter to Brenda, concluding that was the easiest way to explain the situation to her.

She read the letter twice before handing it back to Don. Her eyes reflected more pain and sadness than anger. "You mustn't send this letter," she said. "I know you're angry. I am too. It's so unfair. But life can be unfair. There are times it's important to fight back and there are times when you just have to take the shit, however hard it might be. I know how much you want to leave the club because of that son of a bitch, Dilbert. But you shouldn't, because of Huggie. She's having more fun than at anytime in her life. She doesn't understand the significance of winning, but she loves the excitement. If she can't swim in the first meet of the summer next Friday she'll be a disappointed little girl. You go with her. I'll be waiting for you when you get home, and ready to celebrate with you."

THE SWIM MEET WAS UNEVENTFUL. No one asked for proof of Huggie's age, and all of the club swimmers, including Huggie, won without difficulty. The opposing club did not have a full team of swimmers and forfeited several events. In those they did swim, they were not competitive. The result was that the meet was less exciting than practice had been.

When Don and Huggie got home, Brenda was waiting for them on the front porch. Huggie jumped in her arms. When asked about the meet, Huggie didn't seem interested in talking about it. She was more excited about going to Hardees for supper.

They sat in Hardees enjoying their hamburgers. "There may be an opportunity to get Huggie into something she would enjoy more than swimming at the club," said Brenda. "Have you ever heard of the Special Olympics?"

"Seems like I have." Don said. "Wasn't it a program started by some of the Kennedy family for athletic competition among handicapped or retarded children?"

"Children and adults," Brenda replied. "Here, look at this information I got off the Internet."

Don put down his half-eaten hamburger, took the paper from Brenda, and read it with interest.

> *"Everyone should have the opportunity to feel good about their abilities and compete where they have the opportunity to succeed. The vision is to bring all persons with developmental*

disabilities into larger society under conditions whereby they are accepted, respected and given the chance to become useful and productive citizens. The purpose is to provide year-round sports training and athletic competition in a variety of Olympic-type sports for all children and adults with developmental disabilities, giving them continuing opportunities to develop physical fitness, demonstrate courage, experience joy, and participate in a sharing of gifts,, skills, and friendship with their families, other Special Olympians, and the community. The Special Olympic Oath is: "LET ME WIN, BUT IF I CANNOT WIN, LET ME BE BRAVE IN THE ATTEMPT."

Brenda watched the excited expression on Don's face as he finished reading. "They have more than one million athletes from over 100 countries involved," said Brenda, "and training opportunities in over 2500 communities in this country."

They looked at each other, both knowing that Huggie would be a perfect Special Olympian!

The following day Don dictated another letter, simply saying:

I hereby resign my membership in the Magnolia Country Club in Florence.

Chapter 21

NOT SINCE BRER RABBIT was thrown into the briar patch, had anyone adapted quicker or better to an environment they were forced into. Sabrina loved New York and nothing about it disturbed her— not the noise, the odors, the crowds—not even the short tempers of some of the taxi drivers and other motorists.

"I can't believe she has no complaints. For the first time in my life, she seems to be enjoying herself." Jeff was speaking to his sister on the phone.

"Maybe if she had been born and reared in New York rather than in the sand hills of South Carolina, our lives would have been better," Megan replied.

It took Sabrina little time to learn her way around the subway system. Jeff wouldn't let her ride uptown by herself at night, but on Wednesdays, she caught the express subway to mid-Manhattan where she spent the day walking around Times Square or up to Central Park. She would usually have lunch in the park or at a deli on 47th Street near Seventh Avenue. Sometimes she would visit a museum or just hang out in the Algonquin Hotel Bar, sipping tea and watching people, sometimes eavesdropping on their conversations.

Jeff practiced during the day, but was usually home for dinner. Sometimes Sabrina shopped and prepared dinner, but most evenings they ate at one of the moderately priced restaurants around Washington Square.

SHORTLY AFTER RETURNING to New York, Jeff had a bottle of wine and a thank you letter delivered to Ernest Fletcher. Fletcher called to thank him and to invite him to dinner at Le Cirque. Jeff politely declined, using an excuse he hoped Fletcher would interpret as saying, "Thanks, but I'm really not interested." He didn't, or if he did, he ignored it and called again the following week.

Jeff didn't want to hurt his feelings by rejecting him outright. "I would love to have dinner with you, but my mother's living with me now and I don't want to leave her alone."

There was a pause before Ernie answered. "I'd love to meet the mother of such an attractive son. So please bring her along."

THE ELEVATOR OPENED INTO A SPACIOUS CO-OP apartment on the top floor of a Park Avenue high-rise. At first glance, it looked more like an art museum than a residence. Elegantly framed paintings covered the walls. To the right was a large dining room table surrounded by a dozen antique chairs. A large silver service rested in the center of the table and a chandelier, resembling the one that comes crashing down in *The Phantom of the Opera,* hung above it. A formal looking sitting area was on the other end of the dining area, complete with a large fireplace. Large windows in the far wall looked out over the East River and beyond.

Six couples were standing around in the sitting area sipping wine and talking. There were equally as many formally dressed servants moving around with trays of drinks.

Ernie greeted Jeff with a warm hug and some trivial chatter before turning to his mother.

Sabrina looked radiant, but Ernie was paying more attention to Jeff.

Ernie was different from the race drivers she had thought so attractive. He was older, six feet tall and slender with silver hair, and a perfectly groomed mustache. She found him gentle and charming. Compared to Ernie, even though Mike and his friends were rich and famous, they were plain and simple.

Sabrina was seated on Ernie's right. She didn't know it was the highest seat of honor for such an occasion, but she knew it was where the male guests could see her in their peripheral vision while pretending to look at their host.

Ernie led the conversation, while politely leaving openings for his guests to talk.

Sabrina hung onto every word, although she didn't understand a lot of what was being discussed. Talk was about artists she had never heard of, the opera, the stock market, politics and sports. When the conversation turned to sports, she thought stock car racing would be a topic she could join in on. Instead it was about the Rangers, the Islanders, and the Bruins, teams she had never heard of and had no idea what sport they played. Nevertheless, she enjoyed every moment of the conversations going on around her.

She listened intently as Ernie talked about his financial success. His father had sold some oil properties to a larger energy company shortly before he died. He took stock in the company in payment. Ernie, as the only heir, inherited his father's stock. It grew rapidly in value from a few million dollars to well over $300 million. He refused to own any other stock, and it was clear that he thought little of one of his guest's suggestions that he might wish to diversify.

"Why would I buy stock in any other company? Look at how Enson's stock has performed. And that's just the beginning. They have lobbyists in almost every state convincing legislatures that regulating public utilities is unnecessary and old fashioned. Leave it to competition and people's rates will go down. Competition will lead to efficiencies that will translate into lower prices. Except Enson doesn't expect competition, because they'll be so large and powerful no other company will be able to compete with them. If there's to be energy in the world, Enson will furnish it, and they'll charge what they want for it. They won't have to worry about anti-trust laws, because they are in with the administration. When the administration was formulating its energy policy, who did the vice president send for to write it for them? Enson's top management!"

Except for Sabrina, the others at the table were becoming uneasy. They hastily changed the subject to the ballet and turned to Jeff to talk about plans for the next season.

Sabrina leaned to her left and whispered to Ernie, "I want to hear more about Enson. When my divorce settlement comes through, I'll have some money to invest."

Jeff and his mother were the first couple to leave the party. The male guests gave Sabrina a hug and told her what a delightful dinner companion she had been. The women shook hands and mumbled something about enjoying meeting her and her attractive son.

Ernie walked Jeff and his mother to the elevator, holding onto Jeff's elbow and telling him what a pleasure it was to have his favorite ballet performer as a dinner guest. "I do hope we can get together soon. I'll call you. Try to make some time available for me."

Sabrina didn't understand why she wasn't the primary object of Ernie's interest, unless he considered her too young for him.

Ernie embraced her briefly in the elevator lobby and said, "Thanks for coming. It was nice meeting you, Sabrina. I already knew one important thing about you. You have a very attractive and talented son."

She waited for him to say he would call her, but he didn't. His eyes were focused on Jeff as the elevator door closed.

JEFF SPENT AS MUCH TIME AS POSSIBLE with his mother, especially on weekends. They went to the theater, museums, restaurants, and even a Saturday trip deep into Brooklyn to Brennan & Carrs restaurant, which was reputed to serve the best roast beef sandwich in the world. It was started before the Depression by the son-in-law of the famous horse trainer, Sunny Jim Fitzsimmons.

As they walked back to the subway in Brooklyn, the Sabbath services were letting out at a large synagogue. Sabrina was curious about all of the men with beards, dressed in all black and wearing black hats. Jeff explained that they were Orthodox Jews coming out of worship services. "That reminds me," he said. "I've been intending to suggest we go to church, just to show you that there are people in the Big Apple who do go to church."

Sabrina wasn't excited by the idea, but she didn't protest.

Jeff considered the old Trinity Church on lower Broadway. The historical old Episcopal church with the grave of Alexander Hamilton in its shadow had a special appeal to everyone, even people with little interest in religion. But he was afraid his mother would be intimidated by the rituals, not knowing when to stand, sit, or kneel. And how would she react to the fancy dressed man walking down the isle swinging a pot of bad smelling incense?

He selected a small Methodist church halfway between Washington Square and the financial district. The church looked like it would hold 400 people, but there were less than a hundred there. Most were over fifty, and at least three-fourths were women likely widows, with Type A Wall Street successes who died young, Jeff thought.

The service started and the congregation was on the second verse of the first hymn when a young lady about six inches shorter that Jeff slipped into the seat next to him. He moved the hymnal toward her. She slipped her hand under the half nearest to her, and grasp the edge with her other hand. Her beautiful soprano voice blended nicely with Jeff's tenor. He didn't have to look to know she was a young lady with class—the sound of her voice, the subtle smell of perfume, fashionable shoes with medium heels—just the right touch. He also noticed that her nails were trimmed neatly and covered with a clear polish.

When they stood to sing the second hymn, Jeff expected her to reach for the hymnal in the rack in front of her. Instead, she stood as if she had not noticed it. When Jeff found the right page, she moved closer and reached for the edge of the hymnal, pulling it so that it was between them. Their bodies were so close they were touching. Neither moved away as their voices again blended beautifully. There was no choir and except for their singing, the singing of the congregation was weak and without emotion.

It wasn't until the Passing of the Peace that they looked into each other's eyes.

"May the peace of God be with you," the woman said.

"And also with you," Jeff replied.

She was not beautiful like Sabrina, or some of the girls in the ballet company. She didn't need to be. There was an attractiveness about her that went deeper than looks.

The preacher had the collection plates in his hands and the ushers were coming forward when he said, "I'm sorry I forgot to ask you at the beginning of the service to pass the fellowship register down the aisle. Those of you sitting nearest the center aisle will find it in front of you. Please sign your name, list your address, and pass it down the row. As it is passed back, take note of those worshiping around you and greet them after the service."

Jeff took the pad from the young lady on his left, and before signing his name, looked at hers. "Bonnie Small." He could hardly believe it. Her address was the apartment directly across the street from his loft.

When the service ended, several couples gathered. The men did most of the talking.

"Welcome. This must be your first time here since I would remember if I had seen you before. Do you live nearby?"

"Please consider joining us."

"I'll get your address from the fellowship register, and be in touch. Is it okay if we visit?"

"Where are you from originally? None of us are originally from around here."

When Sabrina answered, "South Carolina," it brought on more questions and pithy comments.

In the meantime, Bonnie and Jeff were looking at each other, searching for words to say. Finally, Bonnie thrust forth her hand and said with a little laugh, "Hi, neighbor."

Jeff grasped her hand and said, "Can you believe it? We live across the street from each other. Why haven't I seen you before?"

"Oh I don't get out much. It's a rough neighborhood, you know." She was giggling and Jeff was enjoying her humor, but he was more interested in making serious conversation.

"Do you come to this church often?" Jeff asked.

"This is my first time. I must admit I don't go to church often. It's strange. When I went to bed last night and I had no idea I would be going to church this morning. But here I am. If there are spirits, one is bound to be responsible for urging me on. I selected this church at random out of the yellow pages, got here late and slipped into a seat right next to a neighbor I've never met. The Spirit must be telling me something, don't you think."

Bonnie laughed and Jeff knew she wasn't serious. Yet, it was a coincidence. He continued the banter. "Oh, it was meant to be. Didn't you study Calvin? "Whatever will be, will be, even if it never does be."

Bonnie laughed. "But this is a Methodist church. Isn't predestination a Presbyterian doctrine?"

Before Jeff could answer, he felt his mother pulling at his arm. The spouses of those who had descended on her had finally pulled their husbands away and headed out the door.

"Mom, meet Bonnie. She lives across the street from us."

"Then, why doesn't she join us for lunch?" Sabrina said, without first speaking a word of greeting to Bonnie.

The three walked together the block and a half to the nearest deli. All the tables were filled. When their tuna sandwiches were ready, there were still no vacancies.

"Why don't we take the sandwiches to my apartment," Bonnie said. "It's a short walk, and I have plenty of soft drinks, chips and pretzels to add to our lunch. I also have some baked fudge that I made myself. And oh yes, I have a bottle of Washington State's finest and its neck hasn't yet been wrung."

While walking to Bonnie's apartment they engaged in small talk.

Sabrina was excited to learn that Bonnie was a stock analyst. "I'm going to have some money to invest soon," said Sabrina, "and I'll need some help. Can I call you?"

"Please do," Bonnie said as she handed Sabrina her card. "As an analyst, I research and analyze a certain group of stocks and follow the companies. I'll be glad to give you some of my research. I'm not a broker and don't sell stocks, but I can put you in touch with some of the most skilled of any in the city."

When Bonnie learned that Jeff was a ballet dancer, she almost screamed. "My childhood dream was to be a ballerina! I took ballet lessons from the time I could walk until my senior year in high school. I never got over the disappointment of having to stop. Not that I would have succeeded in getting to New York like you have."

"Why did you stop?" Jeff asked.

"I broke my ankle while skiing during Christmas vacation my junior year in high school. It was six months before I could dance. So I concentrated on my studies and did well enough to get into an eastern school. I came East to go to Brown and have been here since."

BONNIE'S APARTMENT was a notch below Jeff's loft. It was in a small warehouse that had been converted into apartments. Hers was on the second floor and was reached by walking up outside stairs that also served as a fire escape. There was a small but nicely decorated living area, with a U-shaped kitchen on the end. A small table surrounded by four chairs sat between the kitchen and living area. A door opened from the right of the living area into a bedroom. A single bath was located at the end of the bedroom.

Framed pictures of Bonnie and her family at a ski resort sat on each table at the end of the sofa.

Jeff recognized the pictures from pictures his sister had sent him. "Big Mountain, Montana," he said, as he picked up the picture and held it closer. "My sister lives and works there. She's an accomplished snowboarder, and her apartment mate is terrific skier. In fact, she's a professional instructor."

"My family goes to Big Mountain every year during the Christmas holidays," Bonnie replied. "We hire our own instructor for the full week. Her name is Samantha, but she prefers to be called Sam."

"What a small world. My sister's apartment mate is named Sam. She's got to be your instructor. It would be too much of a coincidence for there to be two female ski instructors called Sam."

Bonnie knew that Sam and Jeff's sister were gay partners, because they made no effort to hide it. If there had ever been any doubt, it was cleared up when Bonnie's older brother got a crush on Sam, only to learn that she was already committed...to a girl named Megan.

Bonnie looked at Jeff, wondering if there could be two gay siblings in the same family. Jeff was somewhat effeminate, and wore a gold bracelet and a chain around his neck. I'll take my chances, she thought. At least he isn't wearing an earring, and I trust he has no tattoos. With handsome looks, a good personality and no tattoos or body piercing, I can probably get him past my family's threshold.

Chapter 22

THE SEPARATION AGREEMENT was ready for Sabrina and Don's signature near the end of the fall, less than a year after Sabrina left home. The key to obtaining an early agreement was agreeing to pay Dawg Brinson the exorbitant fee he requested and that Don was willing to give in to all of Sabrina's demands. Fortunately, his own lawyer stepped in to object when Dawg made demands that his client wasn't entitled to, such as a share in property that Don had inherited or otherwise acquired before the marriage.

Don didn't worry because he knew he and Huggie would have enough to comfortably live on. He planned to continue practicing dentistry until his age or declining health required him to retire and he would likely never marry again. Under the worst of circumstances, he would be able to give Megan and Jeff significant cash gifts each year, and with the money and property he had left and proceeds from large insurance policies his life insurance agent friends had persuaded him to purchase, the trust established for Huggie would receive substantial amounts when he died.

Sabrina was interested in cash, not property. Without worrying about questions of ethics or conflicts of interest, Dawg agreed to purchase the property she received under the agreement. He had the properties appraised by three appraisers, all close friends, and agreed to pay the amount of the highest appraisal. Since the appraisals were slightly higher than the tax valuations, Sabrina thought her lawyer was being overly generous. She didn't know the fair market value was much greater.

The issue of custody of Huggie was left open. Sabrina wanted Don to have custody, but for reasons she didn't understand, Dawg insisted the custody agreement remain silent. Don's lawyer didn't push the issue.

Finally, the agreement contained terms stating that a divorce decree would be entered with the agreement of both parties as soon as the period of separation permitted it.

SABRINA'S EIGHT MILLION DOLLARS gave her the false confidence that she could run with Ernest Fletcher and his wealthy friends. She didn't realize that while it was a lot of money in the sand hills of South Carolina, it would not sustain a lifestyle in New York like that of Ernie Fletcher and his friends.

Soon after Ernie's dinner party, Sabrina called and invited him to a dress rehearsal of Jeff's ballet company, to be followed by dinner at a nice restaurant. At first he thought he had a conflict, but when she told him Jeff would be joining them for dinner, he called back to say the conflict had been resolved. Afterwards, Ernie invited them to dinner to return the hospitality. But Jeff wasn't available and only Sabrina could go. To avoid having to spend the evening alone with her, Ernie invited some of his friends to join them. They were so complimentary of his "beautiful young friend," that he realized that like expensive jewelry, the striking blond was an impressive appendage. So he started calling her from time to time when he needed a female guest for a social occasion.

With a recommendation from Ernie, Sabrina was approved to purchase a small unit on a lower floor in the co-op where he lived. It cost over a million dollars, and with Ernie's help, she decorated it herself, spending nearly half a million on furnishings, including designer drapes.

Sabrina knew little about art, but she knew it was important to Ernest Fletcher and his friends. So she asked him to help her select some paintings for her new apartment. Touring the galleries, where Ernie was welcomed as a close friend, was exciting, and she was pleased with his selections. He had a way of making her feel they were her choices, and reflected her superb taste. With the exception of a Marc Chagall original selected for one of the bathrooms, all paintings were by contemporary artists, most of whom Ernie claimed to know personally. He convinced Sabrina that each piece was a masterpiece that would grow in value. "You watch. They'll go up in value like the stock of my company, Enson."

Over half of Sabrina's eight million dollars was gone within a few weeks. Not gone, she convinced herself, but wisely invested in assets that would increase in value. She had no idea that taxes, owner's dues and insurance on her co-op unit and its contents would cost more than her remaining income from Enson stock. And of course, there was the car: the largest and finest BMW made, which cost over $100,000. The cost to park it in a garage near where she lived was more than the rent on Jeff's loft apartment.

JEFF HAD NEVER HAD SO CLOSE A FRIEND as Bonnie. For the first few months after they met, they were together every evening he didn't have a performance. Some evenings he cooked in his apartment; some she cooked in hers. Occasionally they sent out for pizza, which they ate with a beer while listening to music. They enjoyed the same music and the same television programs. They also enjoyed walking to a favorite deli or one of the many restaurants around Washington Square. On Sundays, they often attended a church selected at random.

As close as they were, Jeff showed little affection. Bonnie wanted more. When they sat together, she would move close, and sometimes as they walked she would clasp Jeff's hand. Jeff wouldn't pull away, but he did nothing to indicate he wanted to move closer. This bothered Jeff as well as Bonnie. He looked forward to coming home in the evenings, knowing he would have the company of someone he loved being with. But he knew the relationship could not endure without some feeling of passion and intimacy on his part. He didn't want it to end, but he couldn't muster the feeling necessary to move him closer.

When Bonnie mentioned she was going to fly home to Seattle for the week before Easter, Jeff had a sinking feeling. She had become so much a part of his life that it was hard to think of a week without her.

The weekend before Bonnie was to leave; she and Jeff met Sabrina at a Midtown restaurant for dinner. Ernie was invited, but chose not to come when he learned Jeff would be with a lady friend. Jeff was pleased that his mother seemed to like Bonnie.

Sabrina asked about Bonnie's family And Bonnie loved to talk about them.

"My father has his own stock brokerage firm in Seattle. He's quite successful. My mother stays busy as a volunteer in all kinds of civic projects in the area. They didn't want me to come East, and they constantly beg me to return to Seattle and join the business. I have an older brother who has a degree from Stanford and an MBA from the University of Washington, not that any of that matters since he's a stock broker at my father's firm. Relationships are the most important part of that business, and he excels in relationships. He's very popular. In fact, he and a close friend are considered the most eligible bachelors in the area. They're both thirty five."

As Bonnie talked, Jeff had his head down, his eyes staring at his soup.

Bonnie continued. "I don't have to worry about security. I have an excellent job, my family is well to do, and my professional future is bright. So if Mr. Right never shows, the only question will be whether I'm willing to enter a marriage with someone I have no romantic feeling for, so I can have a family, or have children as a single mom, using the sperm of an anonymous donor"

Jeff pretended not to be interested, but he was hanging onto every word.

The conversation got more interesting when his mother said to Bonnie, "Perhaps you've already had the opportunity to marry?"

"Yes. David has been my brother's best friend since they were in grade school, and our parents are friends. When my brother and David were in high school, I tried to tag along wherever they went. The more I could annoy them, the happier I was. David called me the neighborhood pest. So I was surprised when I came home from college for Christmas vacation my freshman year and he asked me for a date. Well, to make a long story short, we've seen each other a lot since then. He now calls me his favorite little pest. Half the eligible ladies in Seattle would give their chance for a place in heaven to have his interest. But, I'm not certain I can ever see David as anyone other than an adorable older brother. Maybe that's enough. We agreed during the Christmas holidays not to see each other again until Easter. Before that, David was flying to New York quite often. We plan to spend most of Easter week in Victoria. If I make the decision he and my folks are expecting, I won't be coming back to New York."

Jeff's heart was racing and he began to perspire. He didn't want to hear any more and said in a shaky voice, "Bonnie, I've been intending to ask you, for mom's information, what you think about her stock in Enson Corporation."

The question was so out of context from the discussion she and Sabrina were having that Bonnie had to take a few seconds to gather her thoughts

"I don't follow it professionally so I don't know a lot about it. Of course, everyone knows it's had a fabulous run. It could be at the high range of where it will ultimately go. Some of my analyst friends who follow it have reduced their recommendation recently from buy to hold. Nevertheless, I would recommend to anybody that if they like that stock, or any other stock for that matter, they should diversify."

Sabrina blushed slightly, but did not respond.

JEFF HAD DINNER WITH HIS MOTHER and Ernie the evening before he was to leave with the company on a tour. He looked forward to getting away. The week without Bonnie had been difficult. If only he had competed for her affection. He had managed to kiss her good-bye, but he feared it wasn't the sort of kiss she expected. She just said good-bye and left. She didn't say, "I'll be in touch," or anything else.

As Jeff walked home from the subway station, his heart skipped a beat when he saw a light in Bonnie's apartment. He reasoned she probably left it on when she left and he had not noticed it because he didn't want to look at her apartment. He resisted the urge to knock on her door.

It was eleven o'clock when he finished packing for an early morning departure. He knew he would have trouble going to sleep, so he went to the refrigerator and took out a half bottle of chardonnay. "Might as well finish it off," he said to himself as he poured the remaining wine into a tall glass. Etiquette isn't important when you are alone, he thought to himself.

He ran his thumb down his large collection of CDs. It passed quickly over the ballets and after slowing at the operas, he continued. His finger stopped at a recording of sacred arias by Andrea Bocelli. After placing it in his Bose, he kicked off his shoes and pushed back in a comfortable chair with his feet resting on an ottoman.

He blamed himself for being sad and melancholy. There was so much to be thankful for. The time he and Bonnie spent together made wonderful and lasting memories. They had had so much fun shopping together, going to shows, preparing dinners, and chatting on the phone for hours at a time.

He was also thankful his mother had stopped drinking and for the first time in his life she was enjoying herself. He was pleased that the settlement between his parents was amicable. No one had to tell him that the reason the settlement was reached so quickly was that his father had given in to every one of his mother's attorney's demands. His father was the most unselfish man he knew. Don always put the needs of his family before his own, unless their wishes conflicted with his family's welfare.

The wine was taking effect and Jeff was feeling mellow. Thoughts of his father brought a lump to his throat and feelings of guilt. His father's love and care for his children had made it possible for them to endure their mother's selfishness and cruelty.

What had he or Megan ever done for their father? He was bound to crave the love of his children, confirmed by their attention, their open affection, their show of concern and interest, but as much as they loved their father, they had essentially ignored him. Thank God there was Huggie. How would he survive without her?

His father had never mentioned grandchildren, but Jeff knew nothing would make him happier. Not that he craved one to carry on the Hazelhurst name like his brothers undoubtedly did, but because a grandchild would be a creature he could shower with love and affection. But how could he look forward to a grandchild? Because of her chosen lifestyle, Megan was unlikely to ever have children, and Huggie couldn't. That left only Jeff. And as much as Jeff wanted a child, he had no confidence that he could produce one.

Jeff closed his eyes and tried to get his mind off his father. He was almost asleep when he became aware of Bocelli's wonderful tenor voice singing *Pannis Angelicus* by Caesar Franc, one of the most beautiful arias ever written.

As he dozed off to sleep he heard a knock at the door. Jeff looked at his watch. It was 1:30 a.m. He opened the door to find a shivering Bonnie standing there. She wore a trench coat pulled up under her chin with the collar turned up to cover her ears.

"I got up to let my cat in and saw that your light was still on," she said. "I just needed to come over and be with you this last night. I know you leave on tour tomorrow, and when you return, I may be gone."

Jeff didn't actually invite her in. She walked in, took off her coat and threw it across a chair. She wore only a flimsy gown that barely covered her bottom. She took Jeff by the hand and led him into the bedroom where she pulled him down beside her on the bed and buried her head in his chest.

Making a baby might not be such a hard task after all, Jeff thought as he pulled her closer.

Chapter 23

BRENDA WAS GLAD WHEN THE ALARM CLOCK sounded at 6:30 a.m. the morning after Christmas. She had tossed and turned most of the night, and when she finally drifted off to sleep she had a haunting dream.

There was a fire, lots of fire engines, policemen and ambulances. The beautiful old house where Dr. Hazlehurst lived with his daughter was burning to the ground. Firemen were just standing around watching. Brenda saw neither Dr. Hazlehurst nor his daughter. The thought that they might be in the burning house was like a blow that penetrated her stomach and then exploded, sending poison throughout her body. A child was sitting on the limb of a tree, high above the ground and sobbing. It was Huggie. Brenda tried to reach up to her but the limb was so high that there was no way Huggie could have climbed up there on her own.

When Huggie looked down and saw Brenda, her fear turned to anger and she began cursing, using profanity Brenda knew Huggie had never heard. "Where were you? Why did you let this happen?" she cried.

Brenda tried to answer, but as often happens in dreams, she couldn't talk. She wanted to run away, but her feet were glued to the ground and she couldn't move them. She looked up to the limb where Huggie was sitting and was shocked to see that the creature sitting on the limb was no longer Huggie, but a huge cat, growling and showing its fangs. Suddenly it leaped from the limb with sharp claws outstretched and headed directly to Brenda's face. Just before the outstretched claws reached her face she woke up.

When she awoke, Brenda's arms were covering her face and her entire body was shaking. She felt damp, and soon realized that she had perspired profusely during the horrible dream. Her pillow and bed sheets were soaking wet, as was her nightgown.

As she rolled out of bed, she slipped out of her nightgown, letting it drop to the floor. She put on a dry gown and climbed in the opposite side of the bed where there was no dampness. She had just drifted back to sleep when the alarm sounded.

Christmases had usually been followed by several days of feeling depressed, or as the old folks said, "feeling blue." Psychologist friends had told Brenda that such feelings are not unusual, but she didn't recall why. As a child, when Christmas was over she was always anxious to get back to school.

This particular Christmas had been especially difficult. Don and Huggie were in New York to attend Jeff and Bonnie's wedding. Christmas dinner with her mother and siblings had been pleasant, but she was glad to get home to her cats. She had not bothered to get a tree or to decorate. The only suggestion in her place that it was Christmas was an unopened package she had received from Huggie two days before. Brenda laughed as she opened the box to find a similar looking necklace as the one Huggie had given her the year before.

THE OFFICE WAS SCHEDULED to be closed the day after Christmas and Brenda had no plans. A phone message from Miss

Ginny was waiting when she came home from her family's Christmas dinner. Brinson was ordering all attorneys and the office staff to report to work.

Brenda punched in the answering machine to listen again to Miss Ginny's message. The usual slow, drawling voice of the old lady had been turned up a couple of notches. Miss Ginny was talking so fast Brenda could hardly make out some of her words, but the message was clear. All lawyers and staff were expected to be at the office by 7:00 a.m. the morning after Christmas. There had been an explosion in Charlotte on Christmas day.

Brenda started to turn on the television to get more details, but then decided not to. First, she needed the effects of her dream to subside. She took a box of dry cat food from the kitchen cabinet and shook a generous portion into each of the cat bowls. Sinbad, Simon and Simmie bounded from the foot of her bed. It took them only a couple of leaps through the den before they had their heads buried in their bowls, eating as if the food would disappear before they got there.

Brenda looked at her cream-colored Siamese cats. None looked like the cat that Huggie turned into in the dream. That cat looked like Huggie's cat, Buffy, but it was much larger than Buffy, and was very mean.

Brenda turned on the radio while she waited for her instant oatmeal to heat in the microwave. The newsman was talking about the Christmas day tragedy in Charlotte.

Five firemen are dead and dozens more injured, several critically. Three have been flown to the Jaycee Burn Center in Chapel Hill with life threatening injuries. Three others remain at the Carolinas Medical Center with third degree burns over more than half their bodies. Several people a block away received facial burns from the hot sodium splashing on their faces. They will be left with disfiguring pock marks, according to doctors.

She turned off the radio, thinking that as tragic as the story was, it did little to take her mind off the dream.

THE LARGE CONFERENCE ROOM was filled with lawyers and staff, everyone connected with the firm except Miss Ginny, who was left to tend the gate and answer the phone.

Brenda expected the meeting to be somber. Five people were dead and more deaths would follow. Dozens were seriously injured. Christmas had been shattered for many people, and it would never again be a happy occasion for the hundreds of surviving families and friends.

The conference room was anything but somber. It buzzed with conversations about the great opportunities the explosion brought to the firm.

"Dawg already damn near owns the railroad," one lawyer said. "By the time he gets through with the chemical company, he'll own it, too."

Brenda listened, catching bits and pieces of several conversations. She whispered to the lawyer sitting next to her, "But it happened in North Carolina. Doesn't that complicate it for us?"

"Naw," the lawyer replied. "The chemical company over in Sumter is one of the parties that left the vat of sodium in the old abandoned building. They didn't warn anybody about it when they sold it. All their operations are here now. They don't have anything in North Carolina any longer."

When Dawg walked into the room the buzz stopped quickly, like a plug had been pulled out of a static emitting radio. He was smiling.

"Folks," he said, "we got the greatest opportunity we've had since the airliner crashed near here ten years ago. As soon as I heard about the explosion I called some of you, and I appreciate your being available, even on Christmas day. Zeb was at the funeral home before the time the first body got there. He's already got some signatures on contracts. We don't know for sure if they are the next of kin, but they're close enough that we think we can get them appointed administrators of the estates.

"I understand the courthouse in Charlotte is open today. Zeb's gonna try to get the administrator appointed today. Soon as he gets that done, I'll file suit in Federal District Court over in Florence. It's closed for the Christmas holidays, but I'll call the deputy clerk. I'm sure she'll meet me there and stamp the papers. Joe's in charge of seeing that the TV folks and the newspaper folks are there. Once we get a case filed, it'll be easier to get other cases. Which means if any of the cases end up with Charlotte lawyers, they'll need to associate us, because the best place to sue the chemical company is right here in South Carolina. Those stingy Scotch Presbyterians in Mecklenburg County make terrible jurors. They treat a defendant's money like it was theirs. People down here enjoy socking it to big corporations and insurance companies."

Dawg paused to take a sip of water, then continued. "Talmadge has investigated this thing and he's gonna brief us on what he knows. We need to know the facts so that when we talk to the victims and their families we can show them we know what happened, who's responsible, and who we intend to make pay."

Talmadge Baker had practiced with Dawg for twenty-five years. He was a meticulous investigator and was well respected in the firm. When he got up to speak he had everybody's attention.

"Five years ago the Aberdeen Chemical Company bought the old Brown Chemical business in Charlotte. It was owned by two brothers whose father started it over fifty years before. People wondered what the chemical company wanted with it. The plant was obsolete and located near what had become the center of the city.

"The brothers wanted to retire so they agreed to sell the business to the chemical company. It wasn't a big deal for the chemical company. It wanted it only to get its customers. It never intended to operate the plant and it didn't. In fact, it closed it and sold it to a developer who planned to tear it down and build condominiums. But when the developer learned that environmental cleanup costs made development uneconomical, nothing was done.

"In the meantime, the roof of the old abandoned plant began to leak and one of the outside walls fell in. The City ordered the developer to repair the building or tear it down within six months. Over a year passed and he didn't do anything and the City ignored it."

Dawg interrupted. "That's all interesting, Talmadge, but this ain't no history class. Tell us only what we need to know."

Talmadge wasn't intimidated by Dawg's impatience and continued. "Unbeknown to anyone now living, in a part of the building that had not been used for years, there was a vat submerged below the floor. It was probably 20 feet by 20 feet and at least 10 feet deep. The covering stuck up a few inches above the floor. Nobody ever bothered to check to see what was underneath the cover."

Dawg became impatient and annoyed. "What the hell was in it, Talmadge?"

Talmadge continued, determined to tell it the way he wanted to. "You remember a few days before Christmas we had some freezing rain that caused some problems in the Charlotte area. Well the rain poured through the roof of the old plant and froze. Ice formed all around the lid on the old vat. On Christmas morning, the ice began to melt. Water seeped underneath the lid on the old vat, causing steam to form and start coming out from under the lid. Someone passing by saw the steam and thought it was smoke. They called and reported that the building was on fire. Within minutes three fire companies responded. Why the hell they sent so many I don't k now. There was no fire. It wasn't smoke, only steam."

"What happened? What the hell happened?" Dawg yelled. "Cut through the bullshit and tell us what happened."

Talmadge paused then continued. "Four of the fireman pried off the lid on the vat. A fifth stuck the nozzle of a hose inside. The water hit the contents of the vat and there was an explosion. The fireman holding the hose had his head blown off. They found it twenty feet away. A French guillotine couldn't have severed it more cleanly. Of course there were bodies everywhere. Most of those still living would have been better off if they'd been killed outright."

The room became quiet and still.

Brenda was remembering long ago in a chemistry class, the teacher dropped a small tablet of sodium in a glass of water. She didn't recall what the experiment was supposed to demonstrate, only that sodium and water do not mix.

"Did you say sodium?" she asked softly.

"Yes!" Talmadge answered.

The others continued to sit quietly. All had heard the news that the vat was filled with sodium that must have long ago been used by the old chemical company. But to most of them, it meant no more than if it had been filled with baking soda.

Dawg broke the silence. "I know y'all are thinking there are all kinds of culprits out there, and you're right: The brothers sold the building without any warning that a vat of sodium was there. The developer is guilty as sin and I don't need to go into details. As for the City, why the hell didn't they go in there and tear down the building when the developer didn't? They knew it was dangerous. That's why they ordered it torn down. And why did they send so many fire fighters to check on what was nothing but some steam? And why weren't they better trained? They shoulda known better than to put water in a tub of stuff when they didn't know what it was. But it wasn't their fault. They shoulda been taught better. I don't know anything about sodium. I 'spect it tastes kinda salty. But I'm a lawyer. I don't need to know nothing 'bout chemicals."

Dawg paused to take a swallow of water, then made eye contact with everybody in the room. "Forget about all the culprits 'cept for one. The chemical company's the one we can get our arms around the easiest 'cause they're right over in Sumter. They got as much money as we'll need. Since they're from Scotland they probably got insurance with Lloyd's of London. As you know, they're easier to pick than cotton. We don't need to go to Charlotte to sue the brothers who sold the plant. They're probably not worth more than two, three million dollars anyway. And I understand the developer's near bankrupt. The City, the fire department, they would raise all kinds of defenses about governmental immunity. We don't want to have to spend a lot of time looking up the law on that, and we don't have to. We got the deep pockets we need right next door."

DAWG STOOD AT THE DOOR as the lawyers and staff left the room. He shook hands with each one and patted them on the back. "Remember you're a member of this team and your assignment means a lot to all of us," he told them.

The staff, mostly secretaries, were women. Each had been given telephone numbers of at least one of the victim's family. They were to call and recite a canned message that had been furnished them by a senior associate whom Dawg had prepare it.

Mr. / Mrs. (insert name of person you are assigned.) I've heard the horrible news and my heart goes out to you. I pray for you and all of your dear family. I'm so touched by your situation that I had to call. It's probably because I went through something like you're going through. I still miss Ralph so. But at least I don't have any money worries. I don't work anymore. I have enough to live well on for the rest of my life and enough to educate my three children. In fact we got more money than if Ralph were still with us.

Now I wish Ralph were still here, even if me and the children had nothing to eat but beans and rice. But since we can't have him, we are thankful we have enough money.

How did we mange this? Well, we didn't. We had this great lawyer. Don't remember his name, but he was called Dawg. I think his name may have been Shrimpson, or maybe it was Brinson. Yes, that's it Dawg Brinson. I expect he has seen about the explosion on television and will have one of his lawyers contact you. Whatever you do, don't sign up with any other lawyer until you hear from Dawg Brinson's law firm.

BRENDA CAME OUT OF DAWG'S office with her assignment.. She needed to be in Charlotte in time for visitation at the funeral home where the body of an African-American fireman rested. It was her only assignment, but it was an important one.

Dawg called to her as she was about to exit the door. "By the way, Brenda, before you go anywhere, take off that God awful necklace you're wearing. I don't usually pay attention to jewelry, but I couldn't help noticing that tacky thing. I don't want you going anywhere representing the firm wearing that thing."

Brenda was taken aback. With the urgency of all that was going on, she had not expected Huggie's necklace to become an issue. "This is a Christmas gift from a friend," she said.

"He must not be much of a friend to give you something like that. You sure he weren't playing a joke on you?"

Chapter 24

THE FUNERAL HOME STILL HAD A DECORATED CHRISTMAS TREE in the foyer. A manger scene was under the tree. Both seemed out of place, even though it was the day after Christmas.

Brenda stood quietly in the long line winding down the hallway past a registry and through several rooms. In the room at the end of the line, family members stood in front of an opened casket and greeted friends. Occasional sobs could be heard over the mournful sounds of organ music. There was a sweet, almost nauseating smell of flowers.

"Are you a relative or a friend of the family?" a soft voice behind her asked.

Brenda turned to see a tall handsome man looking down into her eyes. She was startled, perhaps because he was so attractive. He was trim, athletic looking, clean-shaven and looked a lot like, O. J. Simpson.

"I guess you could say I'm a friend of the family," Brenda replied. "And you?"

"A friend. William and I were guards on the Independence High School basketball team that won the state championship almost twenty years ago. Then we roomed together at Johnson C. Smith

University for a couple of years. He dropped out to join the fire department and I continued. We were both members of the same church and remained close friends."

"What do you do?" Brenda asked.

"I'm a professor of sociology at Queens University here in town. And what about you?"

Brenda wished she didn't have to answer. She would be stereotyped as an ambulance chaser when the young man learned she knew neither the deceased nor any of his family members, nor anyone else nearby. She started to say. "I'm a hairdresser," but she knew that if she lied, she would lose a chance to get to know this attractive young man.

"I'm a lawyer," she said. "And I must admit that my presence here is partly altruistic. My law firm in Darlington, South Carolina specializes in representing victims of catastrophic accidents. The Aberdeen Chemical Company, which sold the old building to the present owner without telling him of the hidden vat of sodium, has a large operation near us. They no longer have a presence in North Carolina, so it's doubtful they could be sued here. Also, the best place in the country to bring lawsuits is in our area. The judges are friendly. So are the jurors. Verdicts there average much more than here. And our firm is the most experienced personal injury, wrongful death firm in the southeast, perhaps in the country."

Brenda suddenly realized she had been talking rapidly, hardly pausing for breaths during her long spiel.

The young man laughed. "You don't need to be so defensive. Even lawyers, I suppose, sometimes serve a useful social purpose." He laughed again as did Brenda.

"By the way," he said as he extended his hand, "My name is Glenn Osborne."

"I'm Brenda Horton," she answered as she tightly held his right hand. "I'm pleased to meet you. I'm with the Brinson Law Firm."

"Is that by any chance the firm of a man they call Dawg?"

"Yes. Dawg Brinson is the person you have in mind."

"People say he's crooked," Glenn said.

"They also say he's successful," Brenda countered. "And to people like your friend's family, that's more important. But please understand, I would never agree that my boss is crooked."

"I don't question his success," Glenn said. "And William's family will need a good lawyer. He left a pregnant wife and twin six-year-old sons. They'll have a lot of support from their many friends, and especially from their church and pastor. But they'll also need financial support."

"Is the widow close to your pastor?" Brenda asked. "Let me put it this way. Often in communities, there's one person, usually a man, who has extraordinary influence. It might be a teacher, a funeral director, even a popular grocer or barber, but most often it's a pastor."

"Oh yes," Osborne said. "Reverend McCullers is the man in our community."

"Is he here tonight? Could you point him out to me?" Brenda tried not to sound excited.

"I'm sure he's here. He's probably with the family. You can't miss him. He's very short, about five feet five inches tall, and he has a gray beard."

"Thanks," Brenda said. "I think I'll go find him and ask that he convey the sympathy of my firm to the family. It's a long drive home and I need to get started. It might take a couple more hours before I reach the family by standing in line."

"I'll be glad to give the family that message for you, if you like," Glenn said.

Brenda politely declined the offer. She planned to ask Reverend McCullers to do more than convey sympathy. She extended her hand and in a warm voice said, "It's been nice talking with you, Glenn. Perhaps our paths will cross again sometime."

"I hope so," he answered.

REVEREND MCCULLERS WAS standing at the head of the receiving line of relatives lined up in front of the open casket. Brenda didn't look at the body, though she was curious as to how an undertaker could make such a badly burned corpse presentable.

As the pastor dropped the hand of one visitor and turned to take the hand of the next, Brenda reached in and took him by the arm and gently pulled him toward her. "I hate to disturb you, Reverend McCullers, but if I could just have a moment of your time. It's quite important and it won't take long."

She led the pastor down the hall until she found a small empty office. They sat on a couch facing a desk with an old upright typewriter on it. A picture of a dark-skinned Jesus hung over the couch.

"I'm Brenda Horton from the Brinson Law Firm in South Carolina. You've probably heard of us, especially Dawg Brinson who's the senior lawyer in the firm."

"Oh yes," McCullers said. "Everybody's heard of Mr. Dawg, even here in North Carolina."

Brenda's spirits rose as she sensed McCullers was enjoying being in the presence of someone who worked for a celebrity like Dawg Brinson.

Then the pastor said, "I know Mr. Dawg's a mighty good lawyer, but we have a couple of lawyers in the church. They've already been through the line and I heard Mrs. Williams promise them she wouldn't get a lawyer until they had a chance to talk with her."

"Oh, I hope you don't think I'm here trying to solicit a lawsuit. That would be unseemly under these circumstances. The reason I'm here is that everyone in our firm is so touched by this tragedy that we want to do something to show our love and sympathy. We know how much you and the church mean to the Williams family, and we want to make a memorial gift of $10,000 in memory of Mr. Williams. Mr. Brinson asked me to contact you personally to find out whether you want the check made out to the church or to you personally?"

McCuller's heart beat faster and his eyes grew wider with each word Brenda spoke. "That's so fine of you folks, especially Mr. Dawg. I sure would like to meet him someday. As for the check, just have it made out to me. I'll see that the family knows about it and I'll make sure the money is used in the right way."

For the next few minutes, Brenda talked about what the firm could do for the family. They would never have to worry about money again. She carefully kept interjecting from time to time that she wasn't trying to solicit the case, but just telling McCullers some things he might be interested in knowing.

Then she added what she hoped would be the clincher. "Should Dawg end up with the case, and I understand it's unlikely he will since you have some mighty good lawyers among your church members, but if he should get the case, he would want you and your church to share in his fee. His donation would make the ten thousand dollar memorial gift seem small." She then pulled a retainer contract from her purse and said, "Why don't I leave this with you, just in case Mrs. Williams decides she would like to have us represent her."

Brenda explained the contract should be signed and witnessed, then said, "Once it's signed, just put it in this addressed stamped envelop and drop it in the mail."

BRENDA SLEPT BETTER THAN THE NIGHT BEFORE. There were no awful dreams. In fact, there were no dreams at all. She awoke later than usual, feeling refreshed and looked forward to the day. The post-Christmas blues had disappeared.

Within less than half an hour upon awakening she breezed through the back door and into Dawg's reception room. "Good morning, Miss Ginny," she said cheerfully.

The old lady, was staring at the computer, and didn't return the salutation, but said, "Mr. Brinson wants to see you."

"Now?" Brenda asked.

"As soon as you get in," replied the old lady, "and it appears you're in!"

"Come in," the gruff voice of the senior lawyer yelled as soon as Brenda tapped softly on his door.

Dawg looked tired. His usually slicked back dyed black hair was uncombed and his clothes were disheveled. He held a mug of coffee in both hands. Brenda could smell the I. W. Harper whiskey in his mug.

"Did you get the contract signed?" Dawg asked.

"I'm confident that it's been signed by now and is in the mail. And by the way, I need a firm check for $10,000 made out to Reverend Richard McCullers. It's a memorial gift we are making to his church in memory of one of the deceased firemen. McCullers is getting the contract signed for us. He was the best way for us to get to the widow."

"Good," Dawg said. "No problem about the check. So far, we have two of the death cases and about half of the others. Some of the badly injured are in intensive care. We're trying to befriend their families, but will have to wait until they recover or die before we can pin their cases down.

"Several of the cases have gone to Charlotte lawyers. I called one and suggested he associates with us so we can sue the Aberdeen Chemical Company here. He said he didn't plan to sue Aberdeen. Claimed that since it's a foreign company it might be too complicated. He thinks they got all the defendants they need right in Charlotte.

"None of it makes any sense to me. Everybody knows Aberdeen is huge. They got plants all over the world, and folks tell me they're in a lot of other businesses, including pharmaceuticals and a fertilizer operation in South America. They may even own North Sea oil reserves. They're bound to be so rich they can pay out a hundred million or so and never miss it. They're just the type of company low country juries like to sock it to!"

Dawg paused, waiting for Brenda to agree with him. But she had some concerns. She knew it would be better for her to ignore them, but she knew she couldn't, which is one of the reasons she fitted with the firm like a square peg in a round hole.

"Dawg, I've been thinking," she said. "Maybe we should do some research before we file to make sure we have the proper party. Foreign corporations are sometimes organized in complex ways. The entity that bought the building might be a shell corporation loosely affiliated with its parent, the Aberdeen Chemical Company. Suing a defendant corporation that's chartered in a foreign country is not like suing the railroad. At this point we don't even know that the name Aberdeen Chemical Company is that of a legal company. It might be just a trade name. We don't want to sue the wrong party and be embarrassed."

"What do you mean embarrassed?" Dawg replied. "We gonna serve papers on the manager of the company over there in Sumter and the company's lawyers will come running with barrels full of money. They don't want one of my juries telling their client how much they gotta pay. Everybody knows it was the Aberdeen Chemical Company. Don't matter what name they put on the deed, they owned the building and are responsible. If they come before one of my judges and try to deny it 'cause of some technicality, they're gonna be in a heap of trouble.

"Braveheart, Rob Roy and Robert the Bruce all together couldn't protect them Scots once they're caught trying to be cute in this state. The judge'll shoot those pigeons before they can get off the ground. That vat of sodium was like a Bengal tiger. I don't remember much from law school, but I do remember the doctrine of strict liability. If you got a Bengal tiger caged up on your property and he gets out and eats somebody, you're strictly liable. You may show that he was there when you bought the property and you didn't know it. You can show you took every precaution possible. You can claim you did a better job of keeping him locked up than the zoo or the circus would.

"The plaintiff can agree that you were not negligent. It don't matter. You're responsible for whatever that tiger does. That vat of dangerous chemicals is just like that tiger. Once it gets out and hurts somebody, everybody that ever owned it and left it there is liable."

"That's right," Brenda said. "The plaintiff doesn't have to prove a lack of due care on anybody's part. But he does have to prove the right owner of the property where the tiger was kept. And it doesn't do any good if the plaintiff thinks it was one person and sues him, but it turns out to have been his brother. I wish it were as simple as an escaped tiger, and it may be, but horrible possibilities keep running through my mind. Suppose we have process served on the manager of the plant over in Sumter. We wait and no one comes running with barrels of money. Thirty days later we get served with a special appearance and motion to dismiss. The papers are signed by lawyers with a large New York law firm specializing in international law. Of course, they'll have to have South Carolina counsel also sign the papers, but the New York law firm will handle the case, and they have years of experience cruising in the murky waters of international law."

Dawg was mad and ready to kill the messenger, or in this case the person daring to suggest adverse consequences. But he was also concerned. The only issue he usually had to deal with was the amount an insurance company would have to pay his client. Questions of proper parties, jurisdictional issues, and problems of unraveling foreign corporations with multiple subsidiaries were never encountered in his practice.

"Why the hell you trying to get me antsy about the biggest case this law firm ever had?" he asked. "You know damn well the judge ain't listening to any lawyers who ain't from around here."

Dawg reached for his bottle of I. W. Harper whiskey. Could it be that the mad dog, capable of ripping defendants apart, was feeling ripples of uneasiness running through his belly?

Chapter 25

BRENDA GOT TO CHARLOTTE two hours before the ten o'clock service started at Reverend McCuller's church, or more accurately, she got there an hour late for his seven o'clock service.

Why didn't I know that the first service would have to start before eight if the second was to start at ten, she asked herself. She remembered that her mother used to say, "White folks complain if their preaching goes longer than an hour. If their picture shows lasted only an hour they'd think they're cheated. Our preaching is more entertaining than picture shows and we like for it to last a long time."

Going to Charlotte to attend church and meet with the firm's most important client was Brenda's idea. She had repeatedly expressed concern to Brinson that their explosion clients would become impatient if they continued to hear nothing from the firm.

How was she to kill two hours in Charlotte? She thought of finding an IHOP where she could sip coffee and read the Sunday Observer. But that wasn't appealing since she had stopped at Hardees for a sausage biscuit and two cups of coffee. She was interested in seeing where the African-American people lived, but didn't know where to look. She was sure it was not in Myers Park or Eastover.

She soon found herself driving to the old chemical building. It was on South Boulevard and easy to find. Parking wasn't easy because worshipers at a large church across the street had taken all of the parking places near the old building. She parked in an empty parking lot three blocks away. People arriving for church looked at her suspiciously as she made her way to the old building. It was still surrounded by yellow police tape and numerous signs warned: "Trespassers will be prosecuted."

She went to the back of the building where she could not be seen by the church-goers, and ducked underneath the police tape. Doors to the old building had been bolted, but she easily climbed through a window that had been broken out, probably by vandals.

The room where the old vat had been stored was like the rest of the building: dark, dirty and lonely. But nothing about it suggested that two months before it had been filled with badly burned bodies. The vat, now empty, looked harmless enough. It would be easy to ignore it if you didn't know what was in it. But this was an abandoned chemical plant. How could knowledgeable people not suspect that it contained toxic chemicals?

As she wandered about the old building, she found herself in what must have been an office. Papers were scattered everywhere. They had likely fallen out of desks and filing cabinets as they were being removed. She picked up a handful and glanced at them. They were insignificant. I'm sure they shredded all sensitive material, she thought.

As she dropped the papers back on to the floor her eyes spotted what appeared to be a handwritten memorandum. Handwritten, she thought. Interesting. It wasn't signed and it appeared to be from one of the brothers to the other. When she glanced at the memo she was overcome with anger. The brothers needed to be punished.

REVEREND MCCULLER'S CHURCH was on a street corner in an old neighborhood mixed with commercial and residential occupants. Brenda assumed the church was probably also racially mixed. The building was old, made of red brick, and built close to the street. There was no side yard and only a small yard in front of the three steps that led to the front door. Painted glass windows blocked the view of passing traffic.

Brenda estimated that over three hundred worshippers were packed into the sanctuary. If the first service was as well attended, the Reverend was to be commended for having such a vibrant church. Her heart started beating faster when she saw Professor Glenn Osborne in the bass section on the back row of the choir.

Although McCullers was small, he had a strong voice and was a powerful preacher. He stressed the choices people have between Heaven and Hell. He didn't say much about the former, but he described the latter in vivid and frightening detail. I wonder if that's from the Bible, Brenda thought. Sounds more like Milton's *Paradise Lost*.

It was Brenda's first church experience since she was a child. Her father never attended church and after she moved in with him, she didn't go because there was no one to take her. Later while in college, she lost interest in religion and didn't expect to be attracted to it again. Yet, as she sat in Reverend McCuller's church, listening to the music, the prayers, and even the hell fire and damnation sermon, she was touched. She was especially moved by the prayers of the people. Rather than praying silently, each person prayed aloud an individual prayer. With all talking at the same time, it wasn't possible to distinguish what anyone was saying, but the spirit of the prayers was moving.

The communion was served in little holders of Welch's grape juice, while loaves of stale bread were passed down pews for each person to tear off a piece. Brenda hesitated to participate since she didn't belong to the church. But she did, and like the others, lowered her head and closed her eyes after taking first the bread and then the grape juice, all the while feeling her spirits rise.

After the service, Brenda waited outside the front of the church while Reverend McCullers greeted each of the worshipers as they came out. One of the last to come out was Glenn Osborne. When he saw Brenda, he walked over to her. She extended her hand and he took it in his and said, "I'm Glenn Osborne. Do you remember me?"

"Of course I do. It's good to see you again. I'm Brenda Horton, the lawyer. We met a couple of months ago at William Williams' visitation."

At that moment an ambulance siren sounded in the distance. Brenda put her hand to her ear and pretended to listen intently. "Pardon me. I think there's somewhere I need to go." She made a fake move as if going to chase down the ambulance.

Glenn laughed. "I understand the urgency, but I'm sure some of our Charlotte lawyers will beat you to it. Why don't you let them have this one while I buy you lunch."

Before she could answer, Reverend McCullers came over with two women. He greeted Brenda with a hug. "I'm glad to see you have met Professor Osborne. He isn't much of a bass singer, but we're glad to have him in the church." The two ladies giggled softly. Glenn smiled.

Reverend McCullers introduced his wife, Sarah, an attractive lady several inches taller than her husband. Her high heel shoes made her still taller. She grabbed Brenda's hand and squeezed it tightly. "I'm so glad to meet you, Miss. Horton."

"Call me Brenda."

"Reverend McCullers has told me about the generosity of your law firm to our church."

Glenn listened, curious as to what kind of generosity, but suspecting it was given for some reason other than kindness.

The second lady stood quietly. She was showing several months of pregnancy.

Brenda extended her hand. "Mrs. Williams, it's so good to meet you. Our firm is happy we can be of service." Then Brenda gave her a warm embrace, being careful not to put pressure on her extended stomach.

"Oh I apologize," McCullers said. "I had forgotten you two had not met. Alice, meet your lawyer." He then turned to Brenda and said, "I hope you can join us for lunch?"

"It will be my pleasure to take you to lunch," Brenda replied. She was embarrassed she had not thought to call and invite them to lunch, and to make reservations. She had no idea where to take them, and worse still she had no way to transport them. Oh my God, she thought, what will they think when they see that my sports car has room for only one passenger?

Glenn stood quietly by while introductions were being made. "May I invite myself to lunch with you? If you let me go along, I'll pay. And I have room for everybody in my SUV."

"I would love to have you go along," Brenda replied. "And I'm sure the others would, too. I'll tell you what. You drive and I'll pay."

Glenn took them to an upscale restaurant with white tablecloths located in South Square Mall. He did most of the talking and charmed the others, especially Brenda. She learned that the sprawling shopping mall sat on what was once Governor Morrison's cow pasture. Prize bulls used to roam the area.

Glenn leaned over and whispered to Brenda, "Alice has been anxious. It's been over two months and she's meeting one of her lawyers for the first time. Some of the other victims' families have already received good settlements."

"I understand and I apologize," Brenda replied. "We'll stay in closer touch from now on. It's important to remember we're going after the chemical company that is chartered in Scotland. It will take us a little longer. But that's where the big money is. The claimants have only one chance to recover. They don't get a second bite at the apple. So it's important that we get the most we can, and not jump at the first offer. It'll be worth the wait, I promise."

Glenn then talked about his family, especially his father, who had been a political activist preacher in the northern part of the city. "Any politician who had the support of Reverend Osborne could count on a thousand vote majority from his precinct. The results would be like 1200 to 6, or 900 to 3. He would laugh and say he didn't want it to be unanimous. People might accuse folks in his precinct of block voting."

"How could he get a thousand people to vote the same way?" Brenda asked.

"People wanted to vote for the candidate who would best serve the interest of the black community, or as more likely the case, the candidate who would do them the least harm. They trusted dad to know. On Election Day, three ladies from his church would sit at a table and hand out sample ballots that were marked. Other candidates would have tables, some with sample ballots, but everyone knew the right table. Some people probably made mistakes and marked the wrong names, but out of over a thousand voters, the opposition vote was never in double digits."

Other customers had finished eating and the restaurant workers had stacked chairs on the tables and were mopping the floor. Their stares showed that they wanted the last table of people to leave.

"Oh my goodness!" exclaimed Alice. "It's almost four o'clock. I need to go rescue my mother. She's looking after the twins."

Glenn dropped the others off first and then took Brenda back to the church for her car. As they approached the church, he said, "If you don't have to leave right away, I would love to show you around Charlotte."

It was almost four o'clock and Brenda had planned to be home by five. "I would love to see Charlotte," she replied, not trying to sound too excited. "And I'd love to hear more about you and your family."

They drove down McDowell Street near it's intersection with Second Street and parked in front of several of the four-star hotels facing McDowell.

"Let's go sit in the park," said Glenn. "You can see a lot of Charlotte from there and it'll be a good place for me to deliver my lecture."

"I'll listen to your lecture, Dr. Osborne, but please, no pop quizzes."

"I promise," he said with a laugh. "If you prefer, you can read my book and skip the lecture."

"Book? Where can I get a copy?"

"I haven't written it yet, but I will, even if I have to publish it myself. It'll be about this very place where we now sit, or more about the people who used to live here. My people. Our People."

It was a beautiful area. Several blocks of neatly manicured lawns, shrubs and trees, obviously the right species, arranged according to the plan of a skilled landscape designer. There were inviting benches and beautifully lighted fountains. Across the street was a row of first class hotels and office buildings. The city and county governmental complex of attractive modern buildings faced Fourth Street. on the other side of the park. On the far side, six or eight blocks away, the skyline was beginning to light up as darkness settled over the city.

"This beautiful spot was once called Brooklyn," said Glenn. "It was one of several slum areas close to the affluent homes surrounding the business center of the city. Blacks had to live close enough to the white residents for them to walk to their homes to work. Another slum area, on the other side of the boulevard that winds past was called Blue Heaven. I don't know how either of the areas got their names. You can see where Blue Heaven used to be. It's been replaced by parks and modern buildings. See the church steeple on the other side of what was once Blue Heaven? The view of the slum area was blocked from the church by a row of office buildings, but the afternoon shadow of the church's steeple used to fall across part of the slum. People worshipping there probably didn't know that within a stones throw of the beautiful church, hundreds of people were living in squalor.

"Houses in both areas were so close together you could barely walk between them. They were all alike and had never been painted. The roofs needed repairs and the steps of most had fallen in. Each had three rooms, one behind the other, which is why they were called shotgun houses. Coal was the source of heat during the winter. See how clear the air is? You can see the lights from the skyscrapers uptown. Forty years ago, we couldn't have because of the thickness of the smoke from the burning coal.

"In the summers, heat and humidity were unbearable. Most of the houses had ten, twelve, even more people living in them, and on weekends they would spill outside to escape the heat. They would be shoulder to shoulder and the slightest incidental contact or insult would result in violence. Some tried to escape their misery by drinking white liquor, which was sold throughout the area in fruit jars. It was so cheap that even people in the slum areas could afford it.

"The place was a powder keg. Murders, rapes, assaults, occurred in this area, less than a block from the police station across Fourth Street. On weekends, pistols carried by at least half the men and a lot of the women, flashed. But they weren't the only weapons. Sticks, broom handles, frying pans, anything people could get their hands on were used. For many, razors and knives were the weapons of choice and blood flowed.

"National studies showed that the area where we now sit was the bloodiest four-block area in the country. A news reporter researched the causes of some of the killings. Most were over trivial matters. An argument over a twenty-five cent debt, a botched shoe shine, a critical remark about somebody's dog. And women. Fights over women were the number one cause of death. But the root cause of all of the violence was misery, helplessness, and living conditions as bad as those on slave ships.

"In the 1960s, urban development cleared out Brooklyn, Blue Heaven and the other black slum areas separating the city from the beautiful and affluent residential areas developing south and east of here. Some people objected, claiming it involved the wrongful taking of privately owned property. The owners of the property, all white, objected the most. They would be paid for their property, but there were few places they could get as good a return on their money as from the weekly rents they charged the black tenants."

Brenda pulled her trench coat tighter around her neck in an effort to keep out the chill. Glenn wore no topcoat or jacket but seemed comfortable in the coat and tie he had worn all day. Brenda assumed his passion for this subject kept his mind off the chill.

After a few quiet moments Brenda spoke in a soft voice. "Where did all the people go? What happened to them?"

"That's the right question!" Mike exclaimed. "Everything about this property is insignificant in comparison to the question of what happened to the people."

"It sounds like a good topic for a book."

"It's the book I plan to write. It'll take a lot of research and I'll need some grants, but I'll eventually get it done,"

IT WAS WELL PAST MIDNIGHT as the BMW Z3 arrived home to Darlington. Memories of the events of the day flowed through Brenda's mind. Discovering the handwritten memorandum in the old chemical plant was worth hundreds of trips to Charlotte. And she had patched things up with the firm's client, Mrs. Williams, at least for now. But the most significant event of the day was running into Glenn Osborne. She could live without knowing what happened to the people who moved from Brooklyn and Blue Heaven, but she was overwhelmed by Glenn's passion about the subject. She wondered if it were possible he could be passionate about other things, such as attractive and intelligent young people of the opposite sex, which she hoped to find out.

Chapter 26

SEVENTEEN MONTHS AFTER Mike McMillan's arrest, he pleaded guilty to careless and reckless driving, and misdemeanor possession of a controlled substance. All other charges were dismissed in an unscheduled hearing thirty minutes after the completion of the criminal docket late on a Friday afternoon. Court had been closed, jurors had been dismissed, and all reporters had left. Only the judge, clerk, bailiff and assistant district attorney remained.

As soon as the courtroom cleared the assistant D. A. said, "Your honor, I see there's a case that was inadvertently omitted from the printed docket. Could I respectfully request that court be reopened to dispose of it? I understand that the defendant and his lawyer are here. It's a guilty plea so it won't take long."

Dawg Brinson and Mike McMillan entered from a rear stairway where they had waited out of sight until summoned by the bailiff. The clerk cried the court back into session.

The assistant D. A. read a stipulation of facts and announced the remaining reduced charges. Dawg entered a plea for his client. Mike sat silently; barely aware of what was going on. Dawg introduced a stack of twenty or more affidavits describing Mike's exemplary conduct since his arrest. He then made a statement, more for the benefit of the record than to persuade the judge. The charges were consolidated for judgment, and without comment, the judge entered a sentence of eight months confinement, suspended upon the payment of a fine of $1000, payment of court costs and supervised probation for a year.

The hearing was over in twenty minutes. Several weeks would pass before reporters became aware that the high profile case had been disposed of without an active sentence. By then, it would be stale news and get very little play.

A HALF HOUR AFTER THE HEARING, Mike sat across the huge desk from Brinson. Dawg pulled a half-empty fifth of I. W. Harper from his desk drawer and took two huge gulps.

"Sorry Mike, but as long as you're on probation you're not to take a drink outside your house, and if you drink there, don't leave the house until after you're cold sober. Do you live with someone who can hold a gun on you and shoot you if you start out the door drunk?"

Mike laughed. "We haven't talked in a long time, Mr. Brinson. My wife and I are back together. She's too nervous to pick up a gun. But don't worry. Neither of us drink. We're born again Christians. The Lord works in mysterious ways, Mr. Brinson. My wife happened to show up at my church. She was pregnant, and has since had a baby. Little Mike is perfect. Some day he'll replace me on the circuit. You know, Mr. Brinson; the first six months in that church were hell. But then Jesus Christ came into my heart. I prayed and He sent the greatest blessing I ever had: my wife and future son. Are you born again, Mr. Brinson? Has Jesus ever come into your life?"

Dawg was disappointed. Someone drunk on religion like Mike was not who he needed for what he was going to ask him to do. Jesus might not approve. On the other hand, there was the poor widow with the starving children. Maybe Jesus would be sympathetic, and cut Mike a little slack.

"Naw," Dawg said. "I've never been much on religion, but I took a philosophy course in college. I member there was this famous philosopher who once said, 'Everbody has to think something, and I think I'll have another drink.'" He turned up the bottle of I. W. Harper and took a large swallow. "He's always been my favorite philosopher."

Dawg sat quietly, enjoying the mellow glow he was getting from the whiskey. He was glad he never had any children. Life is complicated enough. Who would have thought Mike McMillan would end up back with the woman he once hated and raising a kid that's not his. He probably continues to deny to himself that he fathered that funny looking kid that's being raised by the dentist. Dawg wondered what Jesus thought about that.

DAWG REMEMBERED THAT Angela McMillan, noticeably distressed, showed up in his office shortly after her husband's arrest. "Mr. Brinson, I know from the news account that you represent my husband. I've heard that he broke up with that Sabrina bitch he'd been shacking up with for so long. Well, he has another problem. His wife's pregnant. Although we've been separated for over two years, we aren't divorced, and I'm still on his medical insurance. I'm also told that the child will be considered his although it obviously isn't."

"Then who's the pappy?" Dawg asked.

"I'm embarrassed to say I don't know. It could be one of three guys. I'm not sure I want to know which one. I just don't see how this could happen to me. I was on the pill. Never missed a time."

"I guess you come to see me to find out where you can get an abortion. I can give you some names, but if you got a personal doctor, he'll probably do it for you. Getting an abortion ain't that big a deal any more. Just about any doctor will do it for a fee."

"Oh no. I didn't come to ask your advice about an abortion. I don't want an abortion. I want Mike back."

She dabbed at her eyes with the edge of a tissue. Then the tears began to flow so fast that she was wiping them from her cheeks with the back of her hand. "I know you think I'm nothing but a lowly whore, but remember Mike gave me plenty of reasons to be unfaithful. I'm willing to give him another chance. He's bound to need someone to lean on through the trouble he's going through. I guess the tough question is whether he'd be willing to give me another chance."

"I'm sorry I ain't a marriage counselor. Maybe you should talk to a marriage counselor, a preacher, or a psychiatrist…somebody in the business of making people feel better. I've never thought very highly of those folks. One time a marriage counselor told a client of mine and her husband to never go to bed mad. So they didn't. They stayed up and fought. The husband was winning until my client reached in a drawer one night and pulled out a pair of sharp scissors. They more than equalized things. Tell you what, Mrs. McMillan, Mike has joined that big Baptist Church between here and Florence. You might check with the preacher there. Maybe he can get you two back together. It would help Mike's case for him to be a family man."

DAWG HAD NEVER MENTIONED TO MIKE the conversation with Angela. He hadn't learned that they were back together, nor did he see any reason to discuss it with him now. It would just waste time.

"I'm happy for you, son," said Dawg. "I know it means a lot for you to have a boy who can carry on the McMillan name in racing, and to be shed of the responsibility of supporting that poor kid you had with Sabrina. By the way, do you know whatever happened to her? I haven't heard from her since I got her all that money in the divorce settlement. She didn't even call to thank me."

"Oh yes. A couple of my racing buddies keep up with her. As you know, she went to live with her son in New York. Everybody always thought he was queer like his sister, but he married a woman they tell me makes money hand over fist. She works for a brokerage firm as a stock analyst. They say people who are good or lucky at picking stocks can make as much money as a 300 hitter with the Yankees. Maybe that's why Sabrina's boy married her. He's a toe dancer and probably doesn't make much money himself.

"Anyway, bout the time Sabrina got her divorce, she moved into a fancy condo to be close to this wealthy Texan she got the hots for. The old man was more interested in her son than he was in her, but he liked to parade around with a trophy blonde on his arm, so he started taking her to fancy parties, shows, things like that. Even took her to Aspen to visit with the man who ran the company that was the source of the old man's wealth. It was mighty high cotton for the daughter of a low country tenant farmer. Listening to all those folks talk about getting richer as their company's stock kept going up got her to thinking that she'd like to have some of the action. The old man convinced her that the company's stock was a no risk deal. Everything he had was invested in the company. So Sabrina put everything she had in the company's stock. She even leveraged it to the limit so she could buy more. Her daughter-in-law tried to get her to…what do you call it? 'Versify.'

"Yea, something like that," Dawg said.

"Anyway, something happened at the company. Stock went from around eighty dollars a share to less than a dollar, almost overnight."

Dawg interrupted. "You ain't talking about Enson, are you?"

"Yeah, I think that's the name of the company. It started out as a small oil company of some kind and grew into a large energy company."

Dawg's face turned red with anger. "Those sons of bitches! They cost me over a million dollars. I bought some of their stock when I heard how they were taking those stupid ass folks in California for damn near all they were worth. But while they were stealing out in California, some of their folks back in Texas were stealing from the company. My little investment went up to a million dollars before they started uncovering all that shit. Then it dropped to near nothing. The company big shots claimed they didn't know what was going on. I'd of been embarrassed to admit I was in charge and didn't know what was going on. If it had been me, I'd have said, 'Hell yes, I'm guilty. I just didn't know how to steal so it would stay stole.' I'd rather people think I'm crooked than that I'm a dumb ass."

Dawg reached for the I. W. Harper bottle. "You know, there're all kinds of sons of bitches; ordinary sons of bitches, first class sons of bitches and even fourteen karat sons of bitches. Them Enson folks are in a class by themselves. They're eighteen karat sons of bitches."

He turned up the bottle until it was empty and then shook it over his up turned mouth to make sure he got the last remaining drop. Then he angrily threw it into the trash can where it crashed against an empty bottle from the previous day.

"So tell me," said Dawg. "What's Sabrina doing now that she's broke…that is until she finds another turkey to support her?"

"Last I heard she was living with her son and his wife in one of the queer sections of New York. The old man that got her into that Enson stock killed hisself; jumped off the balcony of his apartment and splattered all over the sidewalk.

"I expect I'll be hearing from Sabrina one day soon," Dawg said. "She'll want to milk the dentist some more."

MIKE WANTED TO GET back to the business at hand. He knew Dawg was going to charge him more money. "Do I owe you any more, Mr. Brinson?" He asked.

Dawg was offended. "Do you owe me any more! Son I saved your ass. But for me, your ass would be in prison, trying to keep away from them big horny apes wanting some of you. But for me, you'd never race again. You'll make, what, four or five million over the next year or two? Ever time you get a check, just remember that old Dawg ought to get a part of it."

Mike braced himself for what he expected to be an exorbitant demand. He was willing to pay another hundred thousand, but the way Brinson was talking, he was afraid he would demand more.

"But let's not talk about money," Dawg said. "There's something else I want to discuss with you."

Chapter 27

A WEEK AFTER MIKE MCMILLAN settled his account with Brinson, lawyer Jacob Seigal sat in the reception room waiting for his appointment with Dawg Brinson. He leaned forward on a cane, which he clutched with both hands. Under his right arm was a thin legal size folder, which he squeezed tightly against his body. Scleroderme, the deadly arthritis disease he was diagnosed with five years before had progressed, leaving him with serious deformity. His partners had encouraged him to retire, but he refused, though he now needed help in moving around and could not grasp a pen or pencil in a single hand.

"Good to see you, Jacob," Dawg said as Seigal's associate helped him into a straight chair in front of Brinson's desk "I'd heard about your health problems. Thought you might have turned your Lloyds' clients over to somebody else in your firm. I'm glad to see you're still active, but I hate what I'm gonna have to do to you."

Seigal got right down to business. "Lloyds' American counsel in New York sent me your summons and suggested I meet with you before you file a complaint. I'm not authorized to offer you anything at this point, but if you are seeking only a nominal sum, I can probably get my folks to pay something to close the file. It was a tragic accident, but the evidence seems clear that there was nothing the truck driver could have done to avoid it."

"Nominal amount!" Dawg said, faking annoyance. "If what you mean by nominal is two or three million dollars, we can talk. If less than that, you might as well get your ass back to Columbia."

Seigal struggled from his chair and turned to leave.

"Wait," Dawg called after him. "I don't want to hurt your feelings. We started out together in law school, Jacob. You were at the top of the class and I was at the bottom, but we've both done all right."

You have been a state senator, a position that you have often abused, Seigal thought to himself, and you have become wealthy, largely in ways that should be embarrassing to our profession. But I have a hard time thinking you are successful according to any reasonable criteria for success.

Dawg continued. "Since me and you are friends, I'm gonna share with you the affidavit of the only eyewitness to the wreck. Any jury in this state'll believe ever word of it, and they'll punish the beer company for trying to cover up what happened so's not to have to pay the poor widow and her starving children."

Seigal sat back down. The paper, which Dawg had handed him, slipped from his crippled hands. Dawg went around the desk to pick it up. "I'll read it to you," he said.

Seigal listened as Dawg read the affidavit as if reading it to a jury. He showed no surprise because he was not surprised. He had expected to hear a prefabricated story based on perjury. He couldn't wait to cross-examine the witness. By the time he got off the stand, he would be screaming for mercy and shouting, "Dawg made me do it!" It would be an opportunity to get Brinson disbarred.

"Three million," Dawg said as he handed the copy of the affidavit back to Seigal.

Seigal started shuffling toward the door to the reception room where an associate waited to assist him. Only the cane kept him from collapsing on his face.

"I know it ain't the strongest case I ever had," Dawg shouted. "If it were stronger, I'd be asking many millions more. And just remember if I happen to get a runaway jury, I might get twenty million."

Brenda was coming in the door to the reception room as Seigal was being helped out by the associate. She instinctively reached out to give her former boss and mentor a hug but stopped abruptly when she saw his fragile condition.

"Mr. Seigal, I'm so sorry. I didn't know."

Seigal ignored her words of sympathy and said, "Great to see you Brenda. This is Harvey Howe. He has your old job of carrying my brief case. But if you'll come back, I'll fire him."

The young man laughed as he and Brenda shook hands and exchanged pleasantries.

"Is there some place we can go for a cup of coffee?" Seigal asked Brenda.

"I'll have someone stir up a cup of instant, if that's satisfactory."

Miss Ginny looked up in surprise as the three made their way back to Brenda's office. Seigal and Howe sat in straight chairs across from Brenda's small desk.

"Brenda, I don't want any coffee, and Harvey here is a Mormon and doesn't drink coffee," said Seigal. "What I want is to talk to you about leaving this firm. I regret I didn't do more to persuade you not to come here. You're working for a crook and it's just a matter of time before he gets into bad trouble. The more money some shyster lawyers make the more they feel they're beyond the law and beyond the reach of professional disciplinary bodies. When the net falls on Brinson, I don't want you to be caught up in it."

Brenda wanted to agree and assure Seigal that she was looking for a way out. But she knew that as long as she worked for Brinson it would be inappropriate for her to bad-mouth him. "I understand your concern," she said, "and I appreciate your continuing interest in me and my career." Then she abruptly changed the subject and asked, "What brings you here, Jacob?"

"To meet with your boss," Seigal said. "But it's probably better that you not know why. I hope your hands remain clean of the matter I'm here about."

He didn't have to explain. Brenda knew Seigal represented Lloyds of London, the insurance carrier for the beer company. Cole finally signed the affidavit, she thought.

Before Seigal left he handed Brenda his card. "As you know, I'm still head of the State Bar Ethics Committee. As a lawyer and officer of the court, you have a duty to report any matter you become familiar with. Just send me a confidential memorandum and I'll do the rest."

A WEEK LATER, SEIGAL got a call from Scott Peterson, Lloyd's American counsel in New York.

"Thanks for faxing me a copy of the affidavit and Brinson's offer to settle for three million dollars," Peterson said.

"Well, I hope you agree with me that we should reject the offer and defend the case." Seigal said.

There was a pause before Peterson said, "As you know, Mr. Seigal, we coordinate the defense of cases all over the country. We know, as do most lawyers, the prejudice a large corporation can face when defending against someone who has suffered catastrophic injuries or death of a family member. Consider also that this case would be tried in one of the most unfriendly jurisdictions a defendant like a beer company can face, and the plaintiff's lawyer has a reputation. Well you know him better than we do. Here we have a dead father and dead children with a surviving widow struggling to care for her destitute family. The issue of legal responsibility is like a small pebble lying on the beach hoping to be discovered."

Seigal was disappointed. The case was likely to be his last chance to rid the profession of Dawg Brinson.

Chapter 28

BRENDA WAITED FOR HALF AN HOUR BEFORE Dawg got to the office. She pretended to read a newspaper while trying to think of a way to break the thick block of ice enclosing Miss Ginny. The old lady had not answered when Brenda said, "Good Morning," only nodded slightly and cleared her throat.

Brenda glanced over her newspaper and saw Miss Ginny staring at the blank computer screen, and occasionally striking a few keys on the key pad, pretending she was working.

Brenda walked over to her desk and picked up Dawg's appointments calendar. There was the name of a man she recognized as a runner. He was probably coming by to collect for the last case he ran down for Dawg. Brenda wrote her name above his.

Miss Ginny snatched the book from Brenda's hand and pointed to the name of the runner.

"Sorry," Brenda said. "He'll have to wait. There's an important matter I have to talk to Mr. Brinson about. I know he'll want to hear it first thing."

The runner came in and approached Miss Ginny. "How's the keeper of the gate," he asked, trying to be cheerful. When he noticed Brenda sitting on the far side of the room, he said, "Hope you put me down first like you said you would."

Miss Ginny leaned over and whispered, "I did put you down first, but that black girl is a lawyer here and claims she has to see Mr. Brinson first thing. He'll have to decide who he wants to see first."

When Dawg came in the door and saw Brenda, he walked past his runner, mumbling, "Good morning, John Richard," and went immediately to Brenda. He dreaded talking with her, because when she came to his office it was usually to agitate him about something.

"You wanna see me?" he asked.

"If you could spare me a few minutes, it shouldn't take long."

Dawg stood aside to let Brenda enter the office first, then followed and flopped his heavy torso into the huge judge's chair behind his desk. As he was getting settled, Brenda tossed an envelope on his desk.

Dawg made no motion to pick it up and look at its contents. "What's this?"

"My resignation."

"Why you quit'n?"

Brenda didn't know where to start. She wanted her departure to be as smooth as possible, because there remained the question of which files he would agree she could take with her.

Before she could reply, Dawg asked, "It hasn't got anything to do with the Smith case, has it?"

"No. I've tried to create a Chinese wall between myself and that case, so I can say I know nothing about how it was terminated. But what you were trying to get me to do in that case convinced me that I should start thinking of leaving the firm. I've been considering it since our first conversation about it."

"Well," Dawg said, "it's settled. The Smith widow's happy. The insurance company and the beer company are happy 'cause they know they got off light, and I'm happy. The Smith's will be paid $25,000 a year. They'll get a check every month for as long as the mother lives, and whatever's left will be distributed to the surviving children."

Brenda was doing the calculation. The settlement must have been for two million dollars. Dawg's million would be paid up front. The Smith's portion would be paid in installments over many years, so its present cash value would be much less. But Dawg would see nothing wrong with pocketing more money than his needy clients.

"I'm pleased that everybody's happy," Brenda said. "But I'd prefer to hear nothing more about the case." She changed the subject back to the original question. "The reason I'm leaving is that I'm moving to Charlotte. I've met someone there. He's a college professor."

"You can't practice law there, you know, unless you pass the North Carolina Bar examination, and I hear it's harder than ours."

"I'll take the exam as soon as I've satisfied the residence requirement, and I'll pass it. Until then I'll work with the Hudson Law Firm. One of their lawyers will appear with me whenever I try a case, and I can participate as long as I'm a member of a Bar somewhere. There are some cases I would like to file right away and try as quickly as possible."

"I don't understand what you talking about. What kind of cases?"

"The sodium explosion cases."

"The what!" Dawg shouted. "You crazy woman. Them cases are worth a lot of money, and they're my cases. No way the clients would want an inexperienced lawyer handling their cases."

Brenda responded quickly. "The cases are worth nothing as long as you have them and won't file suit in North Carolina. It's been a year and a half and you're no closer to getting service of process than you were the day you filed suit. Many of the claimants in Charlotte have already received good settlements. As for your second point, our plaintiffs have never met you. I'm the one they know and trust. My significant friend grew up with the victims and their survivors. I'll call him when I leave here and tell him my resignation is complete. He has papers that I prepared, releasing you and naming me as their sole attorney. All of the plaintiffs will sign them. And by the way, I'll reduce the fee changed from one-half to one-third if the cases are tried and one-fourth if they're settled."

Dawg was furious, but he needed to be cautious. Unless he associated a lawyer experienced in suing foreign corporations, he might never be able to get service on the Aberdeen Chemical Company. He had never associated other counsel and would rather lose a case than admit he needed help. But with North Carolina lawyers getting good settlements for their clients, losing was not an option. One way to save face might be to let Brenda have the cases.

He buzzed for Miss Ginny. She appeared moments later and set half a mug of steaming coffee in front of him. Neither she nor Dawg offered coffee to Brenda. Dawg pulled a full bottle of I. W. Harper whiskey from his desk drawer and finished filling the mug. Brenda was wondering if the fifth would last him through the day.

"I like my coffee half and half," Dawg said as he took two large gulps. His face flushed as the whiskey struck the pit of his stomach and sent sharp sensations throughout his body.

He finished his coffee mixture and filled the mug with pure whiskey. His words were slurred, but there was no mistaking his rising temper. "I'll decide which cases you take with you and it won't be the sodium cases."

"Okay, Okay, Dawg, calm down, and let me tell you what I plan to do. I'll file a petition for plaintiffs asking the court to release them from their agreement with you on the grounds you've ignored their cases. We'll cite the success of the other plaintiffs and allege you have yet to find a proper party to sue. Each time you've directed a summons at a company, it's turned out to be one that doesn't have a presence in the state."

"No judge in this state's gonna pay attention to bullshit like that," Dawg asserted.

"You may be right," Brenda said. "But it'll be written up in all the papers, and lawyers everywhere will laugh and say, 'Ole Dawg finally got a case that needs a lawyer, not just a windbag that can persuade a friendly jury to relieve some deep pocket defendant of a lot of money.' And you know what Dawg? It'll get worse as time passes and you are unable to latch onto the right defendant. You'll have to associate someone who knows what they're doing and there will go what you think is your reputation. Or you can continue to go it alone until the statute of limitations runs. Then you'll be in deep trouble. It'll be easier to let me have the sodium files. You can keep the rest of mine. We can say that is our dissolution settlement. I took the few files of people who are from North Carolina. It should make sense since I'll be living there."

By the time Brenda got up to leave, Dawg was drunk to the point his words were unintelligible. Brenda was nevertheless confident that he understood what she was saying.

"MISS GINNY," BRENDA SAID as she came out of Dawg's office. "Mr. Brinson isn't feeling well and wants you to cancel the rest of his appointments for the day. "

Miss Ginny, sensing the problem, turned to the runner and asked, "Would it be convenient for you to come in tomorrow?"

Brenda saw that Miss Ginny's right hand was shaking so that she had to hold it with her left hand so she could make the change on the appointment calendar. It was not until after the runner had left that she noticed that Brenda was still there. Brenda pulled a chair up to the edge of the old lady's desk and looked her directly in the eyes.

"There's something I need to tell you, Miss Ginny. I've just told Mr. Brinson. You'll be the second person to know."

Miss Ginny tried to appear uninterested. She picked up a pencil and started to doodle on a legal pad. When she realized her shaking hand was noticeable, she dropped the pencil on the desk and took her shaking right hand in her left, trying to hold it still. But her left hand was shaking too, so she dropped both hands in her lap where they would be out of sight.

When it became obvious that Miss Ginny was not going to speak or acknowledge any curiosity, Brenda said, "I'm leaving the firm. I won't be here to annoy you anymore."

Miss Ginny's breaths started coming more quickly and Brenda hoped the slight change in her expression came from a touch of sorrow. But the old lady still didn't speak.

Brenda continued. "I'll still stop by to visit whenever I come to Darlington, and I'll send you my address and telephone number so you can get in touch in case you ever need me. And by the way, Miss Ginny. Should you ever have a question about anything going on here in the firm, there's a person you can confide in." Brenda took Jacob Seigal's card from her pocket and handed it to Miss Ginny. She made no movement to reach for it, so Brenda put it on the desk in front of her.

"Mr. Seigal heads the State Bar Committee on Professional Ethics. The committee looks into questionable practices by attorneys licensed to practice in this state."

Miss Ginny still didn't speak but changed her expression in a way that suggested she was offended.

"Please understand," Brenda said, "I'm not saying there's anything going on here that should be reported, and that's not why I'm leaving. Also, I know you would never want to be a snitch, especially should it involve someone like Mr. Brinson. But Miss Ginny, sometimes when lawyers get older they have lapses in judgment, and take chances, maybe for what seems good reasons, such as to help someone who needs help. But for whatever reason, their actions can get them and people who help them in serious trouble. Lying under oath, or suggesting that somebody else do so, is a felony carrying a substantial prison sentence. Anybody working for a law firm who knows that's occurring has a responsibility to report it."

Brenda felt a lump in her throat as she turned and quickly walked away. As she passed out the door she thought she heard a faint, "Good-bye."

Miss Ginny picked up the Seigal card, looked at it, and tossed it into the trash can beside her desk. Later, as she was leaving for the day, she scratched around through the trash, found the card, and put it in her purse.

Chapter 29

TWO WEEKS LATER, BRENDA RETURNED to Darlington to take care of tasks she had neglected, such as leaving a forwarding address with the post office, canceling her newspaper subscriptions, and redeeming her utility deposits. She would be in Darlington only for a day, and her most important stop would be in the evening when she would go to Florence to have dinner with Don and Huggie, and to tell them that she had left the Brinson firm and moved to Charlotte. But first there were two other stops she needed to make.

Brenda rang the doorbell three times at Brantley Cole's residence before anyone came to the door.

An elderly lady holding a cane with one hand to steady herself opened the door. "Yes?" is all she said as she gazed at the young African-American lady, as if to ask, "What in the world would you be doing here?"

"I'm looking for Mr. Brantley Cole," Brenda said.

"Don't know nobody by that name," the old lady replied. "My daughter and son-in-law moved in here 'bout three months ago. I live with them." She paused briefly, but before Brenda could say anything the old lady added, "Could be the man you looking for lived here before we moved in. I don't think so though 'cause only white people live in this neighborhood."

Brenda didn't explain that Brantley Cole was white, and said, "Sorry to have bothered you," and walked away. On reflection she wasn't surprised the Coles had moved. They probably took the money Dawg paid Cole for his false affidavit and moved someplace where they could spend it without people being suspicious as to where they got it.

Next, she drove to the house where Maybelle Smith had lived with her children. It was vacant, and in such terrible condition she wondered how anyone could have ever lived there. A woman sitting on the porch of a nearby house eyed Brenda suspiciously as she approached. This house was in little better condition than the one the Smiths had vacated.

"They done moved to Webber City," the lady said in answer to Brenda's inquiry. "The beer company what killed Maybelle's husband paid them a heap of money. They now living high on the hawg. Don't come around here no more. Can't says I blame 'em."

Webber City was a small section of Darlington inhabited mostly by black families with modest incomes. Brenda was directed to the Smith house by the first person in the neighborhood she asked. She knew that everybody around likely knew who they were and where they lived. A damage suit settlement of the size they received would make them a notorious family.

The house was brick and looked large enough for two, perhaps three small bedrooms, a kitchen and a living room. It sat back no more than thirty feet from the street. The small yard was a neatly mowed ground cover of Bermuda and crab grass. There were no trees or shrubs on the lot. A graveled one-lane driveway beside the house was long enough for one car.

When Maybelle Smith saw Brenda standing outside the door she quickly pushed open the screen door and rushed out to grab the young woman in a tight bear hug. "Laud have mercy. I'm so glad to see you, Miss Brenda. Where in the world you been? We've missed you. The children, they working or in school. Wish they could see you. They talk about you all the time. You were so kind to us. Then all of a sudden we never saw you again."

"I've been busy," Brenda said. "And I've moved to North Carolina. I wanted to come by and say good-bye while I'm back in town to clear up some loose ends."

"What you say, child? You ain't gonna leave Mr. Dawg, are you? He the finest, most Christian man I've ever known. 'Cept for him we still be living like we was last time you saw us." Maybelle continued. "Come in. Let me show you how we live now, all 'cause of Mr. Dawg."

She led Brenda through the living room into a small kitchen. As they passed through the living room, Brenda noticed a couch that looked like it could open as a bed, two large upholstered chairs, and a television set about nineteen or twenty inches in diameter. The furniture may have been used, but it was luxurious when compared to what the Smiths had before.

Maybelle led Brenda to a small utility room that opened from the kitchen. "An automatic washer-dryer. Can you believe that?" She pointed to a white porcelain washer and separate dryer. "This is the first neighborhood I've ever lived in that don't have clotheslines. My mama washed clothes for white people all of her life, scrubbing 'em till her knuckles bled. She'd be so proud to know her daughter just drop 'em in this white tub, sprinkle a little powder over 'em and push a little button. Then, when they clean, put 'em in this other white tub, turn it on and in an hour they dry. It's a miracle, Miss Brenda, a show nuff miracle, all 'cause of that precious Mr. Dawg."

Maybelle walked to the refrigerator and opened the door. "Fridgerator," she said. "Who woulda ever dreamed? And we always got food in it. Look. Cold milk, eggs and bacon. Not fatback, but real bacon with strips of lean."

Brenda said little, but was almost overcome with emotion as she followed Maybelle oohing and ahing over the comfort that was now the fortune of the Smith family. How could it be wrong for this family to be lifted out of miserable poverty to a tolerable life? Brenda quickly suppressed thoughts of such a question.

When Brenda started to go, Maybelle grabbed her in a bear hug. "I don't want to let you go," she said as she squeezed tightly. "You such a precious child. I sorry you leaving Mr. Dawg. I know you must have good reason. He too kind to fire anybody. He an angel if there ever was one."

Brenda told her she was not fired and that she was moving to Charlotte to live with her boyfriend. She didn't respond to Maybelle's praise of Dawg Brinson, though she wanted to say, "Look honey, if Dawg Brinson's an angel, he's an angel from hell."

THEY HAD PLANNED TO GRILL HAMBURGERS by the pool, but a late afternoon thunderstorm drove them inside. Huggie was disappointed but understood, especially when a ball of lightening, accompanied by a deafening clap of thunder, split a pine in the back yard down the middle and set it on fire. The rain, coming down in sheets, quickly put out the fire but left the pine smoking. Don and the girls stared nervously out the kitchen window.

"This is a bad one," Don said.

A second nearby flash and loud clap of thunder near the street was followed by a loud boom sounding like cannon. The lights went out without flickering.

"It got a transformer," Don said. "May be awhile before we have electricity."

"Does that mean we can't have hamburgers for dinner?" Huggie asked.

"We'll figure something out," her father replied. "In the meantime we need to round up some candles before it gets dark".

The three sat close together on the couch with Huggie in the middle. The lightening flashed and the thunder roared, but with the warm bodies of her father and her dear friend pressing against her, Huggie wasn't frightened.

As is typical during hot humid summers in the low country, the storm passed quickly, leaving blue skies and temperatures in the low seventies.

"The charcoal's so soaked I could never get it started," said Don. "And with no electricity we can't cook the burgers in the house. I'll run down to Hardees and get us a bag of burgers."

Huggie was hungry but she didn't complain.

When Don returned half an hour later it was almost dark. Brenda and Huggie had lit a couple of candles and placed them on the kitchen table.

"Sorry, but no food of any type. The power's out all over town. All restaurants are closed. Power lines are down everywhere. I doubt that we'll have power before morning. Fortunately, the Seven-Eleven was open. I bought some dry charcoal and some starter. We'll cook out after all."

Huggie jumped and clapped. It would be special with candlelight.

"Are you sure you have enough charcoal starter?" Brenda asked sarcastically as Don removed the third can from the bag.

"Everything's so wet and humid," Don replied. "I wanted to make sure I could get the coals started."

DON AND BRENDA SIPPED GLASSES OF WINE as they sat in the darkness on the couch in the den. A candle on the hearth flickered as it neared its end. Huggie had gone to bed.

"I can't believe I didn't get more candles and some flashlight batteries while I was at the Seven-Eleven," Don said.

"Don't worry. You got the essentials," Brenda said. "These were the best charcoaled hamburgers I've ever eaten. And didn't Huggie have a good time?"

Brenda had two flashlights with fresh batteries in her car, but wasn't ready to mention them. If the darkness became unbearable she would "suddenly remember" and go get them. But for now, she wasn't going to do anything to interrupt the evening and the ambience produced by the storm and darkness.

"Don, there's something I need to tell you. I've resigned from the Brinson Law Firm and moved to Charlotte. I'm living with Glenn Osborne."

Don had a sinking feeling like he felt when he opened the letter from Sabrina's lawyer. He wanted to respond but he didn't trust his voice to conceal his emotions. It wasn't that he had not heard of Glenn. She had talked a lot about the handsome professor, and Don had suspected that her absence from the area on weekends was because they were together. But to know, rather than to suspect, is different. He wanted to ask, "Does this mean you plan to marry? Will Huggie and I not be seeing you again?"

Before he could speak, Brenda interrupted his thoughts and said, "I'll come back to visit, and if things work out, I'd like Huggie to spend some time with Glenn and me this summer. There are a lot of fun things to do in Charlotte. Maybe she can come up after we go to the Special Olympic Games in Columbia in August."

Don's spirits were lifted, knowing Brenda still planned to go with them for the weekend of the state Special Olympics. It was something to look forward to.

"You've meant so much to us. If you hadn't come into our lives, Carol wouldn't have gone to a school for mainstream children or participated in Special Olympics. We might not have a computer. There'd be no gold medals for swimming and track, and Huggie would not be nearly as advanced."

"I love her dearly," Brenda said. "Both of you mean a lot to me. I doubt there's another white person in Hazelboro who would so openly accept an uppity black girl like me. You and Huggie even came to Mama's funeral. She had slaved for half the white families in town and helped raise a lot of their children. But you and Huggie were the only white people there. It meant a lot to me."

Don walked Brenda to the door. She stopped and turned toward him. "You don't need to walk me to the car," she said, knowing that they were going to have a good-bye embrace that would raise the eyebrows of people driving by. The embrace lasted longer than usual, like neither wanted to let go. But after a moment, Brenda pushed back and moved out the door and down the driveway.

Don watched as she disappeared into the darkness.

Chapter 30

"I BEEN EXPECTING YOU," Dawg Brinson said to the beautiful blonde sitting across his desk from him. "Ole Dawg did good by you. Got you all that money and I hear you've pissed it away."

Sabrina wasn't offended. Dawg was talking in a teasing voice. Whatever his opinion, she knew she could handle him. If she couldn't wrap him around her finger during the next hour or so, she had really lost it, and she wasn't about to believe she had.

"I do need your help," she said. "And I promise to be wiser this time."

"Well don't feel bad. A lot of us got took by that bunch of Enson bastards. But it weren't that big a deal for me. What's a million dollars here and there to ole Dawg?"

"I was very foolish," Sabrina said. "This friend I trusted insisted it was a sure deal. Now, he's dead and I'm destitute, living on what my children can scrape together for me. They want me to go back to their father, at least let him know I need help, but I can't do that. He's been nothing but kind to me, but I hate him. It's strange isn't it? How you can intensely dislike someone who would do anything in the world for you. Why do I dislike him so? Simply because he exists. I can think of no other reason. As long as there's a Don Hazelhurst, I'll want to throw up when I think of him."

"I understand," Dawg said. "I got so I felt the same way 'bout all my wives. I just got rid of the third one. Paid her a bunch of money and sent her off to West Palm. I don't intend for there to be any more."

Dawg was looking at the crossed legs of Sabrina and fantasizing about what must be between them. "Don't get me wrong. I'm not done with women. Just done with marrying 'em. You know I've always been hot for you. I'd like to get close to you. Maybe take a cruise, or a road trip somewhere."

Sabrina quickly seized the opportunity. "There could be something better than that. You live in a huge house by yourself. I could move in with you and you'd have someone to come home to."

Dawg was almost salivating. Surely she would not expect him to keep his hands off her. "None of the bedrooms in my house have doors that lock from the inside," he said.

Sabrina smiled. "Oh, I wouldn't need a separate bedroom. There'd be no point in having two beds to make up in the mornings."

Dawg reached in his desk and pulled out a nearly empty bottle of I. W. Harper whiskey. He was so excited that the bottle of whiskey was shaking all around. He asked Sabrina if she would like a drink. There were no glasses in sight so she presumed he was offering her a drink straight from the bottle.

"No, thank you," she said. "I don't drink anymore. I quit without any help. Didn't have to go to any of those silly meetings."

She paused a moment long enough for Dawg to turn up the bottle and empty it with three large gulps. His face, which was always red, turned a deep purple, and he coughed for a few seconds while trying to speak. "Had to take a drink in celebration," he said.

Sabrina continued. "It's not completely truthful that I quit drinking without any help."

She held up a couple of pills the size of an aspirin. "These little fellows and several of their cousins helped. You get a similar effect, and they don't put on the pounds."

"Drugs?" Dawg asked. "I don't know much about drugs. They were never all that fashionable when my generation was getting into beer and liquor. I don't like to be around them much. I'd rather you go back to drinking."

Sabrina changed the subject. "Any ideas how I can get back in the pockets of my ex?"

"I've been thinking about it since I knew sooner or later you'd wash back up on my shore begging for help," Dawg replied. "It won't be easy 'cause the court signed off on your separation agreement and you got a final divorce. We can't open it back up. Going after your former husband would be like going after a complete stranger. But soft hearted as the old fart is, he'd probably support you if you asked him, or if you let one of your children ask him. Whatever he thinks of you, you're still the mother of his children, and he'd never let the mother of those he loves go hungry."

"I know," Sabrina said. "But I'd rather die than have him think he's being kind to me. I don't know why, but that's the way I feel. Strange isn't it. It's like knowing a victim who would give you money if you ask, but you would rather knock him down and take it away from him."

"Well as I was saying, I've been giving it some thought and I have a suggestion. You know how much he loves that kid...what's her name?"

"Carol, but most people call her "Huggie Bear or just "Huggie."

"Yeah, Huggie. Well we can ask for custody of Huggie. I 'spect I can dig up enough dirt on Hazelhurst to take the youngun away from him."

"Don't count on it. He's squeaky clean. Anyone that boring is not going to do anything risky."

"Then I might have to create a little dirt. I've got some ideas. Just trust ole Dawg."

"I don't want custody of Huggie. We should have put her in an institution when she was born."

"I know." And since you'll be living with me, you should know that I don't want her around either. I don't like younguns of any type, and meaning no disrespect to you, I especially don't want to have to put up with an ugly, dumb kid. But it wouldn't be for long. Her daddy would have visitation rights. We'd let her visit with him all the time, so long as he continued to make the support payments to you. It'd kinda be like a kidnapping, 'cept legal."

DAWG BRINSON'S PERSONALITY underwent an abrupt change after Sabrina moved into his house. He came to the office every morning with a smile on his face and stayed cheerful all day. He complimented his associates for their work, and even brought flowers to Miss Ginny and hot donuts to the staff. Associates and staff debated among themselves as to whether the change would last. The consensus was that it would last only until Dawg got enough of another beautiful, dumb blonde companion.

At home, Dawg stayed busy arranging for decorators to refurbish the huge home to match the tastes of the lady living there with him. He hired two full time domestic workers, Agnes and Isabel, both African-Americans. Agnes' duties were to keep the house clean and follow the instructions given her by Sabrina. Isabel did the cooking. The yard took on a new life. A landscape service was hired; the pool was drained, painted and refilled. All of the trees and bushes were pruned. The grass was reseeded, fertilized and rolled. Two Mexican immigrants were hired to care for the lawn and run errands for Sabrina.

Sabrina loved the life style, except at night when a slothenly drunk Dawg tried to make love to her. Sometimes at night, after he had exhausted himself trying to perform, Sabrina would stay awake for hours, listening to the obnoxious creature snore. During those moments, probably more than at any time in her life, she would do a lot of thinking.

PEOPLE LIKE SABRINA SELDOM THINK. Thinking about anything but the present requires a certain depth, a feeling of purpose and direction. Sabrina never thought much about the future—where she wished to be in five, ten, or perhaps more years. It was like a journey across country without a mind picture of what was at the end of the journey, or even about points in between. All she could see was the next point, like a curve in the road, or a large truck in front. But her thoughts began to stretch, to wonder how long she would need to serve the interests of Dawg Brinson. Fortunately he was so old, overweight, and drunk, and she was usually high on pills, that sex was not that much of a problem. After a few minutes of trying, Dawg would fall asleep. The next morning she would assure him that he had been terrific. He would smile, puff up like a frog and giggle as if to say, "And what would you expect from the great lawyer, senator and lover, Dawg Brinson?"

Only occasionally did Sabrina's thoughts turn to Jeff, Megan and Huggie, and when they did there were questions: "Why did come into a world where I don't fit? I never planned to have children, but the few times I imagined I might, I envisioned them normal. Girls would like boys and boys would like girls, and there would not be one unusual like Huggie. Who's to blame? Is it pure chance? Is it

God, or is it that non-entity of a man I married? And why does he see Huggie, as different as she is, as such a great blessing?"

BRENDA WAS A FEW MINUTES early for her appointment with Dawg Brinson. As she pulled into the parking lot, she saw a shiny new Cadillac in his parking space. So, he's already here and it's not yet 9:00 in the morning, she thought. He's probably armed and ready. She was there to get the sodium explosion case files. She expected trouble, even though she had agreements signed by all of the plaintiffs releasing Brinson and employing her as their sole counsel.

Miss Ginny greeted Brenda with a little grunt and nod. Brenda walked over to her desk and started to hold out her hand to shake. Then she remembered that Miss Ginny was embarrassed by the uncontrollable shaking of her hands, so she withdrew hers.

"It's good to see you, Miss Ginny. I've missed you during the three weeks I've been gone."

In a shaky voice, Miss Ginny replied, "He's expecting you. Go on in."

When Brenda walked through the door, Dawg got up and came around his desk to greet her. She walked into his outstretched arms for a brief hug. This is not the Dawg I remember, she thought. He looked younger and happier and the smell of cologne coming from his face and neck partially obscured the odor of whiskey and coffee.

"Great to see you," Dawg said as he motioned for her to sit down. "We've missed you even though you've been gone only a few weeks. We'd love to have you back."

"Thanks." Brenda said, but didn't add that she had missed the firm or would ever consider returning. She noticed a stack of files on the corner of the desk and recognized them as the sodium explosion files.

They were amazingly slim considering the seriousness and complexity of the cases, and the length of time they had been opened.

Dawg pushed the files toward her. "They're all yours and I wish you luck with them. It works well for me. I'm gonna slow down and live a little."

"Can you tell me who she is?" Brenda asked with a little laugh.

"The most beautiful and wonderful woman in the world. I may even rethink my resolution to never marry again."

Brenda didn't press him for further identification. She couldn't care less. No matter what kind of transformation Dawg had undergone because of his new relationship, she was glad to be free from the firm and its domineering owner.

AFTER LIVING WITH SABRINA for only three weeks, Dawg was ready to marry her. His proposal was enticing: Luxury living, travel, cruises, unlimited spending money. "And the inheritance of millions should I ever die."

If only he didn't come with the deal, Sabrina thought. "I'm honored," she told him. "Give me some time to consider it. But in the meantime, let's proceed with our plan. I'd like to gouge Donald Hazelhurst one more time."

"Will do," Dawg replied. "And remember, Dawg never loses and I won't lose this case. It might be my last one. I want to retire and spend my last years enjoying the company of my lovely wife."

Sabrina did not respond.

Dawg started talking even more excitedly. "Why don't we plan a big party for this fall when the weather cools off? Maybe we can announce our marriage, or at least our engagement. We'll invite everybody who is anybody. It'll be the biggest barbecue and pig picking these South Carolina sand hills have ever seen. We'll add in a little Brunswick stew and enough chicken bog to feed an army. And of course, there'll be plenty of bourbon and branch water."

Sabrina's mind wandered back to the party at the Hazelhurst home after she had finished decorating it. There had been waiters in formal attire, flowing champagne and food prepared by the best caterers available. And it was on that night that she slept with Don for the first time. Would an evening after Dawg's party be as revolting? She started to take issue with the kind of party he was describing, but didn't say anything. She was willing for Dawg to have his way, feeling that a time would come when she would be in control.

Chapter 31

BRENDA LOST NO TIME in getting back to Charlotte with the sodium explosion files. It was almost seven in the evening and the offices of the Hudson Law Firm were empty except for a couple of associates working in the library. She did not go to the small office the firm had provided for her, but to a large conference room off the reception area. She spread the files out on the conference table and started making notes.

First, there was the question of parties. At the Brinson firm they were referred to in general terms such as the chemical company, the brothers and their corporation, and the developer. From the sketchy information in the file, Brenda learned that the brothers were John and James Brown. They had inherited the Brown Chemical Company from their father and had operated it for twenty years before retiring and selling the company to the Aberdeen Chemical Company. The same day the stock in the Brown Company was delivered to the Aberdeen Company, Brown executed a deed to the old plant and property to Quest Corporation, a subsidiary of Aberdeen. There was no evidence Quest had any other assets or was engaged in business of any kind. It was simply a shell subsidiary, apparently created by Aberdeen for the sole purpose of taking title to the old plant, which it turned out was home to the dangerous vat of sodium. Quest sold the property to the Myers Development company soon thereafter. It was owned by Myers when the explosion occurred.

IT WAS AFTER ELEVEN O'CLOCK when the door to the reception room opened. Brenda's heart beat faster as she heard steps across the marble floor to the conference room. She breathed a sigh of relief when she saw it was Tony Rustler, one of the firm's trial lawyers who had been assigned to help with the case. His responsibility would be little more than signing the pleadings and taking care of the formalities of moving Brenda's limited permission to appear in the case as an out-of-state attorney.

"Hope I didn't frighten you," Rustler said. "Had to get a late flight from Chicago and just got in. Came by the office to check my emails. What're you doing here so late?"

Brenda waived her hands over the spread out files. "I picked up the sodium explosion files today and I'm outlining what has to be done. I'll need you to assign me at least two associates. The tasks ahead are monumental. Lot's of discovery must be done. We'll need chemical engineers and experts on damages. We also need to keep in close touch with the plaintiffs and consistently update the medical condition of those injured. And of course, we'll need to obtain documents for review and take pre-trial depositions."

"You should think about negotiating a settlement," Rustler said. "You can spend countless hours preparing for trial and trying the case, and still not recover what the cases are worth. I understand most of the insurance money has already been paid out. The Brown brothers long ago put everything in their wives' names. Getting any of that reversed won't be easy. Myers Development has already divvied up most of what little it had. It still owns the old chemical plant, but it's so contaminated it's more of a liability than an asset.

That's why it was never put in the Aberdeen Chemical Company's name."

"What about that company and Quest, its subsidiary?" Brenda asked.

"Aberdeen is chartered in Scotland. I'll bet its organizational chart looks like a Charleston family tree. It wouldn't be like filing a case against the railroad. And Quest has already been dissolved. It'd do no good to resurrect it since it never had any assets anyway."

THIRTY DAYS LATER, Brenda had most of what she needed, though some answers would have to await depositions. The stock transfer agreement and the transfers on the stock certificates were dated the day after the date appearing on the deed to Quest. Brenda knew all documents had probably been signed at the same time, but the deed had been back-dated to make sure the old plant was not still an asset of the Brown Corporation when it transferred its stock to the Aberdeen Company. But wait! The date stamped on the deed indicated it wasn't recorded until the day after the stock transfer. Apparently, a secretary or maybe an attorney associate had not promptly made it to the courthouse.

"MR. ARNOLD, YOU ARE the moving party, so I'll hear from you first," said Judge Melton, who was hearing the motion filed by Arnold to dismiss the action against his client, the Aberdeen Company. It was his contention that his client had never owned or had possession of the old plant.

Malcolm Arnold was in his early 60s, handsome, courtly and suave. Other lawyers were fond of saying he could strut while sitting down. He was one of the state's most respected trial lawyers and a senior partner in one of its most successful law firms. He had charmed many judges and juries, and had a way of making opposing lawyers feel small and insignificant without uttering an insult or raising his voice. One lawyer had said of him, "Don't listen to his flattery. He can have you believing he thinks you are a wonderful lawyer and person, but by the time he has finished his argument, you know the sweet son of a bitch has ripped your guts out."

Arnold stood. "Your Honor, Mr. Taylor will present our opening argument."

A young African-American man, barely out of law school, rose to speak. Brenda suspected a strategy, or perhaps a ploy. Put up an inexperienced young lawyer to make the first argument. It would suggest confidence in the matter, and what harm could he do. Since he was young and inexperienced, the judge would likely defer his tough questions for Arnold who would have the final argument. Moreover, an African-American on his side made it easier for Arnold to "put down," an opposing lawyer of the same race.

Taylor's short argument might have received a B- in a second-year law class on jurisdictional conflicts. It lasted barely three minutes and was obviously canned. The judge took notes and appeared to listen intently, but didn't ask any questions.

Brenda rose to speak. "May it please the court? I'm Brenda Horton, attorney for the plaintiffs. I'm licensed in South Carolina and appreciate the court permitting me to make a special appearance here. I intend to seek licensing here as soon as possible.

"The affidavits and exhibits show that Quest Corporation was a puppet of the Aberdeen Chemical Company, obviously created for the sole purpose of attempting to shield the company from responsibility for the contaminated old plant owned by the Brown Corporation which it was acquiring. The companies should be viewed as one. Moreover, when the Chemical Company acquired the stock of the Brown Company, it acquired the liabilities as well as the assets, notwithstanding an agreement by the parties to the contrary. There is still a third point that has not heretofore been addressed.

"In North Carolina, insofar as third parties are concerned, title to real property doesn't vest until the deed is recorded. So, when the Aberdeen Company acquired the Brown Company through the transfer of stock, it acquired the chemical plant, at least until the deed to the Quest Company was recorded the following day. As owners, they were under a duty to remove any hazards from the property, even though the time of their ownership may have been brief."

Brenda argued for thirty minutes. Judge Melton listened intently and didn't interrupt her.

Malcolm Arnold rose to speak. "The lady has indeed made a most ingenious argument, Your Honor, an argument that would not have occurred to me, nor I submit to any other lawyer in this state. Miss Horton, of course, is not yet a member of the Bar of this state. I heard her say she aspires to be, and I wish her well. I'm sure she will be a distinguished member.

"But at this point, all of her legal experience has been in a sister state. Perhaps it was her experience there that suggested to her the very ingenious, but highly technical and flawed argument she makes here. There is no doubt that there was a meeting of the minds of the parties when the deed was executed and delivered. Equitable title, if not legal title, passed at that time. The Aberdeen Company did not need the old plant, did not want it, and it never accepted title to it."

Judge Melton interrupted. "Was there a relationship between the now dissolved Quest Company and your client, Mr. Arnold?"

"The Quest Company, named in the deed, was a subsidiary of a company in which my client owned stock. As a stockholder of Quest's parent company, my client is of course not liable for any action or failure to act by Quest any more than I as an owner of a few shares of General Motors stock, am responsible for its actions."

"How much of the stock did your client own?"

"I'm not sure, Your Honor, but it really doesn't matter. The corporate shield stands between the companies."

"You've heard of the doctrine called piercing the corporate veil, haven't you?"

"Oh yes, Your Honor, but it's not applicable here. My client had no relationship with subsidiary companies here. It owns stock in several companies. They are all domiciled off shore. Such methods of operation are not unusual in other countries."

"What are the purposes of all these subsidiaries, Mr. Arnold? Do they have employees? Do they conduct any business? Do they have officers and directors, and if so, by chance are any of them also officers and directors of your client?"

"I'm not sure I can answer any of those questions, Your Honor, but does it really matter? The Aberdeen Chemical Company is entitled to the limited liability afforded by corporate structures. And if I might add, it's one of the most outstanding corporate citizens in the entire world. It's held in the highest esteem in all of the many countries in which it operates, including this country."

There was a brief silence before Arnold proceeded.

Judge Melton interrupted with more questions. "Mr. Arnold, let me ask if you are familiar with the Super Fund or other environmental regulations?"

"I'm somewhat familiar, Your Honor, though as you know, I'm not an environmental lawyer."

"Well, since most environmental laws are federal laws, I'm not all that familiar with them either. But I've heard of cases where all owners in the chain of title to a contaminated site have been made to clean it up, even when they didn't know it was already contaminated when they acquired it. The management of a large worldwide chemical company would surely suspect that an old building used for more than half a century to manufacture various kinds of chemicals might not be as clean as the sands of the beaches of the Atlantic. Who could blame them for not wanting the property in their company's name?"

Arnold had a pleasant expression on his face as it appeared the judge might be sympathetic with his client.

The judge continued. "The Aberdeen Company could have purchased the assets of the company except for the old plant, and there would have been no risk. But it would be reasonable to suspect that the sellers didn't want the old plant either. They could have insisted that it pass with all of the other property."

"All of that is interesting speculation, Your Honor," Arnold said. "But there's no evidence at this point of any of that. And even if the speculation is correct, Aberdeen still had the right to arrange the transaction in a way that would not subject it to liability for an environmental problem it had no part in creating."

"Perhaps," the judge replied. "But they had to do it right. I deny your motion, Mr. Arnold. Draw an order, Ms. Horton, setting forth findings of fact consistent with the denial and I will sign it."

DEPOSITIONS OF THE BROWN BROTHERS were held five weeks later in the main conference room of the Hudson Law Firm. All defense attorneys were there. Malcolm Arnold arrived early and asked to speak privately with Brenda before the examinations began.

They went into Brenda's office. Arnold entered last and closed the door behind him. He had filed an appeal of the judge's order denying his motion to dismiss his client from the case, and Brenda thought that might be what he wanted to discuss. But instead, he wanted to talk about the possibility of a settlement.

"Ms. Horton, your cases are the last of the explosion cases," said Arnold. "All others have been settled, and these should be also. The community needs to get this dreadful event behind it. I'm not authorized to make an offer. But if you'll give me a ballpark figure, I'll take it up with my client and the lawyers for the other defendants."

"I can give you a precise figure. With the help of an economist, my clients have each agreed to the amount of damages they have suffered. I can assure you that there is no embellishment in any of the figures. The total is twenty million dollars."

"I appreciate your candor, Miss Horton, but unless I'm free to make a counter offer, I don't think I better mention that figure to the others. I don't like being laughed at."

Brenda was tempted to point out the reasons Arnold should want to settle, but she knew he was bright and experienced enough to recognize the risks. If the case went forward, and it turned out the assets and insurance of the other defendants were exhausted, the Aberdeen Company could have to pay all damages awarded. And if a trial was held and all of the facts revealed, Aberdeen would also have to deal with the question of clean-up costs. There was also the possibility of embarrassment to Arnold's firm for not having timely filed the deed from the Brown Company to the Quest Corporation.

BRENDA SOUGHT TO HAVE ONE BROTHER sequestered while the other was being examined, hoping to catch them in contradictions. But their lawyers pitched a fit and she didn't pursue it.

John Brown, the older of the brothers at age sixty-five was the first to be examined. His brother sat on one side of him and his counsel on the other.

Brenda spent the first twenty minutes asking routine questions about the history of the plant, what was manufactured there, the number of employees, and changes made when the brothers took over the business from their father. Both brothers appeared bored until the vat of sodium was mentioned. Then they become somewhat antsy. John testified that the vat had been locked in an unused room since before the brothers became active in the business.

"You are testifying under oath that for all of those years neither you nor your brother ever went in the room containing the vat of sodium, that you didn't know what if anything was in there, and never inquired?"

"I'm testifying that I don't recall that part of the plant being used or the door to the room ever being opened. That area of the plant wasn't needed. After Daddy died, we curtailed our actual manufacture of chemicals. It was more profitable for us to purchase wholesale and deliver to our customers. Our large base of loyal customers was what made our business valuable."

Brenda continued to ask softball questions, but in the process got some useful information. The Aberdeen Company wanted to purchase the stock rather than the assets because it was the simplest way to do the transaction. "But the company didn't want the old plant, and suggested we find a buyer for it. Myers Development was interested."

Brenda prefaced a question by pointing out that the lack of tax stamps on the deed to Quest Company indicated that little or no money was paid for the old plant.

"I'm not sure I can explain," said John. "And I'm not sure why Aberdeen wanted us to deed the property to Quest. I think it was the lawyers who decided how to do it. We just did what we were told. Since we got a good price for the business, including the old plant, we didn't care how it was handled."

"I only have a few more questions," Brenda said. "But first, why don't we take a short break."

Arnold and the other defense lawyers chatted cordially as they dispersed, some to make phone calls, others to the men's room. They were pleased with the way things were going.

THE HANDWRITTEN MEMO had been locked in a safety deposit box since the day after Brenda found it on the floor of the old plant, except for the time it took to make copies. The original still remained there.

Brenda handed copies to all counsel.

The attorney for one of the Brown Brothers glanced at the memo and immediately said, "Wait a minute! If the original is something that's been fabricated, somebody's going to be in trouble!"

"And if it hasn't," Brenda replied, "then somebody is going to be in deep trouble. Lying under oath, fraud, deception, conspiracy. Why don't we just ask the witness? If it's not the copy of a memorandum he sent or received, he can say so. He knows he's under oath and could be in deep trouble if he lies about it."

For the next five minutes, a heated discussion among defense counsel ensued.

Finally, Malcolm Arnold said, "Why don't we let her ask some preliminary questions? If the witness says he's never seen the original copy that should end it."

But Brenda didn't ask Brown if he had ever seen the original, nor did she hand him a copy. "What do you call your brother and what does he call you, Mr. Brown" she asked.

"He's J. A, and I'm J. O., you know James and John. We've called each other by the first two letters of our names since we were kids."

"Are you familiar with a company called Bowen Environmental, Inc.?"

"I don't know of any company around here by that name."

"I didn't ask you about 'around here.'" Have you ever heard of a company by that name located anywhere?"

Counsel for each of the Brown brothers spoke simultaneously. "Why don't we take a break?"

"But we just took a break," Brenda said slyly. Then she nodded to the reporter to be at ease.

The Browns and all lawyers retired to a conference room and locked the door behind them.

The note, faded but still readable said in scratchy handwriting:

> *"J. A.,*
> *The Bowen Company from Richmond quoted a god awful high*
> *price to remove the vat of sodium. I suggest we let some future*
> *owner worry with it."*
> *J. O.*

Conversations in the conference room grew louder and louder. The Brown Brothers were arguing with each other, as were their attorneys.

The younger brother said to the older, "Our reputation will be ruined and it's because of your carelessness."

After an hour, the conversations grew quieter.

Brenda glanced at the phone and noted that lights to all the extension lines from the conference room were lit. They remained lit for over an hour.

It was almost six o'clock when Arnold came out and said to Brenda, "Can you meet me for breakfast at Anderson's restaurant in the morning?"

Brenda smiled. She knew she would sleep well that night.

Chapter 32

HUGGIE PROUDLY WORE both medals while she, her father and Brenda had dinner at a fast food restaurant in downtown Columbia. The gold was for being on the winning swim relay team. The bronze was for placing third in the 50-meter freestyle. She was in several events where she did not get a medal, but enjoyed those just as much.

Huggie finished her hamburger and was chatting with a young Olympian man sitting across the aisle with his parents.

"Special Olympics has been such a blessing to Carol Ann," her father said to Brenda. "We have you to thank for finding out about it and getting us involved."

"It's meant a lot to me," Brenda replied. "And Huggie's involvement has meant so much to the program and the other participants. She's always so lovable, win or lose."

They had finished their dinner and appeared to be waiting for Huggie to return to the table. But they were really waiting for one of them to suggest where they would go from there.

"Do you have plans for the evening?" Don finally asked.

"I should drive back to Charlotte. Glenn and I usually go out to dinner on Saturday nights. But he's flexible. If I call and tell him I want to stay over, he'll understand."

"Huggie'll be disappointed if her roommate leaves," Don said. "But you've already given us so much of your time, and Glenn deserves to have his future wife with him for what remains of the weekend. What do you want to do?"

"I want to stay with you and Huggie. But if I leave, Huggie can move into your room. That would save some money."

As soon as she said it, Brenda realized how ridiculous it was. Don was rich. So was she. Her success a month before with the sodium explosion case had left her a rich woman with four million dollars. A night's expense for a hotel room should not be a factor in the decision for her to stay or go.

AFTER DINNER AND a leisurely walk around the capital grounds, and a portion of the University of South Carolina campus, they returned to the hotel and the room that Huggie and Brenda shared. Room service brought cokes and chips, and they watched movies Don had taken of the Olympics.

Huggie followed the film excitedly for the first half hour. Then she began to nod off. Brenda helped her into her nightgown and tucked her into her side of the Queen-size bed. As soon as she was asleep, Don turned off the TV and packed up the film.

"Remember I said I would teach you to dance?" Asked Brenda. "I know a good place for your first lesson."

"I'll do whatever you suggest," Don said.

THE LOUNGE ON THE MEZZANINE of the hotel was empty except for a single man sipping a beer at the bar. A nodding piano player was playing, *Bring on the Clowns,* not the best dance music, but Brenda took Don by the hand and led him onto the dance floor.

"But you haven't taught me how to dance yet," Don protested.

Brenda didn't answer, but snuggled close to him. He put his right hand on the small of her back, and with his left held her right out to the side the way he recalled seeing others do it. He was struggling to remember the Cotillion lessons his mother made him attend when he was an early teen. Slow, slow, quick, quick, slow, his feet seemed to recall, though it had been half a century ago.

"But you can dance," Brenda said as she skillfully moved in rhythm with his movements to the slow music. He pulled her close. She nestled her head below his chin with her lips almost touching his neck.

"You fit in my arms so perfectly," Don whispered.

Brenda laughed softly and moved closer so the fronts of their bodies were pressing firmly against each other. Both wanted the moment to last, but it didn't. The piano player switched to a very fast tempo, which neither could follow.

Don relaxed his grip around Brenda's waist and led her to a table for two in a dark corner of the lounge. She noticed the single man who had been at the bar returning to his beer, after a likely men's room break. He was tall, about six feet-four inches, and though she could not see his face in the dimly lit bar, for some reason she pictured it as being pock marked.

For the next two hours, they talked while they drank their beers.

Brenda told Don about the explosion cases and how they had made her rich. He was happy she had negotiated such a good settlement and wondered why she seemed to have guilty feelings about making so much money. Without her skill and a lot of hard work, there would have been no recovery.

"This is just the beginning for you Brenda. You've made your reputation. I'm sure injury cases will flock to you now. You'll become richer than Dawg Brinson!"

"I'm not sure I want to continue as a personal injury lawyer," Brenda said. "I don't feel I'm cut out for it, even though I was successful with my first big case. I'm thinking about wills and estates. Lawyers who practice in that area can make a good living, and at the same time, enjoy helping people plan and shape their affairs in ways that will care for those they love, long into the future."

Don wanted to tell her about his estate plan, but instead chose to talk about something of more interest to him.

"I assume you and Glenn will marry someday?"

Brenda didn't respond immediately. It wasn't a question she could easily answer yes or no. "Perhaps," she said. "There are good reasons why we should. We respect each other and we also care deeply for each other. We could probably go through life enjoying each other and being there for each other in time of need. I trust him completely and have willed him most of what I have." She paused before adding. "But there's an important ingredient missing."

"Sex?" Don was shocked to hear himself ask.

"Yes. My memories of the experience with my father return whenever I get close and I panic. I've had counseling, read books; done everything. Nothing works, and I don't want to marry someone I can't love in a physical way. Glenn says he's willing to live without sex, but how can I be sure?"

They had finished their third beer and were preparing to order another when the lights began to flicker and the music stopped. It was time to leave.

As they made their way to the elevator, Brenda said, "Don, maybe it's the beer making me so bold, but I'm going to say it. I love you. I have since before I first saw you. The first night, when I brought Huggie home, she talked about you constantly, and something deep in my soul said, 'You will love that man.' During the times we've been close, I've asked myself, 'What is it about this shy, plain looking man that attracts me?' It doesn't have to be anything identifiable, Don. I believe there's an unknown spirit that touches your heart when you meet someone and causes the electricity to flow, lighting up your whole life. I believe it because that's what happened to me."

Don was too stunned to speak, but at the same time, he felt a warm glow flow throughout his body. He took Brenda's hand and they started moving toward the elevator.

Brenda had second thoughts about being so candid. What would happen when they got upstairs? It made sense for her to sleep in the room with Don and not risk waking Huggie. But what if Don made a move and she had the same withdrawal compulsion. He would be humiliated. But even worse, what if they made love? Whichever way it turned out would be wrong. Suddenly, it was as if she had awakened from a deep sleep to realize that, while sleeping, she said something she would might regret. She pushed the down button in the elevator and said, "The night is young and there's a place I've always wanted to go. We can go together."

Standing in the door of the hotel as Brenda pulled Don outside was that man. He was smoking a cigarette and pretending not to be aware of them as they passed. As Brenda had thought, he had a pock marked face. He made her nervous. She knew she had seen him before, but couldn't recall where.

It was well after midnight and the streets were empty except for a lone taxi parked half a block away. The Off-Duty sign was up and the driver was asleep inside. Brenda knocked on the window. A third, hard knock aroused the driver enough for him to point to the Off-Duty sign. Brenda pulled a one hundred dollar bill from her pocket and held it against the window. The window slowly rolled down.

"The Dew Drop Inn," Brenda said.

In broken English that was hard to understand, the man tried to explain that he didn't go to that part of town, even when he was on duty.

"I'll pay you twice what the meter says," Brenda promised in a pleading kind of voice.

The driver wasn't interested and started to roll up the window. Brenda stuck one arm in the window and with her other hand waived the hundred dollar bill and said, "You get this for taking us and bringing us back."

The driver continued to hesitate, but finally, overcome by the chance to make so much money on such a short trip, he reached back and unlocked the door behind him. Before he had time to nod for them to get in, Brenda opened the door and pushed Don ahead of her into the back seat.

The drive was less than five minutes, but it was like moving from Palm Beach to the heart of Citi Soleil. Houses were a lot like those in the old slum areas of Charlotte that Glenn had described. Although it was after midnight, people, including some children, still wandered around the narrow streets.

The Dew Drop Inn was an old building that looked like it had once been a tobacco warehouse. As the taxi pulled in front, a group of men stumbled toward it shouting vulgar words that were meaningless. The driver pointed to the meter, which registered eight dollars. Although he was as black as any of the men surrounding the taxi, he was nervous and wanted to get out of there. He was talking hurriedly in a language neither Don nor Brenda understood, but it was clear he was trying to say he would settle for eight dollars and not have to come back.

Brenda quickly ripped the hundred-dollar bill in half and handed a half to him. "You get the other half when you come back to this very spot exactly two hours from now."

While the driver protested even more vehemently, Brenda pulled Don from the cab. "He's probably from one of the islands," she said. Some African-American men dislike islanders."

The crowd lingering outside the club parted to make a path for them, and watched curiously as Brenda made her way to the door of the club, dragging Don behind her. They continued to talk to each other in vulgar language, but didn't direct any of it toward Don and Brenda.

Brenda paid a cover charge of a few dollars at the door and pulled Don inside. There was a band and a couple of male rappers on a make shift stage off to the side. The music was strange and deafening. Two female strippers, already down to their g-strings, gyrated on each side of the rappers, but few seemed to pay attention. Except for the stage and room for several bars, the entire area was a dance floor. It was filled with people doing all kinds of things, including a few who were trying to dance.

A hand reached for Brenda and pulled her into the crowd. Don couldn't see the person, but he heard the man say, "Come on, sister. We gonna dance."

Brenda skillfully followed the rhythm of her partner. The crowd moved back to give them some room and then stood watching and clapping. Soon a male larger than the one Brenda was dancing with pulled her away from her partner and deeper into the crowd. They were soon out of Don's sight.

A huge man, resembling Shaquille O'Neal, bumped Don in the side. He turned and held out his long neck Bud. "Hold my beer for me, bro," he said.

When Don took the beer, the man took a large knife from his pocket. He pushed a button on the side and a ten-inch blade popped out. Don stood motionless. Others standing nearby didn't seem bothered. The man held up the knife even with his eyes, and smiled proudly as he turned it from side to side, admiring the tip of the blade. Even in the dark smoke-filled room, the blade shined. He curled the fingers of his left hand downward and started running the blade underneath his fingernails. When he finished, he switched hands.

"Gotta clean my fingernails, bro," the man said. As he closed the knife and put it in his pocket, he said, "You all right, brother? Come with me."

Looking fearful, Don followed the man to the nearest bar. People waiting for drinks stood aside as the man pressed his huge frame against the bar. "Give my friend a belly washer," he said.

The bar tender reached for a fruit jar containing pure liquid. He took one of the tall glasses of beer lined up in front of him and shook a third of it on the floor behind of him. Then he filled the glass with the clear liquid, stirred it with a long teaspoon and handed it to Don.

"How much?" Don asked.

The big man threw a five-dollar bill on the bar and said, "I pay. When Big Max drinks, everybody drinks."

With Big Max standing over him, Don felt he had no choice but to drink it. His fear had shifted from that of being knifed to being poisoned. He had heard of boilermakers, where whiskey is mixed with beer, but he never thought he would ever drink one.

When he finished the drink, Big Max moved on. Don moved over as near against the wall as he could get, trying to separate himself from the crowd. He found a bench that had been pushed against the wall and sat on the end that was empty. He was more relaxed, feeling good and mellow, enjoying the music and watching the crowd. He wanted another drink, but this time only a light beer. But when he tried to stand up, he couldn't.

Shortly before it was time for the taxi to return, Brenda found Don passed out against the wall. "Wake up, wake up!" she shouted as she shook him.

Don didn't budge.

After a few attempts to pull him up, Big Max appeared. "I hep the lady," he said, as he picked Don up with ease and carried him out. As he put him in the back seat of the taxi, he turned to Brenda. "Now that your friend has been one of us on a Saturday night, he ain't ever gonna want to be a white man again."

DON WAS ABLE TO WALK from the taxi to the elevator with the help of Brenda's steadying hand. She got him to his room onto the bed, removed his shoes and socks, and loosened his belt. Don mumbled something unintelligible before losing consciousness.

For the next few hours, Brenda, fully clothed, lay next to him. When it became apparent she would not be able to sleep, she slipped into Huggie's room to pack.

As she came out of Don's room, the door to the room across the hall opened and the man with the pock marked face came out. There was something sleazy about him. They met in the hallway eye-to-eye, almost touching as they passed. Neither spoke nor even nodded.

Brenda was half way to Charlotte when she recalled where she had seen him before. He was the man she saw come out of Dawg Brinson's office when she was last there.

Chapter 33

THE WEEK FOLLOWING the Special Olympics in Columbia was not a good one for Brenda. It should have been because she spent the week planning how to invest her millions. But her thoughts were of Don and Huggie, and she was overwhelmed with feelings of guilt.

For several weeks Don had promised to bring Huggie on Friday evening to spend the weekend, but when Brenda had heard nothing from them by Thursday, she was certain they were not coming. She wouldn't blame him. After what she put him through Saturday night she would not expect him to entrust his daughter to her again.

During dinner Thursday evening, Brenda asked Glenn, "Have you ever instinctively done something completely out of character and afterwards knew you would regret it the rest of your life?"

"I've probably acted instinctively and made poor choices at times," he said. "But I've never done something I regretted for long. Why do you ask?"

"Saturday evening after Huggie went to bed, Don and I had a couple of drinks and I…I told him how much he means to me."

"Well," Glenn said. "They say that sometimes truth is at the bottom of the wine glass. You shouldn't feel bad about that."

"But there's more," Brenda added. "Much more. What if what I said made Don think I wanted to get romantic? What if he made a move that I had to reject? How unfair. He would be hurt and I can't bear to hurt him."

"Well," Glenn said, "you never seem to worry about rejecting me."

"Oh, Glenn, you know I love you and that I'm working on getting rid of my problems about sex. You understand. Don might not."

"So you did something worse than rejecting his passes?"

"Yes. I took him to the Dew Drop Inn."

"You what?"

"I'd always been curious about the place. When you talked about the old slum areas here, Brooklyn and Blue Heaven, and about Saturday nights around McDowell and First Street, I envisioned the area around the Dew Drop Inn as similar. I had this sudden impulse to make sure the evening didn't end in a way neither of us wanted. Going there was all I could think of at the moment."

Glenn sat quietly, wishing they were not having this conversation, but since Brenda had started it, it might be better if he heard the whole story.

Brenda continued. "As soon as we got there I was grabbed and dragged onto the dance floor. Men were cutting in right and left, and more than an hour passed before I could break loose and look for Don. When I found him, he was passed out, dead drunk. He seldom drinks and never more than one or two beers. Somebody had slipped him no telling what. I got him back to the hotel and to bed. I left before he woke up. Since then, he hasn't been in touch with me, and I don't have the nerve to call him."

They sat quietly for several minutes, unable to finish their dinner.

Finally Glenn said, "We may as well forget about having Huggie come visit. It's unlikely her father will ever trust you with her again."

IT WAS LATE FRIDAY AFTERNOON. Glenn was working in his study and Brenda was preparing dinner for four people, though she expected only two.

The doorbell rang and they heard Huggie shouting, "Benda, Benda!" She jumped into Brenda's arms as soon as she opened the door. When Glenn approached she broke loose and gave him a big hug, and said, "You Glenn?"

He knew from her warm hug that he could be added to the long list of people who loved Huggie.

Don followed, carrying a small suitcase in one hand. HeBear was curled under his other arm. He dropped both and gave Brenda a brief hug, more cordial than warm. He didn't notice the dampness in her eyes.

Glenn extended his hand and said, "It's a pleasure to meet you Dr. Hazelhurst."

"And I'm glad to meet you Glenn," Don replied. "You and Brenda are kind to take Huggie for a week. She's talked about nothing all week but getting to spend time with you all. I've never seen her so excited."

Brenda knew Don was there to keep from disappointing Huggie. No humiliation, however bad, would cause him to keep Huggie from this visit.

During dinner, Don avoided eye contact and the few words he spoke were directed to Glenn.

It may take a long time, Brenda thought to herself, but I'll get his friendship back. And when I do….

SATURDAY MORNING WAS SPENT preparing a picnic lunch. Brenda made fried chicken for the first time in her life, trying to remember how she saw her mother do it. Huggie watched every movement and asked lots of questions. Brenda answered as if she were an experienced cook. As they placed pieces of the still sizzling chicken in a picnic basket, Brenda was glad she had not followed Glenn's advice and bought a bucket of fried chicken at the KFC. Part of the fun of a picnic is preparing for it, rolling the chicken in flour highly seasoned with salt and pepper, and dropping it piece by piece into a frying pan filled with piping hot lard. The sound, the smell, the entire experience would be exciting to any young girl.

They went to the park along McDowell Street in the area that was once a slum. Huggie spread the tablecloth, placed the napkins and put out the paper plates. They spread their lunch out on the ground and sat down. Brenda arranged the chicken on a large paper tray and placed rolls, potato salad, baked beans and cold slaw, all from Harris Teeter, around the platter of chicken.

ON SUNDAY MORNING THEY WENT TO CHURCH. Huggie joined in the singing. Her voice rose above all others, but no one stared or seemed to find her presence curious. She dozed during the long sermon, but so did Brenda.

After a quick lunch at Anderson's restaurant, they hurried to Carowinds, the giant amusement park twenty miles south of Charlotte, just over the South Carolina state line. It was to be the highlight of Huggie's visit. She walked between Glenn and Brenda, holding their hands and skipping joyously into the sprawling park filled with people. Glenn had listed the rides they were going on, hoping to avoid any too stressful for the three of them.

Brenda and Huggie both needed to use the restroom. Brenda told Huggie to wait outside the door with Glenn if she got out first. Glenn decided he also needed a restroom break. It would take him less time and he could return before Huggie came out of the ladies room. As he came out of the men's room, a large man with a pocked-marked face bumped into him, grabbed him by the arm and swung him around until they were face to face.

The man held Glenn tight by the shoulders. "Rasheed," he said, "I haven't seen you since we got out of that god-awful prison in Pee Dee."

Glenn tried to break away, protesting loudly that the man had the wrong person.

"Remember," the man said, "you got out first. That's why I let you have the cot nearest the door."

People began to gather, sensing a fight brewing.

The man was laughing and shaking Glenn, claiming he was a long lost friend. A security officer walked up. The man suddenly let go of Glenn's shoulders and said, "Sorry friend, you are not Rasheed." He then quickly disappeared into the crowd.

Glenn rushed over to the ladies room door, feeling it wouldn't matter if he wasn't there when Huggie came out. She would wait and be okay. She could take care of herself as well as any child her age.

Brenda came out of the lady's room when Glenn got there. Huggie was nowhere to be seen.

DON SAT IN HIS DEN after church, listening to Beethoven's Fifth Piano Concerto and tried to read the Sunday paper. He wasn't hungry and had no plans for lunch. He was having trouble concentrating, even on the funnies. His thoughts were of Huggie and how much he missed her. The two days she had been in Charlotte were the longest they had ever been separated. Five more days! He had talked with her the night before and was happy and having fun.

By mid-afternoon Don started to doze in his chair when the doorbell woke him.

A young deputy stood at the door. "Sorry to disturb you, Dr. Hazlehurst. It's unusual to have to serve civil papers on Sunday, but the judge directed that this order and notice of hearing be delivered at this exact time."

Don took the package of papers, but before he could ask what they were all about, the deputy was gone.

The order was the first document to catch his eye. His heart started to race and he felt faint as he flopped into the nearest chair.

In bold print at the bottom of the page it said:

"It is therefore ordered that the custody of Carol Ann Hazelhurst, a minor child with physical and mental disabilities, be vested in her mother, Sabrina Hazelhurst, pending further orders in this cause."

It further ordered Donald Hazelhurst to appear at a hearing set for ten days hence: **"To show cause, if any he has, as to why this order should not be made permanent."**

Don reached for the phone to call his cousin and lawyer, Dwight Andrews. He had second thoughts as he realized he should first review the other papers so he could better explain what was happening. He became physically sick from what he saw.

The motion for custody was based on allegations of unfitness of the father. It was weighted down with affidavits saying Donald Hazelhurst and his consort, Brenda Horton, had left the child unattended in a hotel in a strange city while they went out dancing for most of the night. Photographs were attached to better tell the story. Don and Brenda were shown dancing close together, then getting into a taxi well after midnight and going to a liquor and drug-infested part of town known for pimps and prostitutes.

There were several photos showing Don staggering around in the Dew Drop Inn, obviously drunk. Others showed Brenda being swung around so while dancing her skirt came up almost over her head. Of course, there were photos of big Max putting Don into the taxi. A picture stamped 3:00 a. m. showed Brenda helping Don into his room. Another stamped 7:00 a. m. showed her coming out of his room.

HUGGIE WAS EXCITED to see her mother and ran into her arms. But she became worried when her mother pulled her away and said, "Come with me, darling. There's something I want to show you."

Sabrina had never used such affectionate language toward her daughter, and to Huggie it was unnatural. She struggled as they neared the gate and began to fight once outside the park. A security officer came up.

By then, Dawg Brinson was on the scene and said to the officer, "It happens every time we bring her to Carowinds. She doesn't want to leave. You can see from looking at her that she's retarded. You can't reason with her."

The officer walked away as Dawg forcibly put Huggie in the back seat of the car. The large man with the pock marked face held the door while Dawg and Sabrina squeezed Huggie tightly between them. The man then jumped into the driver's seat and sped out of the parking lot.

BRENDA AND GLENN PANICKED when a quick search of the area revealed no trace of Huggie. Brenda called 911 on her cell while Glenn rushed to find a security officer. No one seemed excited.

"Kids get separated from their parents here everyday," the security officer said. "They wander off. We always locate them, so don't worry.

And with the description you gave me of your child, I'm sure she'll be easy to locate."

"Oh," Brenda said, "I forgot to mention that she's white."

The officer led them to the Carowinds Security office where they were to wait.

The captain sitting at the desk seemed to recognize them. "The child is safely with her mother," he said matter of factly. He then handed them a stack of papers. "I was told to see that you got these."

Brenda needed but a single glance at the papers to know what had happened. Dawg Brinson had orchestrated a perfect kidnapping, and unfortunately a legal one. The ransom would be high. "The son of a bitch," is all she could say.

The call to Don was the most difficult she would ever make. She was overflowing with guilt. Without the Saturday night of the Olympics, the kidnapping would have been more difficult.

Don was devastated, but he didn't lash out at Brenda. In fact, he said nothing to cast blame on her. The only understandable communication was that he had been in touch with his attorney, who told him there was nothing to be done until next week when they would start preparing for the hearing.

When she hung up the phone, Brenda turned to Glenn and said, "I'm going to be with him."

"Why?" Glen asked. "There's nothing you can do except make matters worse. If you move in with him now, it'll seem to confirm what the papers say about you two. And Don doesn't have the guts to tell you not to come."

"At least, I can try to keep him alive until the hearing," Brenda said.

IT WAS AFTER MIDNIGHT when Brenda finished packing and hit the road. Before she was out of the driveway, she noticed she was nearly out of gas. I was too upset to even notice, she thought.

The gas pump at the all-night convenience store would not take her credit card, so she drove to the drive-in window. A lone attendant came to wait on her. No one else was in sight.

Poor guy, Brenda thought. He has one of the loneliest and most hazardous jobs there is.

When the attendant leaned out the window to give her change, she got a good look at him for the first time.

Brantley Cole! she thought. There was so much she needed to ask him, but a car pulled in behind her and the driver, probably needing a quick beer, sat down on the horn. She pulled away.

HUGGIE CRIED ALL THE WAY to the Brinson mansion, begging for her daddy and Benda. Dawg was annoyed and wondered why he ever got involved in the first place.

Sabrina tried to assure Huggie she would be happy at Daddy Dawg's House. She told her that the house had a nice swimming pool, a large screen television and large comfortable rooms.

"A computer?" Huggie asked.

"No computer," her mother replied. "Dawg and I are not into email and that sort of thing."

"Can I bring Buffy over?" Huggie asked.

"Is Buffy a cat?" Dawg was almost shouting. "I'm allergic to cats. Can't bring any cats in the house!"

Sabrina giggled. "The only animals we have are a couple of little pigs in a cage in the back yard." She didn't add that they would be there for only another week before they were to be cooked.

Chapter 34

HUGGIE TRIED TO ADJUST to living with her mother and Dawg Brinson, but it wasn't easy. She missed her father, Brenda, her cat, Buffy, and her computer. And unlike her room at home, the room where she confined herself most of the time was cold and foreign. Hostility toward anyone was not a part of Huggie's nature, but it was hard to feel kindly toward Dawg. When she would ask him a question he would reply. "Ask your momma, kid." He made it clear he wanted nothing to do with her.

Sabrina's conduct toward her daughter wasn't much better. During the day, she was so drugged that she moved around as if in a trance. After dinner, she went straight to bed, followed closely by Dawg.

Two things made life for Huggie tolerable. First, there was HeBear. The day after Huggie's abduction, Brenda brought the stuffed animal and Buffy by. Sabrina met her at the door and rudely rejected the cat. But she did take HeBear to Huggie's room where the child greeted him as if he were a living soul, hugging and kissing the stuffed animal and soaking his face with her tears.

Second, there was the maid, Agnes. She was young and reminded Huggie of Brenda. Agnes let Huggie follow her around and do little things like dusting, patting down the pillows and putting clothes in the washer. The cook, Isabel, arrived late in the afternoons to prepare dinner, but she seemed frightened by Huggie's unusual looks and asked Sabrina to keep her daughter out of the kitchen.

On Wednesday, her third day at the Brinson House, Huggie discovered the pigs enclosed in a cage in the back yard. She named one Piggly and the other one Wiggly, and they soon became pets. When they tried to sleep, she enjoyed waking them by poking them through the wire with a sharp tree limb. She also liked to watch them eat. The yard man assigned to feed them let her stick ears of corn through the wire and into the cage, and tease them by pulling them back as they snapped at the corn. When she tired of that and tossed the corn into the cage, she laughed loudly as they rooted against each other, each trying to get more than the other.

On Friday morning, while Huggie was teasing the pigs, a truck drove up and two men got out and started unloading a large tent. Another truck brought tables and chairs, and a third truck pulled a barbecue cooker up next to the pigs' cage.

Two men got out of the truck. Huggie heard one say, "It'll be the biggest party this town ever seen; tubs of chicken bog, bushels of shrimp and oysters, and the finest barbecue in the state, 'cause we'll furnish it fresh from our ovens in Conway. Our job here is to butcher and cook these fat little pigs, and put one at each end of the table with an apple in his mouth. They are just for decoration, but after the party's over, me and you'll eat 'em."

Huggie ran in the house excitedly crying out to Agnes. "What the men gonna do with Piggly and Wiggly?"

Agnes had no idea the sensitive little girl cared what happened to the pigs. "Oh, they gonna cook 'em. That's why they had 'em caged up for the last couple of weeks. So they get fat for the party tomorrow. Bet they sure gonna taste good."

Huggie ran outside to the pig cage crying loudly. She opened the door to the cage and tilted it over. The pigs spilled onto the ground and took off in different directions. One ran toward the pool. The yard men ran after it yelling and shouting in Spanish. When one of the pigs got to the pool, it couldn't stop. Neither could one of the men chasing it. Both hit the water in the deep end of the pool with big splashes. The man could barely swim and struggled to keep his head above water. His co-worker ran along the side of the pool, shouting in Spanish for help.

Agnes heard the commotion and looked out the window. When she saw what was happening, she dialed 911 and screamed into the phone. "Get police, ambulances, firemen…anybody you can over to Senator Brinson's. Something dreadful is happening in back yard!"

Agnes' screaming woke Sabrina, who was taking a nap.

Huggie jumped in the pool and swam after the pig. She quickly caught up with him and pushed him toward the end of the pool. Meanwhile, the other pig was running toward the partially erected tent. One of the men erecting the tent dove for the pig, and for a moment, got his arms around it, but the pig slipped away like he was greased. Running like a blind little hog, it ran into the center tent pole and knocked it down. The canvas collapsed covering the pig and two workmen. The men scrambled out, but the pig continued to run around under the canvas like a puppy trapped under a blanket.

By then, every dog in the neighborhood was checking out the commotion: Two large German Shepherds, a Doberman, a half dozen mixed breeds, even Amos, an English bulldog joined the chase, his fat, short legs churning as fast as they could. It sounded like a fox hunt as they chased the lump moving around under the canvas, pawing and snapping at it.

271

The pig finally came flying from under the canvas with the dogs in pursuit. It headed to the rear of the back yard and somehow managed to get through a thick hedge. The dogs couldn't get through the hedge so they turned their attention to the other pig, which Huggie was pushing out of the pool.

The air filled with the sounds of sirens as fire trucks, an ambulance and several police cars approached from different directions. Neighbors from blocks around came running, and yelling, "What's going on!"

Ms. Tulula Maybank, a seventy-year old dowager was late for her hair appointment at the "Wash and Curl." She was driving her Cadillac at an uncharacteristically fast speed and didn't see the pig run from underneath the hedge and into the street in front of her. The Cadillac struck the pig with such force it sounded like an explosion. Pig parts flew in all directions. The head crashed through the windshield and came to rest in Ms. Maybank's lap. She fainted as the out-of-control car continued, taking down four mail boxes, hitting a parked car, before spinning around and coming to rest in Miss Katy Pierce's rose garden.

A medic pulled the struggling yard man from the pool and started giving him artificial respiration. As soon as the yard man recovered his breath, he jumped up, and with the other yard man, ran to their pick-up and hurriedly drove away, cursing and vowing never to return.

With Huggie and the pack of dogs chasing, the other pig made it through two neighborhood back yards, knocking garbage cans in all directions. The dogs, except for Amos the bulldog, caught up as the pig reached the Maple Leaf Cemetery. Amos got tired and stopped to rest half a block away.

Before the dogs could pounce on the pig, it ran into the tall thin tombstone marking the grave of Civil War hero, Major James

Broadhead. The old stone shattered as the pig collapsed and the dogs started ripping him apart.

From half a block away, Huggie saw the dogs pounce on the pig. Crying uncontrollably, she ran home and by her mother, who was standing at the back door in a drug-induced stupor. Agnes tried to stop Huggie, but she continued upstairs to her room and locked the door.

An ambulance rushed Tulula Maybank to the hospital. Her physical injuries were not serious, but her pride was shattered. Far into the future, people in Darlington would talk and laugh about the town's leading dowager ending up with the head of a dead pig in her lap.

DAWG BRINSON HURRIED HOME after receiving a call that all hell had broken loose at his place. His tie was loosened and his white shirt was soaked with perspiration. His face, already red from drinking I. W. Harper whiskey all day, became redder as he saw the crowd and noticed the turned over empty pig crate. He didn't need an explanation as to what had happened.

As he stormed into the house, Agnes jumped in front of him shouting, "You be careful what you do to that child, Mr. Brinson."

He pushed her aside and staggered upstairs to Huggie's room. Sabrina was passed out on her bed and oblivious to what was happening.

"Open the god-damned door!" Dawg yelled at the top of his voice.

After banging on the door for several minutes and shouting loudly, he took a few steps back and then lunged forward with his shoulder. The weight of his huge body crashed into the door, ripping it from its hinges. He fell face down onto the bedroom floor. He crawled to the bed, and reached up and grabbed a handful of bedcovering. He tried to pull himself up, but fell back to the floor as the covering gave way to his weight.

He was breathing hard. Overweight, poor physical conditioning and the lingering effects of I. W. Harper whiskey were taking their toll. For several minutes he lay on the floor struggling to get his breath. He heard a child crying, but when he was finally able to pull himself up, the room was empty. The crying was coming from the corner of the clothes closet.

Brinson staggered toward the closet, eager to get his hands on the kid who had caused him more grief that afternoon than he had suffered in all of his life. The great Dawg Brinson was humiliated. People might not laugh to his face, but they would laugh behind his back for the rest of his days. They would not remember his power, his wealth, and his many triumphs over the railroad without also remembering that a handicapped little girl and two pigs once put him in his place.

He reached for the closet door while trying to control his temper enough to keep from ripping Huggie apart with his bare hands. Although it would feel good, he didn't want to spend the rest of his life in prison for killing a child, even one he thought deserved killing.

He snatched the closet door open and saw Huggie in a fetal position on the floor in a corner of the closet, one arm wrapped tightly around HeBear. Her sobs were loud and uncontrollable. Dawg reached down, grabbed the back of her dress and snatched her to her feet. He spun her around so he could look straight down into her eyes.

Suddenly Huggie stopped crying and shouted, "You murderer, you mean man. You were gonna kill my friends, Piggly and Wiggly. I hate you. I hope you go to hell and burn forever!"

Dawg was stunned. No one had ever talked to him like that. He turned loose of her dress and took a step backwards. Once free, Huggie ran to the bedside table and jerked off a lamp and hurled it toward the still shocked Dawg Brinson. He deflected it and it fell harmlessly to the floor.

Looking around for another weapon, Huggie could find only a pillow. She snatched it from the bed and started swinging at Dawg's face. He caught it and with Huggie hanging onto one end, pulled her to him. Instinctively she reached out and put her arms around his neck. Her feet were off the floor and Dawg was holding her up. She started sobbing again, this time more gently, as she buried her face in Dawg's chest. The pillow dropped to the floor and Dawg tightened his arms around the sobbing child, surprisingly trying to sooth her. It felt good to hold her close. Dawg stroked the back of Huggie's head and then with his right hand pushed her head more firmly into his chest. Finally, he gently laid her on the bed. Both were exhausted.

"Would you like some dinner?" Dawg asked.

Huggie didn't answer and he quietly left the room.

IT WAS LATE AND MISS GINNY was in bed. She answered the phone after the second ring.

"Sorry to disturb you Miss Ginny," Brinson said. "But there's something I need you to do first thing in the morning. Get as many of the girls into the office as you can. Divide tonight's guest list among them and have them call and tell all of the guests that the party's been cancelled."

"Cancelled?" She asked. "Are we to give a reason?"

After a moment Dawg said, "No, just tell 'em it's been called off."

"What in the world happened?" Miss Ginny asked, her voice shaking.

"If I told you, you wouldn't believe it," Dawg replied.

IT WAS AFTER MIDNIGHT when Dawg slipped quietly through the doorway of Huggie's room. I'll need to get somebody out here to fix this door, he thought. The room was dark and he didn't want to turn on a light. But he could see the table by the bed, the one where the lamp had been. He placed the tray of food on it, hoping Huggie would find it if she woke up hungry during the night.

Huggie appeared to be sleeping, holding HeBear tightly against her body. Dawg started to lean over to kiss her, but didn't. He tiptoed quietly out of the room. As he did so, he thought he heard a sweet voice say, "Thank you Daddy Dawg."

Chapter 35

SHORTLY AFTER BEING SERVED with the custody petition, Don closed his dental practice, gave his staff generous severance packages and referred all patients to other dentists. For the first time in his adult life he had nothing to do. Some days he didn't get out of bed and didn't eat the food Brenda brought to him. When he managed to get up, he stretched out in his reclining chair and dozed, while melancholy classical music like Dvorak's *New World Symphony* played in the background. Brenda wanted to change it to something more upbeat like Handel's *Royal Fireworks*, but didn't want to upset Don. She was afraid he might be suicidal.

She checked on him several times every night. Usually he was awake, staring into the darkness. The first night she was there, she searched his bedroom and bath and removed all medicines except what she considered non-lethal doses. She left his electric razor, but hid all others.

Don did little to help his lawyer, Dwight Andrews, prepare the case. Andrews nevertheless obtained helpful affidavits from Huggie's teachers, the minister of the First Methodist Church, Special Olympics coaches and several relatives and friends, as well as Megan and Jeff. All expressed the opinion that awarding custody to Don would be in the best interest of Huggie. He also obtained Sabrina's medical records showing her suicide attempt, and her history of drug use. There would be plenty of evidence showing Sabrina was never interested in her children, especially Huggie.

THE MONDAY MORNING FOLLOWING the pigs' wild event was no time to begin a custody hearing, so Judge Weston granted Dawg's motion for a week's continuance.

That afternoon, Dawg came home sober carrying a box containing a computer. Huggie danced with joy before giving him a warm hug. With her help the computer was assembled in a couple of hours, and she showed Dawg how to get online. When her mother came downstairs from her nap she was startled to see the two of them with their heads close together. Huggie was teaching Dawg how to play a video game.

Huggie and Dawg spent a lot of time together when he was home, which was more than he had ever been before. One evening he suggested they all go out for hamburgers. Sabrina didn't want to go so Huggie and Dawg went without her.

While they sat at a booth eating their hamburgers, a couple of Dawg's associates and their wives came by and spoke. Dawg proudly introduced Huggie as his young friend.

When they left, one associate said to his wife, "This is the first time I've ever seen Dawg befriend a child. It must be the kid in the custody suit. I understand she has a gorgeous mother."

ON WEDNESDAY NIGHT after Huggie went to bed, Dawg said to Sabrina, "It's time I got you ready to testify. Why don't you leave Huggie with Agnes tomorrow and come to the office. I'll need to work with you for a couple of hours."

"Testify! What do you mean testify?" Sabrina shouted. "I'm not testifying in any case."

"You'll have to appear as a witness in support of your petition," Dawg calmly replied. "Your custody of Huggie is not permanent, you know. Your ex's lawyer will try to make you out as a drunk and tramp, and claim that you had abandoned Huggie for years. We have to prepare a defense. I don't have any other witnesses to testify that you're a good mother, except for possibly the maid and the cook. And another thing, you shouldn't have any drugs or alcohol for at least three days before the hearing. You may have noticed that I've quit drinking."

Sabrina thought the last time she had answered questions in public was when she was in a beauty pageant many years ago. It had not gone well, and the idea of being questioned by a hostile lawyer, while a judge wearing a dark robe looked down on her, was unnerving.

"I won't do it!" she said. "I can't do it. Why don't we see how much Don will pay us to let him have Huggie back and drop the case."

"It's not that simple. Custody hearings aren't like other cases where you can compromise. Once the issue has been raised, the judge must find what's in the child's best interest. He doesn't have to award custody to either parent, but can order other arrangements."

"Good!" Sabrina said. "Let him order her put in an institution. That's where she should have been all along." She stormed upstairs to her bedroom and slammed the door.

THE FOLLOWING MONDAY MORNING, Don sat with his lawyer, Dwight Andrews, at one of the tables facing the judge's bench. Dawg Brinson sat alone at the other table. Mrs. Ross, the court reporter sat to one side, and Brenda sat in a far corner of the courtroom. All rose when Judge Winston entered and took his seat.

"I see *In re Hazelhurst,* is the only matter on the docket for this morning," said the judge. He glanced first at Dawg and then at Don's lawyer. "I assume counsel and their clients are ready?"

Dawg was on his feet quickly. "I represent Mrs. Hazelhurst, the petitioner, Your Honor. She's ill and unable to be here today. But I have her affidavit and can proceed on her behalf. She has custody pending this hearing to give the respondent the chance to show cause, if he can, as to why the temporary order granting custody to the mother should not be made permanent. I've filed affidavits showing she's a suitable person to retain custody. Of course, there's plenty of evidence to show the respondent is not a fit and proper person to have custody."

"What about the child, Mr. Brinson. I assume you will make her available for the court to interview."

"Your Honor, this is an unusual case in that the minor has what is called Down Syndrome. She's so handicapped and retarded that it would not help for the court to talk with her."

"We totally disagree," Dwight Andrews said as he stood to address the judge. "The child may be somewhat slower mentally than most children her age, but she has sufficient intelligence to lead an almost normal life. We urge the court to talk with her. We're confident you'll find her to be a competent witness. Furthermore, Your Honor, it's most unusual for a lawyer to ask that custody of a child be vested in someone the court has never seen nor heard, and the other party has not had an opportunity to cross-examine. However, my client is anxious to have this matter decided, so I will not ask for a continuance."

"I agree that it's unusual," replied the judge. "But let's start and see how far we get. You are first, Dr Hazelhurst, since you have the burden of showing why the existing order should not be made permanent."

Andrews read into the record the affidavits in support of Don. The judge listened intently. He knew a number of the witnesses and knew them to be credible. He was particularly impressed to learn that Huggie had lived with her father since the separation of her parents, and that her mother had never sought custody, or even visitation privileges, until she filed the petition. But he knew Brinson's response would be that it was not until Dr. Hazelhurst showed his being an unfit parent that night in Columbia that the mother decided it was in the best interest of the child that she take her.

After introducing the affidavits, Andrews said, "Your honor, I'll be glad to call any or all of the witnesses to testify in person if Mr. Brinson wants to cross-examine them."

Dawg, realizing that their live testimony would be even more persuasive than what they had written, responded, "That won't be necessary, Your Honor. I'm sure none of those good people know about Dr. Hazlehurst's shacking up with that colored girl and showing his rear end at that night club in the most drug and crime ridden section of Columbia. I wonder if any would be willing to entrust the care of their child with this man if they knew that."

Don's testimony took the rest of the morning. The judge was impressed with his sincerity and demeanor, and also the fact he didn't try to demean his wife beyond testifying about her disinterest in the children.

On cross-examination, Dawg lost no time in getting to the night of the Special Olympics.

Don didn't try to excuse his conduct and said, "That was the most shameful night in my life. I'll always regret it and I can promise nothing like that will ever happen again."

Dawg was not about to let Don go with a simple *mea culpa*. For more than an hour Dawg led him through every detail of the evening and asked him to explain the photographs.

At the conclusion of Don's cross-examination, Andrews announced that they had no more evidence, but reserved the right to present rebuttal evidence at the conclusion of the petitioner's case.

Dawg presented no live witnesses, but introduced a handful of affidavits. Those of Agnes and Isabel described Sabrina as a loving mother who spent a lot of time with her daughter. An affidavit from a physician friend of Dawg said he saw nothing about Sabrina to suggest she would not be a good mother fully capable of caring for her daughter. However, he neglected to mention that he had seen her only once when she wanted a prescription for a cold.

"We'll take an hour and half for lunch," said the judge. "But before we break, do either of you expect to have other evidence this afternoon?"

"No, Your Honor," Andrews said.

"I think not," Dawg said.

"Well, Mr. Brinson, if you will have the child here after lunch so I can talk to her, we can wrap this matter up in the early afternoon."

"Your Honor," Dawg said, "I again suggest that the child not be interviewed. She's not capable of knowing what's in her best interest."

"I understand, Mr. Brinson. I'll take that into consideration. I won't be bound by her wishes. It's not unusual for me to grant custody to a parent other than the one the child wishes to live with. As you know, the child's welfare is our polar star."

Dawg wasn't pleased with the development, though he had coached Huggie to tell everyone how happy she was living with her mother and her "Daddy Dawg." He worried most about her reaction when she would see her father.

"Your Honor, may I respectfully suggest that I take the child directly to your chambers without bringing her through the courtroom?" asked Dawg.

"Mr. Brinson, I don't understand your concern. I may have some motions to hear after lunch before I get back to this hearing. So, just bring her here and wait until I'm ready to talk with her."

The judge was out of his chair and halfway to the door behind the bench when Dawg spoke again. "Your Honor, I may have an additional witness after lunch? I want to alert you just in case."

HUGGIE, HOLDING TIGHTLY TO DAWG'S HAND, entered the courtroom shortly after lunch. Her mother and Dawg had told her what to say and made her recite it to them several times. "I love my mother and her friend, Daddy Dawg. We live in a nice house. Agnes keeps it clean and Isabelle cooks us good meals. I'm happy living where I do. I want to stay with my mother." She was told not to mention the pigs or her wish to have her kitten.

As they approached the courtroom Dawg warned her again not to run to her father and hug him if she should see him in the courtroom. "Everybody in a courtroom has to be quiet. If they aren't, the judge will lock them in jail."

But when she walked into the courtroom and saw the back of her father's head, she went ballistic. Nothing, not even the threat of jail, could hold her back. She broke loose from Dawg's grip and ran to him, shouting. "Daddy, daddy!"

Don turned around just as she reached him. She jumped into his arms and wrapped her arms tightly around his neck and her legs round his waist.

She was sobbing and could hardly talk. "I miss you, Daddy. I miss Benda, and I miss Buffy! Take me home. Please take me home. "

Don was crying also. Their cheeks were pressed together and their tears were mixing and running down their faces. Mrs. Ross, the court reporter, dabbed at her eyes with a tissue. The judge wiped away a tear with the back of his hand. In the back of the courtroom, Brenda put her head in her arms and wept. Dawg and Andrews were speechless.

The judge retired to his chambers with Huggie.

Dawg raced to the door where a young associate was waiting. "Go get the witness. He's across the street in the coffee shop. Tell him I need his ass in here immediately."

WILLIAM MILLER RANSON, MD, PHD was tendered as an expert witness after testifying as to his experience in matching DNA to establish family relationships.

"Objection!" Andrews shouted. "My client has given no DNA sample. Whatever Mr. Brinson is up to is unusual and irrelevant on the question of what's in the best interest of the child."

Dawg rose and spoke in a manner quieter than usual. "We're not trying to prove that Dr. Hazelhurst isn't the child's father, so it is not necessary to have samples of his DNA. Dr Ransom's testimony will establish who the father is, and it is a person other than Dr. Hazelhurst."

Dawg handed the original affidavit of Mike McMillan to the clerk and copies to the judge and Andrews while continuing to talk. "This man admits parentage and sets forth details of the conception and birth. Dr. Ransom's comparison of his DNA with that of the child confirms that he is indeed her father. Accordingly, Dr. Hazelhurst cannot be."

To Don, the remainder of the hearing was only a blur. Having to listen to the tedious testimony that the DNA of Mike McMillan and that of his daughter was a perfect match was the most painful experience of his life.

"Any closing arguments?" the judge asked.

"None, for the petitioner," Dawg replied.

Andrews rose from his seat and stood speechless for a moment. "Your Honor," he said in an unsteady voice, "we need time to decide how to respond. I need time to talk to my client to see if he wants to continue after the last development. I move for a continuance of at least a week."

"Motion denied," the judge said. "I've heard enough, and I'm ready to rule. The court will recess until half past nine o'clock tomorrow morning. I will have an order at that time."

Don walked from the courtroom in a trance. Andrews stood alone, pondering what had happened. The paternity of Huggie did not surprise him; that it was presented in the case did.

The judge's gavel struck indicating adjournment.

Brenda ran from the courtroom saying to herself, "That son of a bitch will stoop to anything. I'll get him, if it's the last thing I ever do."

Chapter 36

AFTER JUDGE WINSTON FINISHED meeting with Huggie, Benny Meyers, one of Dawg's young associates, took her to a restaurant across the street. No one wanted her in the courtroom while a witness testified that she wasn't the biological daughter of the man she believed to be her father.

Meyers ordered ice cream and cookies, but Huggie refused to eat. She put her head on her arms spread out on the table in front of her and did not look up. Meyers suggested they walk to a park nearby and she followed obediently.

At the park, she sat in a swing, swinging slowly back and forth with her feet still on the ground.

"We better get back to the restaurant where we're to meet your Daddy Dawg," said Meyers.

Huggie didn't protest and followed quietly. When they got to the restaurant, Meyers guided her to a bench where they could see Dawg when he came out of the courthouse.

BRENDA HAD A MISSION, but first she needed to stop at the restroom. She almost ran into Dawg who was rushing to the men's room next door. Neither looked at each other nor spoke.

Dawg walked into a stall and pulled out a miniature bottle of whiskey. He always carried a pocket full of little bottles with him. There was no need to stay sober any longer. The case was over and after the testimony of the last witness, he was sure he had won and it was time to celebrate.

But he didn't feel like celebrating. He had placed evidence on the court record that Huggie was a bastard. She would never know, but he was regretting the action. He had an empty, depressed feeling that liquor could not help. He lowered the bottle and poured its contents into the commode. As he left the men's room, he tossed the empty bottle, along with all the full ones, into a trash container.

Dawg was only a few steps in front of Brenda when she came out of the ladies room. She wanted to jump on his back, reach around his head and scratch at his eyes with her long fingernails. But as she followed him closely out of the courthouse her attention turned to Huggie, who was sitting on a bench in front of the restaurant across the street.

"Here comes Daddy Dawg!" Meyers said to Huggie. She looked up and saw Dawg but made no move towards him. Then she saw Brenda a few steps behind him. She jumped up and ran across the street, crying with excitement. An approaching car swerved to miss her.

"Benda, Benda!" she shouted.

Dawg stopped and watched the little girl, her short legs churning, running toward him. He opened his arms thinking she would run into them, but she ran past him into the Brenda's arms instead.

Dawg and Meyers watched quietly as she clutched Brenda.

"Benda, Benda, take me with you, Benda," cried Huggie.

After a long embrace, Brenda gently pushed the crying little girl back and looked directly into her eyes. "Huggie, you have to go with

Mr. Dawg. Love him and your mother. If you do, they'll love you. I promise."

Huggie spread her arms and moved back toward Brenda. But Brenda held her back.

Brenda continued, holding back her tears. "Huggie, if you love me, and if you love your father, you will go with Mr. Dawg. That's what the judge says you must do and that we must let you do. We will do everything we can to have you visit with us, but for now, you must go to your mother."

Dawg took Huggie by the hand. Brenda bent down and kissed her. "I love you," she said to Huggie, before turning to go.

As Brenda hurried toward her car she could hear Huggie repeating, "Luff you, luff you."

.Huggie walked quietly beside Dawg to his Cadillac. He opened the front passenger door for her, but she crawled in the back seat and lay face down sobbing quietly.

Dawg searched for something to say. The child he had called a funny looking, dumb kid had become the most precious thing in his life. But the main objects of her love and affection would always be Donald Hazelhurst and Brenda Horton. No judge's order could put him on their level. What did he have to offer, wealth? But all the riches in the world could not buy Huggie's love. Throughout his adult life, wealth and lawsuits had been his weapons of choice. But they were worthless to fight this battle. For the first time in his life, Dawg Brinson felt completely helpless.

SABRINA WAS DOZING ON THE COUCH in the den when Dawg and Huggie walked in the door. She sat up and mumbled something unintelligible. Huggie did not speak or glance in her mother's direction, but ran upstairs to her room and closed the door.

Sabrina was so heavily drugged she was hardly aware of Dawg's presence. He ignored her and went directly to the kitchen. Moments later, he emerged with a tray of food.

"Did you win?" she asked, slurring her words.

Dawg walked by her without speaking and hurried upstairs to Huggie's room. There was no response to his knock on her door, so he pushed it open and walked inside.

Huggie lay on her back staring at the ceiling, clutching HeBear close to her side. She did not move or speak as Dawg put the tray on the table beside the bed.

He had planned to give her a puppy, take her to Disney World, and even let Buffy come live with her. But he knew there was nothing that would relieve the child's misery except a reunion with her father and her friend Brenda.

Dawg sat on the edge of the bed and looked longingly at Huggie, who continued to stare at the ceiling. "I know you don't understand what's been going on for the last few days. You must wonder why a man wearing a black robe gets to decide where you live."

Huggie turned her head to the side and looked at Dawg.

Dawg continued, his voice breaking. "It's because there're people who love you, Huggie. I want you to continue to live with your mother and me, but I want even more for you to live where you'll be the happiest. Since that is with your father, I'll ask the judge in the morning to let you chose where to live. He won't be bound to do that, but I can let him know that is what your mother and I wish."

Huggie didn't fully understand, but she understood enough to know that this man loved her and wanted her to be happy. She relaxed her grip of HeBear, reached up to lock her arms around Dawg's neck and hugged him tightly.

BRENDA'S BROTHER, JOHN HENRY, was washing his car when she drove up. An attractive lady about Brenda's height and size was helping him. Brenda assumed she was her brother's live in girlfriend. Brenda waited for her brother to introduce them, but he didn't.

"Great to see you sister," said John Henry. "What brings you to this section of town?"

"I need you to help me with something. Do you still have your locksmith tools?"

"Yeah. They's around here somewhere, but I don't use 'em anymore. Cops call them burglary tools. If I'm ever caught with 'em, I'll be sent back up the creek."

"Well, you won't be caught with them, I promise. And we won't be stealing anything of monetary value. My former boss recorded every word that was said in his office. His secretary dated the tapes and filed them in a vault behind a paneled wall. If I can get a couple of recorded conversations, I may be able to break an evil white man from sucking eggs. I have the dates of the tapes I'm looking for. If you can just get me into his office and open the vault."

"I don't know, Brenda. I've been straight for all of these years. I don't want to break the law again, even for you."

"Please, J. H., trust me. You'll be doing me a great favor. In fact, except for the evil one, you'll be doing everyone a favor. Meet me at ten o'clock at the rear of the Brinson Law Firm over in Darlington."

Chapter 37

AN AUGUST STORM HAD KNOCKED OUT THE POWER and there was no air conditioning. The temperature in the house was in the 80s, but Don didn't seem to notice. Perspiration rolled unnoticed down his face as he wandered into the den and flopped down in his favorite chair.

Andrews had asked him if he still wanted custody of Huggie now that he knew she wasn't his child. Andrews should have known better. There doesn't have to be a blood relationship for parents to love their children. Millions of adoptions prove that. Indeed, people love their pets, which are even of a different species, perhaps not as much as their children, but intensely nonetheless. It's not physical kinship that generates parental love, but a bonding like no other. So how could anyone think Don, who had loved and cared for Huggie since her birth, wouldn't always feel she belonged to him?

Life without Huggie would never be the same. He had not heard from Brenda since she hurriedly left the courtroom. He assumed she had returned to Charlotte, knowing the relationship between them and Huggie had been forever changed.

Loss of a loved one is expected to bring grief, sadness, and depression. Time can be a great healer, but Don couldn't envision the passage of time helping. Life would always be empty and meaningless.

He had lost his wife, his most precious child, his closest friend and everything that made life real and meaning. He no longer had an office to go to when he got up in the morning. There would be no staff to greet him warmly or patients to praise his care. He had no hobbies: What could he enjoy—music, art, literature, beautiful flowers? He struggled to think of something that might add flavor to his future, but he could think of nothing.

He looked at the vase of lovely flowers on the table beside his chair. Brenda had cut them fresh that morning before she left for court, but he saw no beauty and sensed no freshness. He leaned over and tried to smell them. There was no fragrance. It was like a wet blanket had been thrown over his senses. He tried to recall happy times, such as Christmases with Huggie, the cook-out with her and Brenda the night when there was no power, and holding his new grandson, Donald Hazelhurst, II. Visions appeared, but in black and white. He could remember the times, but none of the pleasure they brought. It was as though he were a stranger viewing them from afar without interest.

Depression can be frightening; a feeling of emptiness, a void in which a person can sense no happiness, beauty or ugliness, heat or cold, truth or fiction, where pain of the present is unbearable and thoughts of the future are without hope.

Don desperately needed to escape his world of hopelessness. An hour passed and then another. There was a way to escape but it was unthinkable. The children, especially Huggie, would grieve. So would Brenda. His former office staff and patients would be sad, as well as others. But with his senses smothered by his depression, even thoughts of pain to loved ones seemed unimportant.

He remembered the extra cans of lighter fluid left over from the cook-out on the night the power was out. They could be poured around the inside of the house, and there were knockout pills he had kept hidden for no apparent reason since removing them from a lab during dental school. If only he could find a match.

Don felt an unbearable burden being lifted. The feeling of hopelessness was fading away with the belief that his pain would soon be swallowed up in a peaceful darkness. But first, a task remained.

Walking like a zombie, he went upstairs where Buffy was asleep on Huggie's bed. He gently took the cat in his hands and carried him to the kitchen where he watched him clean an overflowing bowl of cat food and drink a saucer of fresh water. Then he took him to the front door and kissed him before placing him outside.

Don relaxed in his favorite chair, confident the pills he just swallowed would remove him from this world before the fire spread. At first, he saw nothing but darkness, then a bright light that seemed to become brighter. In the light, he saw several figures coming toward him. The one leading the way was one of Huggie, followed closely by Brenda. Other figures approached from each side—Sabrina, Megan and Jeff, Dawg Brinson, and others he did not recognize. They lined up in front of him like actors preparing to take a final bow. As the light became brighter, the figures converged and merged into the figure that had been Huggie. Soon it was no longer Huggie but an unknown figure. Then, as the light became as bright as a thousand suns, Don knew what he saw was an angel standing in the sun.

Chapter 38

JUDGE WINSTON AND MRS. ROSS, his court reporter, remained after the others had left the courtroom. He had asked her to stay so he could dictate an order for her to type.

"Some judge has to preside over domestic cases, but why does it have to be me? Even cases that are easy to decide, like this one, leave me with an emotional hangover."

Mrs. Ross sat quietly. After seeing the dramatic reunion of Dr. Hazelhurst and the child he had raised, she was emotionally drained. Having to type an order that would destroy such a beautiful relationship would break her heart. But the evidence that the child was not his daughter had not been contested.

"Draw up an order," the judge said. "You can put it in legalese better than I can. Just keep it simple. Findings will be that the child has lived with and been cared for by Dr. Hazelhurst for all of these years, however long the testimony shows it's been. No need to refer to him as her father. They're devoted to each other. He's a person of integrity and is a fit, suitable and proper person to have permanent custody. No need to put any of that shit. Excuse my language. No need to mention that Saturday night in Columbia. Hell, if a man in his sixties has had only one bad night, he'll be at the front of the line when the roll is called."

Mrs. Ross broke down crying. She felt like jumping over the bench and giving the judge a hug.

He pretended not to notice her crying and continued. "We better put findings in there about the child's mother. You know, that she's never shown an interest in her daughter and has even said she should be placed in an institution. Maybe we ought to also put in there that she's living with a man out of wedlock, and that no evidence was offered to support a finding that he's of good character and reputation. That'll shake up ole Dawg!"

In her years of working as a court reporter, Mrs. Ross had never been so pleased with an outcome. But she worried about an appeal. "What about the evidence of paternity?" she asked.

"You mean all of that DNA bullshit?" the judge asked. "Whatever the hell that is." He thought for a moment and then said, "Maybe we better put something in the order about it in case ole Dawg appeals, and I expect he will if he knows how. Just say that the petitioner raised an issue of paternity, which the court finds immaterial, since the evidence so clearly shows that irrespective of a possible lack of paternity, the interest of the child is best served by granting custody to Dr. Hazelhurst. Type up the order and have it here for me to sign in the morning. It'll be good to get this one behind us!"

JOHN HENRY HAD NO DIFFICULTY picking the lock on the outside door, nor the one into Brinson's office. Getting into the vault was more of a challenge.

"I'm out of practice," he said to his sister. "When I got out of prison for all the burglaries, I swore I'd never commit another, but here I am. If I'm caught, I'll spend the rest of my life in prison."

Brenda suddenly had a panicky feeling. She recalled seeing Brantley Cole working the night shift at a convenience market in

Charlotte. If he had conspired with Dawg in the Smith case, surely he wouldn't need to do that. What if he were innocent? The tapes she was looking for were from the dates she recalled his having been in the office. But even if Cole had refused to commit perjury, taped conversations in which Dawg solicited him to do so would be incriminating.

Finally the door to the vault swung open. But before Brenda could remove any of the tapes, the door to the reception room opened and she heard steps moving in their direction.

John Henry turned off the flashlight, leaving the room in complete darkness. "I thought you said there would be no security guard," he whispered.

"There wasn't when I worked here," she whispered back. "Maybe it's only a lawyer who worked late and is passing through the reception room on his way to the parking lot."

Suddenly the door to the office opened and the room filled with light as the switch by the door was pushed on. A large man wearing a security guard uniform stood in the doorway. A pistol in a holster was at his side. Brenda, petrified with fear, quickly squatted behind the huge desk.

The guard took a couple of steps into the room. There was a sudden flash of light accompanied by a loud gun shot blast.

The light and noise temporarily blinded and deafened Brenda. As her sight returned she saw the guard lying on his back with blood flowing from his stomach. John Henry was gone.

Brenda ran from behind the desk, stepped over the fallen guard and dialed 911 as she ran to her car. Trying to disguise her voice, she said, "Man shot and down in Brinson Law Office."

BRENDA'S Z-3 SPORTS CAR raced along the highway between Darlington and Florence. She needed to escape, but something was telling her to go to Don's house first. As she approached within a couple of blocks, she saw the flames.

The street was filled with police cars, ambulances and fire trucks. She pulled into the parking lot of the abandoned building that, until a short time before had housed the Hazelhurst Dental Clinic, and ran toward the house.

A police officer tried to stop her, but she dashed around him, and past others trying to intercept her. Hopping over outstretched fire hoses, she continued until she got to where the heat was so intense she thought she could go no farther. Then she saw something that made her go farther--Buffy clinging to the lower limb of the huge oak tree at the edge of the front yard. She could hear the frightened cries of the cat above the surrounding noise.

With police close behind yelling for her to stop, she ran to the tree, jumped as high as she could and wrapped her arms and legs around its trunk. She shimmied up to the lower limb and climbed out to where she could reach the cat. While talking to Buffy sweetly trying to coax him to her, she reached out to grab him. The frightened cat leaped to a higher limb and scrambled higher up the tree. Brenda climbed to the next limb and then the next. Holding to the tree trunk with one arm and reaching as high as she could with the other, she grabbed Buffy by the tail and pulled him toward her. She then quickly grabbed the fur on the back of his neck. As she did, a ladder extending from a fire truck swung into the limbs of the tree and a large firefighter, hanging onto the ladder, seized her and pulled her toward him.

When they reached the ground, Brenda, tightly clutching the cat to her breast, broke loose from the fireman's grasp and ran as fast as she could to her car. The top was down and she jumped in without opening the door. As she pulled away at full speed she glanced in her rear view mirror and saw the tree, where she had been moments before, explode into flames.

THE POLICE WERE TOO BUSY controlling traffic to chase what they considered only a crazy woman trying to rescue a cat, but Brenda knew it wouldn't be long until she was identified as a suspect in the law office robbery attempt. A statewide bulletin describing her and the car she was driving had likely already been issued. Unless she escaped, she would soon be apprehended, but first she had to get Buffy to his owner.

Clutching Buffy to her chest with her left hand and driving with her right, less than a half hour later, she turned into the Brinson driveway.

Huggie answered the door after the first ring. Her mother stood behind her. Brenda quickly handed the cat to Sabrina, so she could return Huggie's warm embrace. Sabrina tossed the soot-covered cat toward the den and stood watching dispassionately as her daughter and Brenda cried softly on each other's shoulder.

Sirens sounded a few blocks away. Brenda expected to be arrested within minutes. With weapons drawn, police officers would seize her, twist her arms behind her back, clamp handcuffs on her wrists, and drag her quickly away. She didn't want Huggie to see that, so she pushed her back and whispered, "I love you dear Huggie, more than anyone will ever know."

As Brenda ran down the walkway toward her car, she heard Huggie say, "I love you, Brenda."

Brenda drove south on I-95 and minutes later exited onto I-20 toward Columbia. Soon the speedometer of the small car was dancing at 110 miles an hour. Sirens behind her were getting closer, but she hardly heard them. Her thoughts were of her destination. She remembered an overpass ahead, with its supporting concrete pillows near the outside lane. Pressing the accelerator to the floor, trying to coach a few more miles an hour out of her Z-3, she expected her nightmare to be over soon.

MISS GINNY WAS UNABLE to sleep, so she reached for the remote beside her bed and turned on the eleven o'clock news. A reporter standing in front of the smoking remains of the Hazelhurst home was saying that it was feared Dr. Hazelhurst had been in the house. It would be morning before the area was cool enough for rescuers to search for his remains.

The anchor suddenly broke in to say there was more important breaking news. He switched to another reporter standing outside the Brinson Law Office.

"Inside this building is where a robbery occurred about two hours ago," said the reporter. "A night watchman was shot and seriously wounded when he confronted two robbers who had broken into a safe in the office of lawyer James Brinson. They apparently removed tape recordings of conferences between Brinson and a client. Brinson told us a few minutes ago that he suspected one of the robbers was a former female lawyer in his office who wanted to use the tapes to try to blackmail him. Officers are searching for Brenda Horton, an African-American female in her early thirties, and her brother, who has a record for burglary."

The anchor interrupted again. "We've just learned that a vehicle, thought to have been occupied by the robbery suspects, crashed and burned moments ago on I-20! We have one of our crews on the way to the scene, but in the meantime, reports indicate that no one could have survived the crash. We are also told that the stolen tape recordings which were thought to have been in possession of the suspects undoubtedly melted in the intense fire that followed the crash."

MISS GINNY WAS FRIGHTENED AND SHAKING ALL OVER. Brenda was dead! The thought overwhelmed her. And the tapes destroyed? She struggled out of bed and crawled to her bureau of drawers. She reached in the bottom drawer and felt around underneath her slips and panties. She relaxed as her shaking hand came in contact with some solid objects.

The tapes had not melted in a fiery car crash. They had not been stolen; indeed, they were not even missing. They were where they had been since the day Mike McMillan signed the affidavit.

Chapter 39

THE BELLS TOLLED AT THE SAME TIME, ELEVEN O'CLOCK ON a Friday morning. Standing near the center of town one could hear the bells of both churches. One was a mainline Protestant church affiliated with one of the nation's largest denominations. Everything about it suggested affluence—the lovely section of town where it was, its expensive pipe organ, cushioned pews, stained glass windows, and even the paved and beautifully landscaped parking lot. For many years Dr. Donald Hazelhurst had been a member of the church choir.

The other church was Pentecostal and not affiliated with any denomination. It was in what was still called the colored section of town. Its piano was old and out of tune. Its hard pews didn't have cushions, and the sand parking lot was bare of shrubs or trees. The mother of Brenda and John Henry Horton was an elder there before her death.

In the white church, a child with Down Syndrome sat between her brother and sister holding tightly to each of their hands. She wept quietly while she stared at the coffin containing the few earthly remains of the man she would always believe was her father. Her siblings sat stoically. The brother was comforted only by the knowledge that his young son, Donald Hazelhurst, II, would carry on his father's name.

Before the service began, people mumbled to each other in soft tones, saying how tragic for such a fine man to die in so terrible an accident. Though there was evidence to the contrary, authorities had concluded that the fire was accidental. They would never suggest that a member of the town's most prominent family would take his own life.

The parking lot surrounding the other church was nearly full when a beat up old car drove in. It bumped into the rear bumper of another car as the driver tried to park it. People watched a shriveled up old lady get out and start making her way to the church. Her hands were shaking and even her head was bobbing from side to side.

"She shouldn't be driving," several bystanders remarked.

People watched curiously as the only white person in the church tried to sign the register. Her right hand shook so the pen wavered all over several lines. Her signature would be unintelligible, but if one of the two people whose lives were being honored had been present, she would have recognized the writing as that of Miss Ginny Beam.

When the service was over, Miss Ginny returned to Darlington and drove up to the mailboxes by the street in front of the post office. She dropped a package in one of the boxes. The address, typed on a white sheet of paper on an old upright typewriter, was glued tightly to the package. It had been copied from the business card Brenda Horton had given her months before, and was that of Mr. Jacob Seigal, Chairman of the Legal Ethics Commission of the South Carolina Bar.

Smiling and pleased with what she had done, Miss Ginny pulled her car into the street without first looking. The driver of the approaching truck had no time to avoid the crash that followed.

Epilogue

IT WAS-MID MORNING ON A COLD GRAY DAY IN JANUARY. A few flakes of snow drifted down outside the townhouse in southeast Washington, D.C., but not yet enough to whiten the soot-covered snow and ice that lined the street outside.

Dr. Glenn Osborne had left home several hours earlier. His six-month-old twin sons were crying in their mother's arms when he bent down to kiss them good-bye.

"Hang in there, honey," he said to his wife. "I'll try to get home early and give you some relief." He had a job teaching at a nearby community college.

Now both boys were napping. It was unusual for them to sleep at the same time, which made their care stressful for their parents, both in their mid-40s. But nothing could dampen the joy these babies brought to their parents. They had been a long time coming.

Brenda whispered a prayer of thanks as she looked in the crib at her beautiful babies. For years she had struggled to get rid of the demons that haunted her since her childhood. She finally overcame them, but an even greater miracle made the birth of her sons possible.

One night seven years before should have been her last. She tried to suppress memories of that dreadful night, but at times, especially on dark and dreary days, the vivid images returned.

There was the speed, the sirens, the fear, and the feeling of hopelessness that had caused her to plan to turn her Z-3 into a concrete bridge abutment supporting an overpass on Interstate 20. She had selected one she remembered as offering the best exposure, but someone had beaten her to it. Black smoke rose from a blazing flame half a mile ahead, and she had to stop behind the traffic backed up in front of her. Troopers she thought were chasing her sped by on their way to the fiery crash. It was an hour later before traffic was able to pass around the smoldering remains. An officer directing traffic looked at her and waived her past without hesitation. Several weeks later, she learned it was because they thought her brother's girl friend and "get away driver" was Brenda Horton. The bodies in the crash were burned beyond recognition and for reasons no one seemed to question, no modern identification techniques were attempted.

The case of the burglary of the Brinson Law Office was closed. The two bodies were buried side by side. The marker at the grave of the female simply said, "Brenda Horton."

It was late on that fateful night when Brenda got to her home in Charlotte and woke up her companion, Glenn Osborne. She expected he would be outraged by her conduct and report her to the authorities. Instead, he simply said, "People will do anything for those they love."

They needed to get rid of the car quickly.

"It'll be easy," Glenn said. "We'll park it on Chavis Heights. By morning it'll have been stolen, dismantled and the parts ready for sale. The serial number will be obliterated and it'll be as if the car vanished from the face of the earth."

Within a few months, Brenda had a new name, a new social security card and a husband. She and Glenn settled in a middleclass neighborhood in Washington, D. C. Since under Brenda's will Glenn had inherited a good portion of the money she received from the sodium explosion cases, they could have lived in a nicer section of town. But they chose to live modestly so they would not call attention to themselves.

After seven years, Brenda still kept a low profile because of a nagging fear that she would be discovered. The Carolinas seemed far away, and were a part of her past she wanted to forget. But, at times her hunger for news of the region drove her to the Internet for information on her former home. It was a good time to look while both boys were sleeping.

On the front page of the state section of the Columbia newspaper the headlines said: *DISBARRED LAWYER DIES IN PRISON.*

Brenda's heart beat faster as she hurriedly scanned the article that followed.

> *Former lawyer and State Senator, James Earl Brinson, died yesterday in Pee Dee prison after serving a little over half of his ten-year sentence. Brinson was disbarred and sentenced to prison for soliciting race car driver, Mike McMillan, to falsely swear that he had witnessed an accident. McMillan confessed when confronted with taped transcripts of a conversation he had with Brinson. He received a lesser sentence for testifying for the prosecution.*
>
> *The tapes were apparently removed from the Brinson Law Firm during a burglary in which a night watchman was shot. He recovered and identified the two suspects from photographs. Both were killed in a car crash while trying to escape. The tapes were thought to have been destroyed when the suspects' car crashed and burned. But several days later they were mailed*

from an anonymous source to the ethics commission of the State Bar.

Brinson's only survivor is an adopted daughter, Carol Ann Hazelhurst, of Whitefish, Montana.

DINNER WAS OVER AND THE TWINS HAD BEEN BATHED AND FED. One was asleep in his crib. Glenn sat in a rocking chair holding the other, pressing a pacifier in his mouth, gently trying to rock him to sleep. Brenda sat on the couch sipping a cup of coffee, trying to relax.

"According to the article, Dawg adopted Huggie as his daughter," said Brenda. "My guess is he married her mother and she likely divorced him when he went to prison."

"Forget the article and put the past behind you," Glenn told her.

Brenda continued. "I'm sure Dawg didn't have a will, so that means Huggie inherited his money. With that, the trust her father established, and money added to the trust under my will, she's wealthy. I hope she's happy and well cared for. Now that I know where she is, I need to find out."

"What? Please, honey! She's in Whitefish, Montana for Christ's sake. You can't get there from here. Besides, what if she or her sister were to recognize you?"

"I would try not to let them see me, but even if they did, Megan wouldn't recognize me after all these years. I was a small child the last time she saw me, and she regarded me as so insignificant, I'm sure she paid little attention to me. And as for Huggie, I would be careful not to get close enough for her to recognize me." She waited for Glenn to protest further, and when he didn't she said, "If I could just see where she lives and maybe get a glimpse of her from afar, I could tell how she's faring. It's my only chance to have peace in my life."

"What if she isn't well cared for? There's nothing you could do about it without risking exposing yourself. Think about our life and the twins."

IT HAD BEEN A LONG DAY THAT INCLUDED a three-hour wait at the Salt Lake City airport for a flight change. Brenda should have been tired, but her adrenalin was flowing, so she hardly noticed the slippery road with six-foot snow banks on each side of the road as she drove her rental car from the Kalispell airport to the little town of Whitefish.

The closer she came to the town where Huggie lived, the more excited she became. But how would Brenda locate her? She was likely living with her sister, but a check of the phone numbers on the Internet revealed no listing for anyone named Hazelhurst.

As it turned out, locating Huggie was easy. Brenda parked the car in front of a busy ski shop in downtown Whitefish and went inside.

"I'm trying to find a young lady who lives here," she said to the young salesperson, fitting a customer with a pair of ski boots. "She has Down Syndrome and is somewhat different looking. She likes to hug people."

The young man looked up from his task and answered immediately.

"Oh, that's Huggie. Works down the street at the Hibernian Restaurant."

A customer looking through a rack of ski sweaters nearby added, "Everybody knows Huggie. She's a sweetheart."

THE NIGHT WAS CLEAR BUT BITTER COLD. The line of people outside the Hibernian restaurant stretched for half a block. It was the height of ski season and most of those waiting were dressed warmly in fashionable after-ski clothes. They talked, laughed, and relived their happy day on the slopes. Some sipped from cans of beer. A party of four openly shared a marijuana cigarette.

Brenda stood among the crowd unnoticed, though alone and not dressed for the extreme cold. She had not anticipated having to wait outside in the cold. She wore simple jeans with no thermal underwear underneath, boots designed for rain, not ice and snow, and a simple cloth jacket over a cotton sweater. A scarf tied around her head could not keep the cold from stinging her ears.

Half an hour passed and the line had barely moved when a hostess appeared at the door and called out, "If there's a single who won't mind eating at the bar. I can seat you now."

Brenda was certain the hostess was Huggie's sister, Megan. Brenda stepped forward when nobody else did and followed her into the restaurant. Just inside the door she stopped abruptly, overwhelmed by the ambiance of the crowded restaurant. It was packed with people colorfully dressed in clothing of the ski country. Most were in their 20s and 30s and the buzz coming from their happy conversations almost drowned out the sounds of the German beer hall music coming from an accordion being played by a young man standing on a table in a far corner. At some of the tables, mugs of beer, some overflowing with suds, were held high and waived about in time with the music. The rich smell of wood oven pizza filled the air.

Brenda's heart skipped a beat when she spotted Huggie cheerfully moving from table to table refilling water glasses from pitchers she held in each hand. She put the water pitchers on the edge of the table long enough to give hugs to a couple who were leaving.

"Follow me," the hostess said impatiently.

308

Brenda followed the hostess to the crowded bar. She shoved aside the menu the hostess placed on the bar in front of her and said, "I'll just have a beer."

"Brand?" the bartender asked.

"Oh, just a small light, whatever you have on draft."

She sipped the beer while staring straight ahead at the mirror behind the bar. Her heart pounded as she watched Huggie in the mirror, obviously enjoying her work. She longed to run to her with open arms, but Huggie believed she was dead. What if she thought she was seeing a ghost and became frightened? People would ask questions. It was easy to tell by the way she was dressed that she was not a skier. How would she explain what she was doing alone in a ski resort three thousand miles from her home?

Brenda watched nervously as Huggie came toward the bar to refill her water pitchers. Huggie glanced at the mirror behind the bar and her eyes met Brenda's. Brenda quickly looked down at her glass of beer, hoping Huggie would continue past, but soon she felt the presence of a small warm body behind her. It was not touching her but she could sense the vibrations and knew Huggie was standing close. She slid off the stool and stood looking down at the small girl.

Huggie looked at Brenda curiously but did not speak. She appeared surprised but not frightened. She spread her arms and Brenda was about to take her into hers when the bar tender shoved two pitchers of water across the bar and said, "Here you go, Huggie." Huggie took a pitcher in each hand and backed away, still looking curiously at Brenda.

Brenda slipped a five-dollar bill under her half-filled glass of beer and turned quickly to go. As she walked toward the door she took one last look and saw Huggie cheerfully moving about among her customers.

As Brenda walked past the cashier, she noticed a large glass jar beside the cash register with a sign pasted to it that said, "Huggie's tips." Then she recognized the lady working as cashier. She was older, and even at a distance and in the dull light, wrinkles could be seen and there was a slight extra chin. But her hair was as blonde as ever.

Brenda watched as a young man still in ski clothes put a bill in the jar while waiting for the cashier to swipe his credit card. The jar was already stuffed with folding money. "I bet you have to empty this jar three or four times a night," the man said.

The cashier smiled, but didn't answer.

The young man continued. "You know this restaurant is fortunate to have that child working here. She makes everybody feel good. And she's a good skier. Passed me today on a black diamond slope like I was standing still, and I'm a fast skier."

"That child's my daughter and she's twenty years old," the cashier replied while holding the credit slip for him to sign.

He nodded to the tip jar and said, "I'll bet she makes enough on tips to support herself."

"I don't know," the cashier said with a faint shrug. "She doesn't keep her tips. She gives them to the Special Olympics."

"But doesn't she need them herself?" he asked.

"Not really," the cashier replied. "This is the most successful restaurant in the state and she owns it."

BRENDA SHIVERED AS SHE WALKED through the door into the cold night, but inside she felt warm and relaxed. The light of a full moon reflected off the mountains in the east. A dull roar of snow cats could be heard in the distance as they groomed the slopes for the avalanche of skiers the next day. Their lights, dulled by the brightness of the moon, looked like tiny glowworms.

Brenda stood for a moment and gazed at the beautiful hills. Then she took a deep breath and stepped into the night. Her thoughts were of twin boys three thousand miles away and she could hardly wait to get home to them.

THE END

LaVergne, TN USA
05 October 2009
159809LV00003B/4/P